Street People

A Novel

David Faulkner

Other novels by David Faulkner

The Oyster Wars

It is a time in our history when, across the Chesapeake Bay, oyster men battled over the "white gold" and young men were shanghaied into servitude to ruthless oyster boat captains. Haynie McKenna's search for one victim pits him against a sharpshooting assassin, a cabal of former Confederate officers and his own family ghosts. Historical fiction.

The Oyster Navy

In 1868, Maryland's embryonic maritime law enforcement agency, the State Oyster Police, set out on its mission to quell the violence on Chesapeake Bay. The force, quickly dubbed the Oyster Navy, met stubborn and often violent resistance. Historical fiction.

Acknowledgements

As always thanks to my family for their support.

My thanks to a good friend, Al DeRenzis, for acquainting me with the mystery and charm of Dickeyville, MD.

I wish to acknowledge the debt owed to Paul Bendel-Simso for the generous application of his editorial talent and wisdom to this work.

Edited by Paul Bendel-Simso

Cover art by Chris Stutz

1

Noah Cassidy wondered what the attraction was. He shouldered his way through the onlookers until he was wedged against the yellow crime-scene tape fluttering along a row of parking meters. Two uniforms and a couple of EMTs milled around a sheet-covered form lying in the middle of the sidewalk. No doubt, they were awaiting the arrival of homicide detectives and the medical examiner, whose office was two blocks away. The older of the uniforms warily eyed the crowd of gawkers. His face was familiar, but Noah could not put a name with it. The uniform motioned to his partner then approached the tape.

"Cassidy, isn't?" he asked.

Noah nodded, trying without success, to get a discrete look at the nameplate.

"My partner and I are curious why an assistant state's attorney shows up at the scene of some street bum's murder. This one of the new man's crime-fighting initiatives, or a play for the bum vote?"

"I left the state's attorney about a year ago."

"I hadn't heard. So what are you doing?"

Noah usually had a response ready for that question, but hadn't expected to need it here, so it took him a minute.

"I'm taking a break from the law," was all he could muster.

The uniform pointed toward the sidewalk. "No. I meant, what brings you here, to the scene of our little street drama?"

The crime scene, in the one hundred block of Penn Street, was surrounded by blocks of buildings housing various branches of the University of Maryland Medical School. Ironically, the deceased lay at the front steps to the Pediatric Ambulatory Center; the school's famed Shock Trauma Center a short block north. Neither of which had done the form under the sheet any good.

"Over at Shock Trauma," Noah responded, "with a friend."

The uniform studied him. "As I remember, you were one of the good ones in that office. I'm sorry to hear you left; still it's good to know they're not sending you guys out every time one bum slices up another one. What a huge pain that would be for all of us." He inclined his head at the sheet. "Besides, it's just a street bum, who gives a rat's ass? Am I right?"

The uniform headed back to the sheet as a medical examiner and two detectives pushed their way through the crowd.

Noah turned and, once away from the crowd, headed along Pratt Street toward his car. He was two blocks from the scene when he heard someone moving up fast and glanced over his shoulder. A young man loped toward him, shouting and waving his arms.

"Mister Cassidy! Hold up for a minute!"

Noah stopped and watched as the man covered the remaining distance between them. This was not the best neighborhood, even without the killing back there, and Noah was eased to see that his pursuer's hands were empty.

If the man hadn't called his name, Noah could have taken him for a mugger; still he might be one of the pesky panhandlers that, of late, seem to be flooding the city's streets. This man looked to be a few years younger than Noah, mid-to-late twenties, wearing a grey hooded sweatshirt with the hood laid back, his face exposed. Another indication that he likely was not a mugger. Still, Noah shoved his right hand in the pocket of his trench coat to foster the illusion that he was armed.

The stranger stopped in front of him, gasping for breath.

In a crisp voice Noah said, "You called my name. If I'm supposed to know you—I don't."

The man gulped more air before saying, "I was standing near you back there and overheard you talking to the cop. After you left, it took me a minute to figure out what to do. Glad I caught up to you."

"Why?"

The man blinked. "Why what?"

Noah looked him up and down.

"Why are you glad you caught up to me? If you are a panhandler, you're going to be disappointed. If you're a mugger, we're both going to be unhappy."

The man glanced around and lowered his voice. "Back there I heard you say that you used to be a prosecutor. … I think I need an attorney."

Taking Noah's hesitation as a good sign he quickly added, "There's a coffee shop in the next block. We could go there and talk, out of the cold."

"I must say, you've put some thought into getting a free cup of coffee out of me."

The man thrust both hands out, palms up and backed away. "This is not about a free cup of coffee. I got money," he added, and dug a few crumpled bills from the pocket of his sweatshirt. "I'll pay. I need your help."

Noah stood his ground. "I wasn't kidding when I said you would be disappointed. Your buddies waiting to rob me are going to be angry with you for wasting their time."

The stranger pointed down Pratt Street. "My name's Corky," he pleaded "The coffee shop, Peace and a Cup of Joe, is in the next block. It's a public place and there's a community outreach police station right across the street. If you feel threatened, just get up and walk out."

"I'm not looking for clients," Noah said, "but I am curious why you think you need an attorney."

The man glanced over his shoulder. "I know something about the dead guy back there. I need to tell somebody, and I sure can't talk to the cops."

"Why not?"

"Are you kidding? Look at me. To them, I'm just another street bum. After they hear my story, it wouldn't take them long to decide it was me that killed him. Case closed. But, what I tell to my attorney is secret. Right?"

Noah nodded.

"And, even though you quit the state's attorney, you are still a lawyer, right?"

Noah nodded again.

"You couldn't tell them about me, or what I told you, unless I say its okay, right?"

"Only if you were my client. But, you're not, so don't tell me anything."

"It's because you think I can't pay. Am I right?"

"That would be a consideration if we were discussing a fee. But we're not. Since you brought it up, why not visit legal aid? It's another free service for you people."

"This is not a ticket for loitering. If the cops come for me, I would need somebody who knows the system from both sides. I heard that cop say you were one of the 'good ones.' That's what I need, one of the good ones."

Noah felt this Corky was being truthful when he said he would need a good lawyer. At least *he* believed it.

Corky shrugged and held out his hands, palms up, as if to say, "What else can I do?"

"I should know your full name," Noah said.

The man, feeling more at ease, smiled. "Corky. My name is Corky Kilmark."

"Alright, Corky Kilmark, here's what I'm willing to do. You give me a retainer of five dollars—you have that much?"

Corky nodded.

"When I have the five we will have an attorney-client relationship for the following purpose: I will listen to your story and what you tell me is protected. If, after hearing you out, I don't like your story, and don't want you for a client, I'll refund your retainer and we will go our separate ways. However I will remain bound by the attorney-client privilege."

Corky pulled a five-dollar note from the bills in his pocket. "When they do this in the movies the lawyer always says 'One dollar.'"

Noah took the bill. "Those are old movies," he said.

"If I agree to take your case there is one other condition; this transaction gives ambulance chasing a bad name. The circumstances of our meeting are never to be spoken of."

Peace and a Cup of Joe occupied a narrow rowhouse wedged between a University of Maryland Medical Center and a boarded-up warehouse.

Corky paid for the coffee while Noah claimed one of the raised pub tables along a wall of exposed brick.

There was no line at the counter and shortly Corky set two containers in front of them. He stirred sugar into his coffee and said, "Should I call you Mister Cassidy?"

"Noah is good."

Noah sipped from his cup and glanced around the cramped shop.

"This is great coffee. How did you find this place?"

Corky hunched forward, speaking in a low voice, as if sharing a secret.

"I understand that you need to know all about me, but this is part of the stuff you have to keep secret."

"You get a one-stop confessional all for the one low price."

"I get it. Bear with me, this is all new." Corky heaved a sigh, blew on his coffee and began. "You were right, I am a panhandler. It's what I do, but I'm not homeless. The thing is, I commute to work every day from Randallstown. Garage parking is too expensive and I finally found a parking spot on one of these side streets, no meters to feed. That is worth the few extra blocks I walk to the Inner Harbor. In fact I'm thinking of selling the rights to the spot to someone when I'm done with it. It's close to Oriole Park yet remote enough there's little chance one of my customers will happen upon me getting into a car for the ride home. My car is a six-year-old piece of crap, still they might not understand. I stop here in the morning for coffee and a roll to go, when I'm finished drinking the coffee I use the cup in my work. If the weather turns bad or I just don't feel like working, I hang out here. It's sort of my office."

Corky took a cell phone from a pocket in his sweatshirt and glanced at the time. "I know the clock is running on that retainer, just give me a second." He punched one number button and put the phone to his ear.

"Hi. I'm caught in town and am going to sit out the rush hour." He listened for a minute before saying, "It's not that. I'll tell you when I get there. … Me too."

He offered his phone to Noah. "If you need to call anyone, use this. We will be a while."

"Thanks. I'm good."

Before his new client could begin, Noah said, "I guess that was your wife."

Corky nodded.

"Does she know what you are doing or does she think you are going to the office every day."

"She knows what I do."

"And she's okay with it?"

He shrugged. "Let's say she's accepted it—for now. This is November—I've been on the street about 8 months. I lost my ninety-five in January."

"Your ninety-five?"

"That's what street people call a regular job. You know, 9 to 5."

Noah smiled.

Corky continued. "I was a hotel desk clerk, well motel, really. Tried acting—I make more at this—sold cars." He shook his head. "Pontiacs, for Christ sake—Pontiacs. Who knew? Anyhow, by April, I was really discouraged and one day, just for the hell of it, I scrawled a sign on a piece of cardboard and headed for the Inner Harbor."

He raised his cup and peered over the rim. "It's a real cheap way to open your own business and—what did I have to lose, right?"

"Were you coming from work, just now?"

Corky nodded.

"So where is your sign?"

"Still checking on me, huh."

Noah's shrug said, "It's what I do."

"I found a place to stash it." He glanced around the room. "I felt funny bringing it in here, besides it costs next to nothing to replace.

My first sign was pretty crude. 'Help! Need money for food.' I had a lot of competition…"

"What's it say now? Your new marketing slogan?"

Corky was chagrined. "It says, '$aving for a beach house. Please help.' It's stupid, I guess, but folks who bother to read it always walk away with a smile. That's usually worth a few coins."

Noah smiled. "Indeed. No more interruptions. Go ahead."

It took Corky a minute to recollect what he was saying. "Anyhow, the summer was pretty good and my wife didn't bitch at me—much. Just asked me to promise I was still looking for a ninety-five, and I did. Promise, that is. I admit, I wasn't looking very hard. Besides, I was easily making above minimum wage—especially when you figure the tax angle—so those jobs were out. But the last few weeks have been real slow and she's pretty fed up. We're lucky; she's a secretary so we got steady money coming in."

Noah drained his coffee. "Tell me why you think you need a lawyer."

Corky nodded and looked toward the counter. "You hungry?" he asked, "I am. How about a sandwich? They got a great turkey club here. Consider it part of my retainer."

Noah shrugged, "I could eat something."

The restroom door was a few feet from their table and Noah was again seated when Corky returned with two stacked club sandwiches, chunks of turkey breast spilling out onto the plastic plate.

Corky wolfed down a couple of bites of the sandwich before resuming his story. "Have you heard of the Road Warrior?"

"The old Mel Gibson movie?"

"No. I…"

"If there's a remake. I missed it."

"I'm serious. I believe the dead guy on the sidewalk is the Road Warrior." Corky stood, "Think about that while I hit the head."

It had grown dark outside; the streetlights were on. Around Noah, the steamy café was crowded with students wearing backpacks, a smattering of nurses and a few smug looking interns. At some of the other tables, folks were engrossed in surfing the Internet from open laptops, a cup of cold coffee or a half-eaten sandwich in front of them.

Corky slid into his chair across the table and Noah said, "I believe you were saying the dead kid looks like Mel Gibson."

"This is no joke. I saw his face before they covered him. I was standing beside you, working up my courage to tell somebody what I knew, when that cop came over. I thought he was coming to take me in, because of the way I'm dressed. Maybe he even thought I did it, and I almost crapped myself. Then I heard you tell him you'd been a state's attorney, but you walked away before I could bring myself to say anything..."

"Still, what does..."

Corky took in a breath. "Look, I'm still shook from seeing him lying there, dead on the sidewalk. I need to tell it in my own way, but I'll get there."

Noah nodded.

"A lot of street people, even the homeless, are capable of surfing the web. A few of them have a laptop or a tablet and anyone can use one of the old PC's at a shelter."

"In addition to a hot meal and a cot, shelters now offer Wi-Fi?"

Corky shrugged. "A few do. They justify the expense by saying it is a cheap and easy way for street people to find work. Anyhow, 'road warrior' is a common term for young streeters, usually teenagers. A few weeks ago, a streeter at one of the shelters was web-surfing and came across a site called 'The Road Warrior.' Most of them, the men anyway, would rather scan porn than look for a job on Monster.com. The streeter who found it probably thought it was a porn site and within minutes everyone was crowded around looking."

"Were you there?"

He shook his head. "It was night. I was home. One of the streeters, Wise Eddie, was there, he told me about it, later. You know what a blog is, right?"

"Yes."

"This Road Warrior wrote a blog about the life lived by street people here in Baltimore. He never says it's Baltimore but the names of the characters and description of locations leave little doubt."

"You've seen this site, yourself?"

Corky nodded. "The day Wise Eddie told me, I went home and logged on. The first couple of weeks Warrior wrote about different places around town where the homeless slept. Under viaducts, library steps, abandoned rowhouses. No street names or landmarks, but anybody from Baltimore could recognize his description of the Enoch Pratt Library.

"He added something new each week, the first week he mentioned Poe and Marvel—and Frenchy. The next week he wrote about Wise Eddie, Skeeter and a crazy old hag everybody calls Mata Hairy.

"Last week Road Warrior starts saying that not everybody who panhandles is poor, some who say they got no food or shelter live in the suburbs and commute into the city."

Noah was beginning to understand why this man might need an attorney.

"How do you connect the dead guy to the blog?"

"The guy under the sheet used to walk around with a cell phone, one with a camera. He roamed around taking pictures and a lot of them appeared on this blog. A page he called Street Scene had shots of the people and places he wrote about."

"That doesn't prove..."

"There's more, and it gets worse for me. A couple of weeks ago, the dead guy strolls up to me and starts asking a lot of questions: How long had I been on the street, where was I from, how did I wind up like this—that kind of thing."

"What was your answer?"

"To steer him away from me, I told some funny stories about a few of the street people. A couple of the stories showed up that week on the blog—almost word for word. I'm sure he was following some of us around to see what he could dig up. I knew he wasn't finished with me."

Noah said, "Assuming for the moment that you did not kill him, I can see why you might need a lawyer. If you went to the cops and told them your story, it wouldn't take them long to find out about your commute and anything else you might want to keep hidden. They may very well stumble across you anyway."

Corky nodded. "I keep thinking about what that cop said, 'Who gives a rat's ass?' If I told them I had been at the scene, they'd say, 'Why look any further, we got our killer-case closed. And there's no way I could prove I didn't do it. Still, I had to tell somebody. You believe me—right?"

2

By the time Noah left Pratt Street, the rush hour was long past and he was home in about ten minutes. Home, for the time being, was a snug apartment on the second floor of a carriage house located in Dickeyville, a historic Baltimore neighborhood. Quaint cottages nestled among white stone and brick duplexes of two and three stories. Each was crowded up against the stone gutters of the narrow, streets leaving the chance visitor with the distinct feeling he had stumbled into a quaint English village. Missing was the ubiquitous red telephone booth outside a local pub.

A new Saab, belonging to the couple living below Noah, was nosed up to the sidewalk leading to their front door. He rarely encountered either of them. The husband works with computers and she is a dental technician.

Noah parked his Saturn Astra next to the Saab and climbed the outside stairway.

Low-watt electric candles glowed in his front windows, casting enough illumination to provide safe passage along the plank balcony to his front door. A seven-inch candle lamp glowed from each of the windows of what he termed his 'great room.' That was his name for the combined kitchen/dining/living room. One additional candle lamp served as a nightlight in his bedroom.

He had been intrigued to find that an electric candle glowing in each window provided sufficient illumination to work at his computer or watch television, which he seldom did.

He initiated low-watt lighting as a way to cut back on his electric bill, out of a pique with the Baltimore Gas & Electric company; not economic necessity. Family money would cover any financial shortfall, at least for the foreseeable future.

Lately, Noah had grown comfortable with the lighting scheme and maneuvered about easily in the semi-darkness. It had occurred to him that, in the unlikely event he brought a woman home, real lights would be required. At least initially.

He first encountered low-watt lighting during the more than two years he had lived with Denise in her Federal Hill townhouse. She had installed flameless wax pillars scented with vanilla and guaranteed to cast a romantic aura over any room. They could be operated with a remote control from a prone position on the carpet or settee, as necessary.

Living alone, he saw no need for scented or remote-controlled lighting. In keeping with the ambiance of the neighborhood, his candles resembled Early American tapers setting on an imitation brass base.

Noah hung up his trench coat, another vestige of his earlier life. Passing the small clear glass computer desk he switched on his Dell laptop. At the refrigerator, he grabbed a bottle of Blue Moon beer while the computer flashed and beeped to life.

After leaving the state's attorney, Noah had secured a brief gig as a DJ on a 50,000-watt Baltimore radio station, 108FM The Crab. When the station went to an all-talk format Noah found himself unemployed again, along with the other jocks and the Crab.

For a while, he kept in touch with one of the jocks, Marty Keegan, known on the air as "The Mad Irishman," a name Noah thought redundant.

For awhile each checked in to see if the other had found work. Both had vowed to plug the other one if he hooked on at another station. Noah hadn't heard from Keegan in weeks and had not bothered to try and reconnect.

It was expected that Keegan, with a big following at 108, would have no trouble finding work. Noah would have heard if the other man were still in town. More likely he had hooked on with a low-watt AM station in Iowa and had no interest in sharing that news with anyone.

Noah maintained email accounts on separate servers, Yahoo for family and friends, Google for Internet purchases and business-related mail.

On Yahoo, Noah had one message from his mother in Wilmington. Was he coming for Thanksgiving? "Where else do you have to go?" she asked.

His clothes, the car and a laptop were all Noah took away from his relationship with Denise. Once Noah had established himself as a first-rate crime-fighting assistant state's attorney, Denise had urged marriage. She chattered about him becoming *the* state's attorney, followed in rapid succession by terms as mayor of Baltimore and governor of Maryland. All this, of course, a prelude to national office.

Noah's premature departure from the state's attorney's office had revealed Denise for the affectation she actually was. She insisted that he use his contacts to hook on with one of the big law firms in town. When he came home and told her he was going to be playing soft rock on local radio, she demanded that he have his things out of her townhouse by the weekend. That was on a Friday.

Noah swigged from the Blue Moon bottle while he retrieved the Google search engine. He entered the site name Corky had supplied, streetsceneroadwarrior.blogspot.com, and patiently scrolled past a list of sites reminiscing about the early Mel Gibson movies. He had forgotten the actual title of the original film was *Mad Max*. *The Road Warrior* was added for the sequel. There was also a site for a Road Warriors pro wrestling tag team and others offering suggestions for weary travelers.

Even though he entered the exact site name, it did not appear until near the bottom of the first screen. The initial edition of The Road Warrior, dated October 1st, was followed by three others dated October 15th, November 1st and November 12th. The last just three days ago.

The blog began as a very amateurish effort. There were no graphics and the two black- and- white pictures in the middle of the page did little to break up a formless block of black text. The Road Warrior had introduced himself by saying:

"Hi Friends,
In the following months those of you who have the stomach for it, will learn facts about the 'mean streets' of Baltimore which no other reporter has the courage to reveal.
I intend to strip away the flimsy façade the city's politicians' have put in place to deceive you, revealing instead a City that is a mere Potemkin Village created to hide the filth, corruption and agony choking our streets. For all you Street People who have asked yourself—
DOES ANYONE GIVE A RAT'S ASS ABOUT ME?
The answer is—I do. If you dare to journey with me, we will walk miles; nay we will walk leagues, in the shoes of other men. For the rest of you—
If you have the courage to know the truth,
Check It Out."

Below this outburst, the Road Warrior had posted a small photo of an ancient bag lady laboring behind a shopping cart piled high with collected debris. She wore a discarded man's overcoat and long strands of greasy grey hair appeared from beneath a knit cap covering her head. Under the picture he had written:

"This lady, and despite her appearance she is as much a lady as any other, is known on our streets as Mata Hairy. The cart she struggles with is not laden with mere junk. Sadly, it contains her heritage."

The other picture was the snapshot of a ragged form of a man staggering across a broad thoroughfare against traffic. The caption said simply:

GOODBYE CRUEL WORLD!

At the bottom of the page, Road Warrior invited all readers to join his crusade by emailing accounts and/or photos of 'The Street Scene' to the Road Warrior at a gmail address.

The blog's second installment repeated the introduction, followed by more photos under the Street Scene banner.

The first photo was a stark picture of the empty space beneath a viaduct spanning a major downtown thoroughfare. It resembled nothing more than a cold and grimy cement vault. Road Warrior had written:

YOU ARE LOOKING INTO SOMEONE'S BEDROOM.

Just below this line appeared a second photo of the same bridge after dark, the empty space now cluttered with pieces of plastic and canvas fashioned into crude shelters. To one side, several men warmed themselves as best they could around flames flaring from a scarred steel drum. Under the picture it read:

IT IS THERE BEDROOM.

Noah smiled. *Well, we know one thing—the Road Warrior was not an English major.*

On the next page, was depicted a harsh street scene of empty and decaying rowhouses, many with sheets of plywood where windows and doors had been.

THIS IS STILL SOMEONE'S HOME.

In the foreground of the accompanying photo, several street people were tearing away at the plywood covering with bare hands.

NOW IT IS THERE HOME.

In the background, two vehicles were parked curbside.

Down the block, the faint image of a man crossing the street, hand in hand with two young children.

The page ended with a repeat of the plea for input from his readers.

Noah wondered why Road Warrior had failed to include color photos that would provide an alluring contrast to the drab pages. The pictures did not appear to be staged and were very likely taken covertly by a cell phone camera, so color would be a ready option. Noah sensed that the drab black-and-white pictures were intended to be consistent with the mood Road Warrior was trying to project. For these people, life was bleak, colorless, and that is the way it should feel to his readers.

The penultimate entry by the Road Warrior was more of the same.

A narrow alley cluttered with dumpsters and over flowing trashcans, followed by:

THIS IS SOMEONE'S DINING ROOM.

Continuing his before and after display, the next photo depicted the same alley with two street people scrounging through the trashcans.

IT IS THERE DINING ROOM.

The last picture was a single shot of a grubby man holding a sign reading 'homeless pleaz help.'

Below it Road Warrior had written,
"Is this man really homeless? More next week."

Noah studied the photo, relieved that the man pictured was not that of Corky Kilmark, his new client.

At the bottom of the page, Road Warrior had displayed, with some satisfaction it seemed, a recently received email. The message congratulated him on his humanitarian effort and requested a face-to-face meeting so that the writer could reveal some vital information. Apparently, a time and location for the meeting was set, though those details, along with the sender's address, had been omitted. Road Warrior signed off with "I'll be there."

The most recent of the posted blogs was dated November 12th and, Noah reasoned, if Corky was right about the form under the sheet, it would be the Road Warrior's final publication.

More depressing pictures of the cityscape preceded an anecdote about Wise Eddie. Corky had not told Noah which of Wise Eddie's antics he had passed on, but this must be it. The Road Warrior's account was rough and lacked detail; merely that it had taken place last summer. According to the story, Wise Eddie kept on the move and rarely slept in the same spot two nights in a row. He spoke of lurking enemies, real or imagined, and thus he took no chances. Wise Eddie scavenged in the neighborhood of a string of rowhouses in the process of being rehabbed. One evening, Eddie rummaged through a rusting green dumpster sitting at the curb. Much to his delight, it contained discarded pieces of lumber, wallboard, paneling, insulation and packing material. All dry, no garbage.

Thrilled with his discovery, Eddie had tossed in the two shopping bags containing his worldly possessions and climbed in after them. He wedged a piece of two- by-four under the lid providing an air space and settled in for the night.

Early the next morning, Wise Eddie was roused by loud banging and quickly realized a trash truck was hoisting his bedroom. He flung open the metal cover, followed his shopping bags over the side and dropped to the ground. He grabbed up his bags and fled down the street, followed by screams and curses from the truck's crew.

Road Warrior used the story to highlight the peril faced by Street People merely to find a safe place to sleep.

The site posted several more pictures, one of which captured Noah's particular interest. A man in a dark suit and matching overcoat was striding fiercely toward the camera. Though nearly half-a-block away, he appeared to be bearing down, angry with the person taking his picture.

This edition ended with a comment directed at the person who had emailed him previously about a meeting.

'Sorry you didn't show. I waited an hour and I'm still anxious to talk. Let me here from you.'
Road Warrior

That night Noah slept in fits and starts, dragging himself out of bed before 7 a.m. After a quick breakfast of juice and Cheerios, he poured a cup of coffee and set about booting up his computer.

Curious to learn what coverage was being given the stabbing, he did not bother with his email, going directly to *The Baltimore Sun* online. As he had anticipated, very little was said. A few lines buried in the Metro section reported that police were investigating the stabbing death of an unidentified male victim around 3p.m. yesterday on Penn Street.

Noah reasoned that if the victim was still a John Doe, it might mean that he had never been fingerprinted, in which case it could be some time before they would learn his identity. Or it might be that no one at *The Sun* had bothered to follow up on the killing. Noah suspected that, given the circumstances surrounding the death, the public had heard the last of this particular John Doe.

3

Corky Kilmark stared into the first cup of morning coffee, his mind in turmoil about his next move. The right move.

The night before he had been met at the door by his wife, Cindy. She followed him into the kitchen, where he went directly to the refrigerator.

"Are you hungry?"

"Thanks, but no. Remember, I got a sandwich at Cup of Joe."

He scooped a couple of handfuls of ice cubes into a pitcher, reached for a lemon, then grabbed a bottle of Coke and proceeded into the living room.

Cindy hurried after him. "Something happened? You're in trouble—please tell me."

Corky stopped at the faux tiki bar in the corner of the small living room, retrieving two tall glasses from the overhead rack.

"I need this first."

She sat at one of the bamboo bar stools fidgeting while he made their drinks.

A few years before, when both were employed, they had planned a visit to Hawaii, a particular dream of Cindy's. Fate, bad luck, karma, whatever you choose to call it, had stepped in as it is wont to do, and they were forced to settle for this imitation island bar from Costco.

For a time, they had sat on the stools, drinks in hand, grumbling about the damn bar being a piss-poor substitute for a visit to The Islands.

Even a dinner at a nice restaurant or an evening at the movies had become a luxury. To their chagrin, this bar had become their sole refuge in an increasingly wretched world.

Corky fixed her drink and slid the glass across the bar before settling onto the accompanying bar stool. Though in no mood for celebration he raised his glass in customary salute.

Her eyes widened as he spoke of happening onto the murder, sparing her the details of the death scene. Corky was proceeding to tell her about his meeting with the former state's attorney when she spoke out.

"Are you afraid that you might be the next one killed? Is that it?"

He drank from his glass and shook his head.

"I really hadn't thought about that."

"Well what..."

"You'll see, just let me tell it."

"Go on" she said, swirling her drink.

He related his theory that the murdered boy was the Road Warrior.

"The cops think it was one bum killing another bum, nothing more. I have a feeling that it was something else. He was digging up dirt and might have stumbled onto something that got him killed. If the dead guy was the Road Warrior, there will be no more blog, so we'll never know what he might have told us."

Cindy Kilmark was petite and outwardly demure, but when she became frightened or angry she could be as scrappy as a woman twice her size. Corky had this in mind when she questioned him about the man he was with at the Cup of Joe. Not in the mood to withstand one of her outbursts, Corky chose to withhold his fear of arrest from the account.

"We were both shook about seeing the man, a boy really, lying there dead, and we were headed in the same direction, to our cars, You're lucky it was a coffee shop and not a bar or I might not have made it home."

Her husband's manner seemed strangely at odds with his words, but Cindy decided to pursue that another time. Instead, she said,

"Assuming the dead man is the Road Warrior, what do you know about him? Did you ever talk to him?"

"I saw him around some, and yeah, we talked a couple of times."

She made air quotation marks with her fingers . "What do the 'street people' have to say about him?"

"It just happened. How is anyone going to know it was The Road Warrior unless I tell them? Even if one of them knew something, they wouldn't say anything to anyone."

She gave him a quizzical look.

"It would get back to the cops that they knew something and they'd wind up in the chair for it."

"In the chair?"

"Not electrocuted. You know, Cind, being questioned about the murder. Maybe even arrested."

Corky saw this as a chance to prepare her, just in case things got worse. He added, "Anyone who maybe just talked to the dead guy could be in trouble."

"Then you must leave those awful streets. Stay home and never go back. Be done with it."

He shook his head. "That's the worst thing I could do. When they find out I disappeared from the street the day after the killing, I'll move ahead of everybody else right to the top of their list."

Cindy said, "How would they know if you weren't there? What's one street bum more or less?"

Corky stood, added ice to his glass, and topped it off with more rum and a splash of Coca-Cola. He nodded to her and she placed a hand over her glass.

Back on his stool, he said, "How would they know? Somebody would tell them."

"Why, would…"

"Think about it. The street will be talking about the murder of one of its own until something else comes along that is more exciting. The cops won't even have to be working on the murder. Streeters are always getting locked up for something. Right away they'll blurt out, 'I got a name for you, officer. Corkscrew hasn't shown up since that guy got stabbed.' Or worse, 'Corkscrew is the guy you want for that knifing on Penn Street.' So you see…"

"Corkscrew? You're Corkscrew?"

"Well, yeah. That's my street name. Nobody on the street uses his given name." Corky looked away. "I had to come up with something and I thought it might make me sound—you know—tough."

Cindy tried to keep from smiling as she pushed her glass toward him. "Corkscrew. That calls for another drink."

It occurred to her to ask, "Is Corkscrew the only name those street people know you by?"

He nodded.

"Think now, did you never tell *anyone* your given name?"

Corky freshened her drink while he spoke. "I don't have to think about it. It never came up. It's been so long since most streeters used their real names they can't remember them and they damn sure don't care what yours is."

Cindy took her glass from him and raised it, returning his earlier salute. "Even if the cops learn that stupid nickname, they can't find you from that. Besides, you said they are looking for another bum. So, even if they somehow found you, once they see you are not an actual bum they'll go away."

Corky shook his head and drank deeply.

Later, he lay in bed staring at the ceiling while Cindy slept beside him, her breathing even. At one point, he was certain that a noise in the street was the police coming for him. That was at 3:30 according to the digital clock. The next time he noticed the time it was 5:42. The interval had passed so quickly that he must have dozed off.

Corky pulled the covers around him and feigned sleep until Cindy left for work. Later, when he walked into the kitchen he found a note on the counter next to the coffee pot.

Corkscrew

Be careful out there!

Love, Me

He smiled at Cindy's quote. One of their favorite lines from reruns of the old cop show *Hill Street Blues.*

Corky shook his head and forced himself to quit staring into his coffee cup. His laptop had finished booting up and he focused on the screen-saver, a colorful wallpaper of all the characters from *The Simpsons.* It lifted his spirits, as it always did, and he reluctantly replaced it with the home page of *The Baltimore Sun* on-line. When the headline he feared, "Corkscrew sought in slaying," did not appear, he scrolled through to the Metro section. The relief he felt when his name was not among the few lines of the story, quickly approached panic, when he heard a car brake to a stop and the slamming of a car door just outside.

Corky found his parking spot, stopped for a carryout at the Cup of Joe and hurried directly to his street corner. The slamming car door earlier had forced him to a decision. The sound had been his next-door neighbor, who sped off mere minutes later, now late for work. A neighbor in a hurry to get to work had frightened him so much that his body shook for several minutes. He would not live his life panicked by life's everyday sounds.

On the drive in this morning, though alone, he spoke aloud about his own cowardice.

"Today should be no different than yesterday. You didn't kill anybody, so why should the fact that you came walking by just after it happened change your life? And don't blame your fear on a guilty conscience. You are not guilty of anything—except being a phony bum—and not telling your wife the real reason you are afraid. Neither of which is a crime. See what I mean? Not only are you afraid for no reason, you're even afraid to tell your wife why you're scared. Such a wuss. Time to man up, Corkscrew."

Corky stood on the corner of Pratt and Howard Streets feeling better about himself. Having donned his sign, he held his empty coffee cup out to strangers. He was at his usual spot, following his daily routine. There was no reason why he should not.

Two street people shuffled toward him. He recognized them as Choo-Choo and Frenchy. Watching them approach, it occurred to him that the young man lying dead on the sidewalk, the Road Warrior, was not actually a street person. The few times that Corky had seen him moving about the city, he was in full stride, a man with a purpose. Street people, having no purpose, no place they were required to be, invariably shuffled about, having no anxiety over being late for a non-existent appointment.

Choo-Choo, though stooped by age, remained a head taller than most others when moving about the streets. He was easily identifiable by the denim engineer's cap and grimy bib overalls that were his uniform.

Frenchy kept her face hidden beneath a silk headscarf tied tight below the chin. She was said to be much older than Choo-Choo, but Corky knew of no one who had peered beneath the grimy scarf to be certain. The pair could usually be found at Penn Station on North Charles Street or the B&O Railroad Museum on West Pratt Street. Corky guessed the museum was their destination this morning.

Choo Choo touched the bill of his cap. "Mornin,'" he said, with the husky voice of a heavy smoker.

Frenchy uttered a few words of gibberish which she imagined was fluent French.

Corky nodded to each one in turn. "Good morning. Nice day for a stroll."

Choo Choo snorted "Better'n yesterday for some. Like the one got stabbed over by the hospital. You know him?"

Corky shrugged. "Saw him on the street a couple of times. Said howdy, nodded to one another. Like that. You got a name for him?"

"Nope. Don't recollect ever seein' him. But, I can tell you for danged certain...sorry." He nodded to the woman, "She don't like me to curse. As I was sayin,' it's for certain he wasn't one of us."

"Why do you say that?"

"'Cause the poleese is out askin' about him. They was up to the Pennsylvania train station early this mornin' roustin' us and threatnin' like they do. They ain't goin' to all that trouble for a actual streeter."

Without waiting for a response, Choo Choo took a few steps in the direction of the museum, Frenchy at his heels. He stopped and looked back. "You the one they call Corkscrew?"

Corky nodded, his throat suddenly very dry.

"They was askin' about you—the cops. I 'spect they'll be calling on you real soon." He put a finger to the bill of his engineer's cap, "Good day, to you." he added.

With no place to sit down, Corky, head spinning, stumbled over to a blue mailbox and clung to it like a drowning man. It was several minutes before he recovered enough to take out his cell phone.

Last night, at the Cup of Joe, he persisted until Noah Cassidy had reluctantly given up his own cell phone number.

"For five bucks I should at least get a damn phone number," he had declared.

Corky had programmed the number into his own phone as Noah spoke, and now he pressed one button.

"Mister Cassidy—Noah! Corky Kilmark. You're still my lawyer, right?"

4

"I'm your attorney, for the time being," Noah answered. "Is there a problem?"

"The kid was no streeter. 'Cause they're out early this morning rousting street people."

"How did you hear of this?"

"Cops asked a couple of other streeters about me."

"That's it?"

"That's it? Isn't that enough? Why were they asking about me? They must've heard something, but I didn't ask Choo Choo what he told them. I thought that it might make me look guilty, someway. You know how on TV the perp always asks, 'What did you tell the cops?' Besides, Choo-Choo asked me if I was Corkscrew, so he couldn't tell 'em nothing. He didn't know for sure who I was."

At the other end of the call, Noah shook his head. "Corkscrew? Choo Choo? What the hell is this?"

"I told you last night, everybody out here has a street name. I didn't really think about that when I first hit the street and somebody asked my name. I got out 'Cork' before it struck me that I didn't want them knowing who I was. I finished with 'screw' that's all I could think of."

"What's Choo Choo's story?"

"He claims to have been an engineer on the Erie Lackawanna railroad. Always wears bib overalls and one of those striped railroad caps..."

"What did you tell him?"

"I was real cool about it. Just said that I had run into the guy on the street and maybe talked to him, just to say hello."

"Then that's what you tell the cops if they ask you. Nothing else. And certainly not a word about your idea that he was 'the Road Warrior.'"

"But, I figure if I was helping, it would look better for me."

"Jesus. I guess you think that because you are not really paying me you don't have to listen to what I tell you, Is that it?"

"No."

"If you don't do what I say now, I won't be able to help you when you need me. The 'Road Warrior' thing is our pocket ace. When the time is right to play that card, it needs to come from me and not you."

"Won't it be better coming from me?"

Noah drew a sharp breath and, after a pause, said, "I know you're scared and not thinking straight so let me explain. You've heard cops on TV say 'whatever you say can be used against you in a court of law'; that's true, but whatever your attorney says can't be used against you."

Corky said nothing and Noah stayed quiet, letting him think it through. When Corky spoke it was in a tiny voice.

"I see what you are saying and I want to do it that way, but I'm not sure I can."

"Why not?"

"Suppose they gang up when they question me. Or, God forbid, take me to the station. I'm not sure how well I will hold up. If I get scared, I might tell them about the Road Warrior to get them to stop." After a moment he said, "What if I tell them to talk to you, or that my lawyer told me not to say anything unless he is there? Then they can't ask me anything else, right? Like on television."

Noah told himself that his client was like a million others whose only experience with the police was gleaned from TV cop shows like, *Law & Order* and *CSI*. Unfortunately, they think that's how it is in the real world.

This must be what private practice is like.

Into the phone he snapped, "What street person has an attorney on retainer? Even if it is only five dollars. You tell them that and the next time we talk it will be in a jail visiting room."

Corky nodded, before realizing that he had to speak to be understood. "I see, you're right, you're right."

"Another thing. They'll ask your given name and where you slept last night. Tell them."

"But, then they'll know I'm a phony panhandler."

"Fortunately for you—and the politicians of America—being a phony is not yet a crime, but lying to the police is. Now, do you want to help yourself?"

"Of course. What kind of question…"

"I scanned the Road Warrior site last night and saw something interesting. Have you looked at it lately?"

"Ya. A lot."

"You remember the picture of a white man in a dark suit and overcoat? Fierce looking, as if he's coming after the person taking his picture?"

"You think he's…"

"You know his name?"

"Uh…no."

"Find out."

5

After Noah Cassidy hung up, he quickly punched in a familiar phone number .

"Baltimore City State's attorney's Office."

"Jen Stambaugh, please…"

"Jennifer Stambaugh's office."

"Helen, its Noah Cassidy. Is she available?"

"Mister Cassidy, nice to hear your voice. Hang on a sec."

He was pleased with the thought that he would not be forced to listen to some God-awful music, just as an obscure country and western song, sung with full nasal twang, assailed his hearing. Mercifully, it was quickly replaced by a throaty voice.

"Noah Cassidy. You must want something."

"Whose idea was it to torture callers with that frightful music?"

"The new man's."

"Must be his plan to reduce the caseload. No one is going to call there once it's known they will have to endure that."

"I'm flattered that out of all of the assistants in this office, I'm the one you called to complain to about our music."

Noah laughed. "Actually, I wasn't certain you would be there. I read where the new man has made some changes."

"What can I do for you?" she said, her voice now sober.

Strictly business.

"I need to speak to a homicide detective and I thought you might be able to get me to the right man—sorry—person."

"I'm terribly busy right now, but I would like to catch up. Do you have something to write on?"

"Yes. Go ahead."

She gave him her cell phone number and rang off.

Noah placed his laptop on a small table and draped his trench coat over the back of the table's lone wooden chair. The table he had chosen was wedged into a front corner of the Cup of Joe, the chair backed against the brick wall. Though not a police officer, he had socialized with enough of them to assimilate their unspoken rule of never sitting with his back to the door in a public establishment.

It was only a few steps to the counter for his coffee, still he maintained a wary eye on his coat and computer, either of which could be a target in this neighborhood.

He was soon back at the table sipping his coffee and watching the occasional truck rumble along Pratt Street while his computer found its way onto the WiFi network offered by the shop. When the Sun's online story appeared, it contained more detail than Noah had expected.

City police have identified the victim of yesterday's stabbing in the one hundred block of Penn Street as Jason J. Jefferson of the six hundred block Southmont Road, Catonsville. Jefferson, nineteen, was a student at the Catonsville campus of the Community College of Baltimore, County. A man answering the telephone at the Jefferson residence said that the victim was "A wonderful boy who enjoyed the support of a loving family and lived at home." The man added that the victim "was certainly not a panhandling bum."

A spokesperson for the Baltimore City Police Department commented that this incident appeared to be a random street killing.

The article ended with the usual line that the police have no motive or suspects, followed by a standard request that anyone with information should call the tip line.

Noah was surprised that the observation about this being a random street killing had crept into the story. Someone from the city tourist bureau would most likely register a strong complaint with *The Sun*. Routinely, if the media could not in good conscience report that the victim was involved in drugs or had otherwise been a deserving target for murder, nothing would be mentioned.

What this piece said to the city's visitors, businessmen and tourists was, "Come to downtown Baltimore and take your chances along with the rest of us."

6

Noah thrust his way through the after-work crowd clustered around a pool table, pausing to allow a player finish his shot. Then he sidled through an array of revelers and greeted the bronze statue of President Ronald Reagan with a passing nod.

The Ropewalk Tavern, situated in Baltimore's tony Federal Hill, magnetically attracted TGIF worshippers who toiled all week a few blocks north on Charles Street.

Noah made his way to the antique back bar, where he claimed the two remaining bar chairs. Once seated, he draped his trench coat over the adjoining chair and waited for Mark the bartender to finish with a customer.

Ropewalk's four spacious bars were spread among several rooms on three floors. Originally a cask and barrel warehouse, the tavern managed to retain the historical nature of the nineteenth-century buildings even amidst the flat-screen television sets mounted around the room.

Walls of exposed red brick encased heavy plank flooring and brawny angular support beams. Numerous statues of cigar store Indians correctly suggested that Ropewalk was a cigar bar, while the life-size likeness of President Reagan proclaimed that Ropewalk was defiantly a Republican bar in a heavily Democratic city. A dot of red bobbing in a sea of blue.

In spite of his bulk, Mark moved along the bar with ease. While drawing a draft beer he caught Noah's eye.

"Blue Moon, Belgian White with a slice of orange on the rim, right?"

"That's amazing," Noah replied.

Mark shrugged. "You haven't been in for a while." He indicated the crowd, two and three deep at the bar. "Sorry, but I can't bring up the name."

"It has been a while. It's Noah," he called as Mark hurried away to the cold box.

When Jen had agreed to meet here, she sounded almost eager at the prospect of seeing him again. Noah had been an assistant state's attorney for almost a year when she came to the office. For a time, they had engaged in some meaningless flirtation. He identified a spark there, but was already with Denise and one day Jen encountered Drew Jordan, a city homicide detective, and any flirtation abruptly ended.

Mark sat the glass of beer with the orange garnish in front of Noah amid inquiring glances from some at the bar. "How does he get special service?" The looks asked.

"Tab?"

Noah nodded. "Yes, thanks. I'm expecting someone, if you could keep an eye on me."

Mark motioned at the sea of faces clamoring for alcohol. "I'll do my best."

Noah dropped the slice of orange into the glass and raised it to his mouth. As he surveyed the boisterous throng, it occurred to him that he was very close to the upper age limit for this crowd. They all appeared to be twenty-somethings, making him almost a senior citizen at thirty-two.

Out of the corner of his eye he noticed men stepping aside as Jennifer Stambaugh made her way toward him. Only moments before, he had been forced to battle his way across this stretch of floor which now parted like the Red Sea, creating a lane for her. She left a wake of admiring glances from the men and looks of envy from the women.

"Sorry I'm late," she said and draped her coat on top of his before sliding into the chair. "Some emergency at work. You remember those days."

"Yes, but not fondly. What are you having?"

"A mojito. Good luck with that anytime soon."

Mark materialized before them.

"Mark, say hello to Jen."

Mark nodded.

"A mojito for Jen and it'll save a trip if you bring me another."

Mark was gone and Jen said, "That was impressive. Getting his attention in this crowd."

"Mark's a hustler."

Jen crossed her legs and swung around to face him.

Noah had almost forgotten how desirable she looked away from the office. He hoped that his feelings were not registered on his face.

She was saying, "Of course, I'm anxious to know why you called, but first let me explain my brusque manner on the phone. The new boss has banned *all* personal calls on office phones. Years ago when he was here as an assistant, someone in the office was selling trial information to some gamblers. He is obsessive about that not occurring on his watch. We never know who might be listening, so I'm all business on the office phone."

"There's always your cell."

Jen shook her head. "Forbidden within the office. Connie, his secretary, conducts spot checks in the ladies room, and his toady Duane patrols the men's."

Noah raised his glass in salute. "Thank you, Jen."

"For what?"

"For affirming my wisdom in leaving that place. How do you do it?"

"Of course I think about leaving. But I love being a prosecutor. Slamming the cell door on the bad guys. And bosses come and go. We were happy when he came now we're hoping he'll be gone after the next election. If you think you might need to call me again, a quick call on my cell and I'll give you my home number."

Why not give it to me now? She wants me to jump through all the hoops. Fair enough.

She sipped her spritzer and smiled. "Enough about that office, why did you call after all this time?"

Noah said, "It can't be work-related, because I don't have any work. Let's say its curiosity-related."

"You must know that this is not good for a girl's ego. What does that mean, curiosity-related?"

"In the first place, with all the eyes following you as you played Moses parting the sea, I think it would be a big step for mankind to have your ego deflated just a bit."

"Sounds like a compliment hiding in there somewhere."

Noah watched for a reaction as he said, "I called about The Jason Jefferson murder."

"I have no idea what that is. Should I?"

"Not from work. It's much too early for homicide to bring the case to your office. I thought maybe Drew had mentioned it."

Jen set her glass on the bar and gave him an appraising look. "Drew and I are not together. Haven't been for almost six months. But, since you didn't know that, you wouldn't have been calling me for anything personal."

She laid a hand on his arm. "I just assumed—"

Noah nodded. "—that everybody knows. I haven't spoken to anybody from the office since—well it's been a long time. And I'm going to assume that you had not heard that Denise and I were split."

"On the contrary. Your life is the subject of much speculation around the office."

Noah had no response and they sat for a moment, until he shook off the silence. "Ropewalk claims the best crab cakes in town," he said. "And it was true the last time I had one."

"Let's find out. Though it doesn't matter. I'm hungry enough to eat the second best."

The hostess led them back through the bar to a dining room, deposited their drinks and menus while informing them that Max would be their server.

Jen raised her glass in salute. "We didn't do this before, but I think it's appropriate."

"I agree," he said and touched his glass lightly against hers. "To friends and lovers."

She returned his gaze. "May we have the wisdom to tell them apart."

They smiled and simultaneously broke the spell to taste their drinks.

"It's much quieter up here. How do you know the bartender, Mark?"

"Denise has a rowhouse—she prefers to call it a townhouse—a couple of blocks from here. I lived there while we were together. I usually came here and I always ordered this." He raised his glass. "Apparently the drink is more memorable than am I. That's what he recalled."

"You haven't been here in awhile?"

He nodded.

"It must not bother you to come here without her?"

Noah laughed. "Actually it feels right. She wouldn't set foot in the place. Said it was too loud. Got on her nerves. I think it was all the younger women who got on her nerves. Anyhow, it gave me a good place to hide out."

Jen sat quietly looking into her glass.

He said, "That's enough about Denise. Are you up to talking about what happened with you and Drew?"

Without looking up she said, "It ended badly. That's all I want to say for now. Later, if it might be important, I'll tell you." She shuddered as she shook off a disturbing memory and managed a smile.

"I just thought of something. A few months after you left the office, I was dial surfing on my radio when I heard you talking about the Doobie Brothers on some FM station. I listened for a few minutes then I had to go to a hearing. I purposely didn't change the station so that I could find you again."

"108FM The Crab."

"But the next time I turned it on; instead of you there was a panel of local pundits sounding off about the political scene in Baltimore. Were you really a DJ? Do they still call them DJs? After all, there have been no disks to jockey for many years."

"You didn't imagine it. And yes, they still call us—them—DJs."

Just then, Max arrived clad in the ubiquitous uniform of a trendy
wait staffer, black pants, crisp white shirt, red bow tie and black vest.
He opened his pad, hesitating when he realized that their menus lay
undisturbed.

"Do you want me to come back?"

"No," Noah said and looked at Jen, who nodded as he spoke.
"We both want the crab cake dinner with the house salad."

Jen smiled approval when he ordered the Gorgonzola dressing.

"Anything to start?"

Noah touched his glass. "Another Blue Moon and a mojito for
the lady."

When Max was gone, Noah drained his glass and returned it
carefully to the table, saying nothing.

"Well?" She said.

"I'm trying to figure out how to answer your question—how did
I wind up as a DJ—without boring you unconscious."

"Thanks for being so considerate. Start at the beginning, I'll
drink while you talk and when I start yawning, you stop."

"Fair enough. I believe you know that I did my undergrad at the
University of Delaware."

Jen nodded.

"The school had a campus radio station which played a mix of
soft rock and light classical music during the evening hours."

She made a face.

"It was supposed to be soothing so as not to disrupt the student
body while it studied into the night."

"Studied its brains out."

"I was billed as 'Hopalong' Cassidy because I—" Noah made air
quotes with his fingers "'rode along' with them every night while
they studied, or whatever it was they might be doing."

Jen was laughing. "Who is Hopalong Cassidy, some cartoon
rabbit?"

"He was a movie cowboy circa Roy Rogers and Gene Autry. We
share the same last name, so Hopalong has been an alias of mine
since childhood.

"I moved on to the University of Baltimore law school and was able to get a couple of fill-in gigs at a local station. So when I left the state's attorney it was a natural segue for me. It didn't last long, as you know. After a few months, 108 went to an all-talk format so I was back on the street along with the Crab. Let's say I'm taking a sabbatical while I explore new horizons."

Noah paused while Max served their drinks.

Jen, amused by the story, waited for Max to depart before raising her hand.

Noah grinned. "Do you have a question or do you have to go to the bathroom?"

"Both, I guess. You can think of an answer to my question while I'm gone. I want the real story behind why you left the office?"

Noah wasn't surprised by the question, only the fact that it had taken this long for her to ask it. Usually it was the first thing anyone familiar with his history said, after "Hello." Well, no matter, he would counter with a question and then provide his customary response.

When Jen returned, she scrutinized his face for an indication of his answer. Getting no signal she said, "Should I repeat the question, or ask a different one?"

"No need for either. I would have been amazed if you hadn't asked. And I will respond, but first I am curious to know what you have heard."

"Those who were present when you came out of her office said that your face was twisted with rage. Almost maniacal. In case you wondered, that's why they scattered and left you alone. Next thing anyone knew you had cleared out your office and gone. As for the rumors, well they run the gamut; you snapped and have been in an institution, you took money to fix a case, you are a racist and or bigot who refused to work for a black woman…"

"That last one makes no sense. She didn't change race and gender after I was hired."

"Are you saying the others do make sense?"

"Well, neither is true, but they are at least plausible."

"One thing that those who knew you agreed on: You were going places."

"I believed that, too, but it didn't take long for me to realize some of them were places I wouldn't want to be."

He studied the empty glass twirling between his fingers. "It's hard to explain and even harder to understand. I am a small-town boy at heart. Probably best described as a naive idealist."

"Even quixotic?"

"Sure. Why not. I came out of law school ready to wield the terrible sword of justice, smite the bad guys and make the city safe for everyone. Well, I charged around on my white horse, much like Hopalong Cassidy saving the townfolk, when suddenly I hit the stone wall that is local politics. I soon realized that some of the places I was headed, I couldn't go and still be me when I got there. I know that it sounds banal..." Noah straightened to make room for his dinner. "Speaking of knights to the rescue, Max is here to save the day."

They had ordered their crab cakes broiled, not fried, and both were pleased with the golden disks set before them. The cakes bulged with succulent lump crab meat and were accompanied by sides of fries and cole slaw. He had purposely chosen the tavern fries, served in a beach cup with malt vinegar and salt; Jen the sweet potato fries, to be shared.

Noah said, "What do you think—best in the city?"

"That's like asking who has the best cheese steak in Philadelphia? Hard to imagine one better, though."

Jen carefully speared a cherry tomato on her salad plate.

"What's next?" she asked. "You must have something in mind for yourself."

Except for his friend Jack Douglas, no one knew about the idea he'd had for some time now. If he and Jen became a couple he would know when the time was right to tell her. In the meantime he gave his stock answer, "I'm taking a sabbatical for a few months while I sort some things out."

Jen offered no comment and they ate in silence. When her plate was empty, she smiled, "I told you I was hungry," she said, sorry that the fries were gone.

"There's always dessert."

She shook her head.

"There was not much conviction in your denial there, counselor. The Rumple Demint sundae tastes better than it sounds…"

"It would have to."

"…And the Apple Pie Funnel Fries are not to be missed."

"I'll settle for coffee."

After the coffees were ordered, Jen said, "We are to the coffee and have not yet spoken about why you to called me. Something about a murder?"

Noah, being intentionally vague, said, "Actually, you have already answered that. I was going to ask you to put me in touch with Drew. It's a low-priority street killing which is likely to appear as a mere blip on homicide's radar. I came along just after it happened and, out of habit I suppose, I came up with some theories and wanted to talk to somebody about them."

"I…"

Noah held up a hand. "I know how overworked they are, and this is a nothing case if ever there was one."

Jen looked away. "Drew and I ended badly," she repeated. After a moment she added, "But there is someone I can call."

"Again, if you want to talk about it. About anything, I'm a very good listener."

"For now I'll just say he seemed to relish knocking around people who couldn't fight back—and he didn't always leave it at work."

"I'm sorry…?"

She held up a hand. "Its history and I'm moving on. If you give me your cell number I'll have the detective call you."

"Someone I might have worked with?"

Jen smiled. "I hope you like surprises."

7

Detective VoShaun Taylor was seated at a table for two, sipping a latte, when Noah approached. She had declined to meet at Peace and a Cup of Joe, opting instead for the Starbucks on North Charles Street. "I need to be downtown," she told him on the phone.

"Detective Taylor?" Noah asked.

"VoShaun's good—Mister Cassidy."

"Noah works for me," he said. "I'll be right back."

I see what Jen meant about surprises. Glad I wore a business suit, he thought, as he waited in line. *She's a classy lady. If I'd worn that ratty sport coat there's a good chance she wouldn't take me seriously. Worse, she might think I didn't take her seriously. Wasn't showing respect.*

He set his cup on the table and took the chair across from her.

"What exotic concoction did you get?" VoShaun asked.

"Just a cup of coffee."

She laughed. "Shocking."

Noah found her particularly stunning when she laughed. Perfect white teeth enclosed by full lips lightly rouged. Captivating brown eyes, accented by skin the color and milky texture of *café au lait*. Her tan pants suit seemed too snug to conceal a firearm. She was saying...

"...I will be candid with you; I am not certain why we are here. It's a nothing case and if Jen hadn't insisted I wouldn't be."

"She insisted?"

"When I took her call, she said right off, 'I'm calling in that favor you owe me, so I had no choice, but to say yes."

"What kind of favor?"

VoShaun watched him and sipped her coffee, as she considered her response.

Noah waved a hand over the table. "Forget it. None of my business."

"It's not a big deal and Jen will tell you if you ask her. As you may have noticed, I'm not a grizzled veteran detective."

"Now that you mention it."

"A few months ago she was prepping me to testify in my first murder trial when we realized I had screwed some of the paperwork. It wasn't terrible—a rookie mistake, but I was scared. If I told the truth, I could be in trouble, still I wasn't going to perjure myself and she wasn't going to let me. Somehow, she worked it out so that I didn't testify about that particular thing. Saved me at least an ass-chewing, and maybe a visit from the suits."

"Jen's a damn fine lawyer."

"She says the same about you. That you are one of the good ones and it was a shame you had to leave over there."

He laughed. "I guess we can agree that she and I are certifiably wonderful and move on to the case."

"Fine," she said, "Tell me your story."

Noah gave her the same edited version he had told Jen. "If I hadn't happened by the scene, I wouldn't give it a second thought. Now I have a professional curiosity to see if my gut instinct is even close. You referred to the killing as a 'nothing case.'"

"That was flip and very unprofessional of me. It is certainly not a nothing case to Jason Jefferson's family, still it is not one I would expect someone with your background to find interesting. Please forgive me."

Noah nodded. "Forgotten."

"After we found out the boy wasn't a bum, we had two teams out talking to every street person we could find."

"Nothing?"

"Pretty much. One thing—we were told of a panhandler calls himself 'Corkscrew.' You won't believe it. He's on the street but is married, lives in Randallstown and," VoShaun wiggled her fingers in air quotes, "'commutes' to work every day."

47

Her mention of his client jogged Noah's memory and he reflexively patted the pocket where he carried his cell phone.

I was in such a rush this morning, I forgot to turn on my phone. I hope 'Corkscrew' didn't get jammed up.

VoShaun was saying, "It doesn't look like a bum killing so much as a college kid on a field trip who got clipped for his smart phone by some punks. So, given our work load, my loo still considers it a 'nothing case.'"

Noah caught himself before asking if she knew about the Road Warrior. Her first question would be, "What do you know?"

Instead, he asked, "Where was he a student?"

"Catonsville Community College. I spoke with a Professor Martin, yesterday. Another dead end."

Noah nodded. "You figure it was a street robbery for his cell. What kind of a phone was it? Mine's worth about four dollars."

"According to his parents, it is the Maserati of smart phones..."

"Jesus. Maserati?"

VoShaun laughed. "The way his folks described it, calling it the Cadillac wouldn't do it justice. It's a Samsung with all the bells and whistles. They gave it to him as a birthday present last September. Since then, when he wasn't in school he was holed up in his room with the phone and his laptop. They couldn't get two words out of him. It upset them at first, and then they decided they should be grateful he was home and not out somewhere doing drugs."

"I suppose, but on the other hand they could be way off base about that. Even though physically in the house, he could be traveling on the Internet to anywhere in the world and hooking up with anybody. And, I am told, social networking can be as addictive as smack."

"Regardless, my lieutenant believes Jason was showing off that phone on the street and someone admired it too much. Loo pointed out that it wasn't so long ago teenage boys were being killed for the Nikes on their feet or the Orioles jacket on their back. 'The punks are high tech and we'd better get ready for it' is how he put it."

"You haven't mentioned your partner, does he—or she—agree with the Nike theory?"

"Loo hasn't given me a partner."

A rookie detective with no partner, that's beyond strange.

Noah chose not to pursue it with her. *I'll ask Jen*, he decided. "Would you mind if I checked out a couple of things?"

"What do you know that I don't?"

"I don't *know* anything. Just have a couple of wild ideas. If I told you, you couldn't act on it without clearing it with your loo and he would say you were nuts. I won't interfere with what you are doing, and in the unlikely event I uncover anything, you'll be the second to know."

"You could hardly interfere, because I'm not doing anything and nobody seems interested in working it. Still, I'd like to know what you think you have."

"I'd rather not—yet. Right now, it's nothing more than a hunch. Either way it works out, I'll tell you what I had in mind."

VoShaun shrugged. "You know what my loo says about cases like this?"

"Who gives a rat's ass?"

"Exactly."

8

Once in his car, Noah activated his cell phone and found the anticipated voice mail message from his lone client. Corky's tone was unexpectedly calm: "It's me. Just to let you know, I talked to the police. It was two uniforms, not detectives, so I figured I'm not too important to them, but I had to answer their questions, right? They did check my ID and I told them the truth about living in Randallstown. They wrote down my address. I said I had seen the kid around for a few weeks and they wanted to see my cell phone. I showed it to them and they left. I did OK, right?"

Noah saw no reason to call him back and headed south on Charles Street toward Interstate 395 and the Baltimore Beltway.

Noah met Professor Arnold Martin in Martin's office in the math and science building on the Catonsville campus of the Community College of Baltimore County. Martin wore a bulky gray cardigan sweater and rimless eyeglasses, a wisp of fine blonde hair atop his skull.

Noah was certain that anywhere in the world Martin might travel, he would be recognized for just what he was: a junior college professor.

Martin offered a limp hand and then motioned his visitor to the molded plastic chair next to his desk. "Mister Cassidy, what can I do for you?"

"Thank you for seeing me with no appointment. I want to ask you a few questions about Jason Jefferson; I understand he was a student of yours."

Martin was understandably guarded. "Yes, terrible thing. What is your interest in Jason?"

"I am working under a federal grant," Noah lied, "studying urban intra-group violence among members of society's economic tiers. I was hoping to get some additional background about the victim of this tragedy."

Martin paused before saying, "Well, I don't know. Have you contacted his parents?"

"Not yet. They are, of course, on my list, but I don't want to intrude on their grief. You will find my questions are quite innocuous."

Martin appeared to waver and Noah forged ahead.

"This morning I met with Detective Taylor of the Baltimore Police, who was quite forthcoming about the investigation."

Martin said, "I have talked to the police, Yes, Taylor that was his name. Seems to be a hard-working fellow."

A test to see if I have really met with Taylor. Not bad for a professor.

Noah smiled, "The Detective Taylor I met with about an hour ago is a woman, one you are not likely to confuse with a man. Perhaps your visitor was an imposter. If you like, we can call her right now and clear up any confusion."

Martin's face grew red. "No, no. That's not necessary. I er, uh, spoke with this detective over the phone which accounts for any confusion. Please, how can I help?"

You barely receive a passing grade for that recovery, professor.

"What course of study was Jason pursuing?"

Martin pursed his lips. "Sociology was his current passion. Jason was a serious student, at least regarding what interested him. Not frivolous, and certainly not carefree. I can't imagine him engaging in whatever it is that today's teens consider fun. He wasn't out there on a lark; it was a three-credit course in social problems that sent him into the street."

Martin hung his head. "Let's be honest," he muttered, "it is what got him killed."

"What exactly was he doing out there, and do you have other students similarly exposed?"

"No one else. It was entirely Jason's doing, though I doubt that upon reflection, his parents will see it that way. They will blame me—and justifiably so I'm afraid."

Noah was growing concerned that the professor would shut down.

No more beating around the bush. I need to know if this kid was the Road Warrior.

"I assume he was to submit a paper, a thesis perhaps, for you to grade."

"Normally that would be the case, but, as I indicated, Jason had his own way of doing things and could be quite insistent. His idea was to create an Internet blog on which he would report his findings and observations. He convinced me to base his grade solely on the work posted there."

Professor Martin's gaze drifted off for a brief reverie. Momentarily he shifted slightly in his chair and spoke.

"It's quite remarkable, when you think about it. Most students that age are timid about their writing efforts. Not Jason. I expect we'll see much more use of his idea; electronic theses if you will, and grading post-publication. I intend to incorporate the concept in my teaching plan." He hastily added, "Be assured, Jason will get full credit for the idea."

"Of course, professor." Noah made a point of pulling a pen and notebook from his pocket. "I would like to see what he had to say. Could I have the web address of his blog?"

"Sorry, I don't have the address at hand. Just type in 'The Road Warrior' and wade through the references to the Mel Gibson movies. Jason's blog is usually on the bottom half of the first screen."

Noah made a show of recording the information and then returned the notebook to the breast pocket of his suit coat.

"Did you mention the Road Warrior to Detective Taylor?"

Martin shrugged. "It didn't come up. If she had asked—but she didn't. Why is it important?"

"That's hard to say at this point. Have you read all of his postings?"

"Yes."

"Did he mention any problems or concerns that street people out there might have resented?"

Martin shook his head. "I'm sorry, but I don't understand. The detective asked about his cell phone. She said it was top of the line, and asked if he bragged about it; flaunted it, that type of thing. She as much as said that he was killed for the phone. Why are you asking about his blog?"

Noah stood handed Martin a slip of paper with his cell phone number and extended his hand. "My research is broader in scope than the focus of one homicide investigation. If you think of anything else, please call. Thanks for your time, professor."

Leaving the school, Noah headed up Rolling Road into Catonsville, intent on stopping at the Taneytown Deli to pick up a Reuben sandwich on his way home. As he drove, he sorted through recent events.

Maybe he was reading too much into this street killing. It is most likely exactly as the police are saying. One street tough admiring that cell phone and getting it the only way he knew.

VoShaun didn't ask Jason's professor about the Road Warrior website, because no one made her aware of it. Even then, it may mean nothing, merely an intriguing distraction.

Noah hadn't mentioned it to her this morning because the source was his client. Now he was free to name Martin as the source. Given the attitude of VoShaun's lieutenant it is doubtful the police would be interested. Even if they were, Noah didn't see how anyone could determine whether the Road Warrior website was significant or not. Still, he would tell her. She should know that he wasn't just talk—he had followed through.

He briefly speculated about Jason's property. His cell was missing, but nothing had been said about what else might be missing. Had anything of significance been found on his person after the stabbing?

In any case, this was all quickly becoming irrelevant. According to Corky's message, the cops were looking for Jason's phone and moved on when he didn't have it. Apparently Corky was no longer in need of an attorney, even a five-dollar one.

The following day, Noah was at his computer early; quickly confirming that the murder of Jason J. Jefferson was no longer newsworthy. Next he placed a call to Detective VoShaun Taylor, hoping to reach her before she left the office to knock on doors.

"Detective Taylor."

"VoShaun, it's Noah Cassidy, do you have a couple of minutes?"

"For you, there's always time."

"That's nice to know. I did a little work on the Jason Jefferson killing and want to pass along what I learned, as promised."

"I'll listen, but that's about all I can do. I'm on a team working two of the three shootings we had last night. If you have a confession and the knife, and are sitting on the killer, I might be able to help out—but don't count on it. With that thought, go ahead."

"I spoke to Jason's instructor at Catonsville. He said he had talked to you."

"That's right. Not much there."

"Probably not, but I thought you might want to add the Road Warrior website to your report."

"I'm listening."

"It's a blog, really. Jason wrote about what he saw on the street, posted some pictures most likely taken with the missing cell phone."

"And?"

"Well, nothing—yet. I thought you would want to add it to your report and I'll look into it a little more, if you don't object."

He could tell she was writing as she spoke. She said, "I'm not going to try and bullshit you. I doubt this blog thing would ever come up, but, if I get a chance, I'll stick it in the file. Well, you know—this covers my ass. Thanks…"

"Don't hang up. I need to ask you one more thing."

"Make it quick."

"Can you get hold of the property list of what was recovered from the body?"

"His property has been turned over to his mother. I have the signed release on my desk. We…"

"Was there anything besides keys and ID?"

The sound of papers rustling carried through the telephone. She spoke rapidly. "The only other things were a pocket knife and a thumb drive for his computer. I've really got…"

"Did you look at the files on the thumb drive?"

"…No…we…"

"Thanks."

Noah dialed Corky's cell phone, which was answered immediately. "Corky."

"It's me. I'm calling about the message you left yesterday."

"Finally. Good thing it wasn't life or death."

"If it was life or death, I would have called you right back. Is there a problem?"

"No, sorry. Guess I felt abandoned."

"It's pretty raw outside. You at your office?"

"For the moment. A day like this is good for business. People feel sorry for us homeless types. The downside is I have to wear a ratty sweater. I'm told you generate less sympathy in a heavy overcoat."

"I see your point. I take it you've had no further contact with the police."

"You'd have heard me hollering before now."

"I figured. Well, I guess you got your five dollars' worth."

Corky hesitated before saying, "I was kind of hoping for a refund."

Noah's response was dead silence and Corky quickly added, "Hey, just a joke. In fact, why don't you come out for dinner some evening soon? My wife would love to meet you."

"I…"

"Thursdays are good. We have Hobo Stew served in an old soup can."

After a moments silence, Corky hastily added, "Just a joke, you know."

"My favorite," Noah said. "Let me get back to you."

"Sure whatever. You can bring someone if you like."

"Sounds good. I'll let you know."

Corky followed another uncomfortable silence with, "It seems like I'm off the hook, so I guess you won't need to get involved after all."

It occurred to Noah that Corky knew nothing of the contacts he had made on his clients behalf.

"Too late. I'm already involved; I wasn't just sitting around raking in the dough."

Noah recounted his meetings with Taylor and Martin and the follow up call to Taylor. When he stopped talking, Corky said, "Sounds to me like you think there is something more to this than the boy getting jacked for his cell. Am I right?"

"Mostly just idle curiosity. I really have no rational basis for that notion and it wouldn't take much to get me off of it. Still, what if there was more to it? It's clear the cops aren't going to pursue it. It's not in my nature to let it go like that; it would haunt me to know that Jason's killer roamed free and I ignored it."

"Can I help?"

"That reminds me," Noah responded, "Did you find out anything about the angry guy in that picture?"

Corky brightened. "Oh yeah. Wise Eddie knows him from the meth clinic on Fayette Street. They've been in the same line for meds."

"Did Eddie give you a name?"

"The guy's known at the clinic as Doctor Musk. It could be his real name."

"Why do you say that? The guy could have been screwing around with him."

"No. No. See Eddie was standing right behind him when the nurse calls out 'Ellis Musk.' Well the guy is furious—Eddie says he always looks like he's about to go postal. Now it's like he's gonna strangle the nurse. Gets right up in her face, he's spitting and yells 'That's *Doctor* Musk, goddamn it! Doctor Musk, you got that nurse?'"

"What did she do?"

"Eddie was laughing at how cool she was. She ignores Musk and calls out Eddie's name, basically sending the 'doctor' to the end of the line."

"Anything else?"

"Eddie didn't stick around, said he whizzed in a cup, gulped down his meds and left. 'Course I had showed him the picture you got from the website. He says that, in the flesh, Musk's suit and top coat are a lot shabbier than they show up in the shot we saw. Remember his white dress shirt was open at the throat—no neck tie? That's what he's wearing every time Eddie sees him. The suit's always wrinkled and the shirt has stains on it. Eddie figures he hasn't shaved since Jason took that picture. Sounds like he might be the guy, huh?"

"Maybe. I'll Google Doctor Musk and see what the Internet has to tell us about him."

Noah was intently reading about Doctor Ellis Musk on the Internet when his solitude was shattered by the roar of a car engine being gunned relentlessly in the driveway below his apartment. Revving the motor was an eccentricity routinely employed by his landlady, Frau Wirtz, in anticipation of propelling her Audi screeching along the macadam driveway on her way out to Wetheredsville Road. This ritual invariably evoked, in Noah, a mind's-eye view of Frau Wirtz careening her auto along the German Autobahn.

She has to frighten even those drivers.

Mostly he was relieved that she had not rapped on his door before driving away.

Frau Wirtz's appearance at his door a few days before had been alarming. As he warily cracked the door open, she had pushed her way inside carrying a plate of warm strudel.

"Ah, *liebchen*," she had gushed. "I'm afraid I have neglected you these past weeks. Come, let's sit and share some coffee and this wonderful *Apfelstrudel*. Just from the oven."

Noah, flummoxed by the intrusion, had groped for a response.

"Missus Wirtz..."

"Please, call me *Frau* Wirtz. The late *Herr* Wirtz, God rest his soul, called me nothing else."

By the time Noah recovered, she had set the strudel on the breakfast bar and was searching the kitchen cupboard for plates and silver.

"Well, yes, all right, *Frau* Wirtz. I have a few minutes—only a few."

She seemed not to be listening and busied herself slicing the strudel and sliding a generous piece onto each plate. It was then that Noah noticed her appearance. Aside from the crimson robe covering a filmy pink nightgown, she appeared groomed for an evening on the town. Her platinum-colored hair was carefully brushed and worn in a pixie cut, in what Noah deemed a failed effort to appear younger. Pancake makeup layered her cheeks, her eyelashes heavily lacquered with mascara; bright red lipstick circled her mouth. A strand of pearls adorned her neck, begging the question: Had she worn them to bed? He had no intention of finding out.

She gently patted her stiff hair. "Do you like?"

"It's very becoming."

Frau Wirtz then perched herself on one of the bar stools while Noah filled two cups with coffee. *Let's get this over with.*

She plucked a sliver of pecan from the slice of strudel before her and held it to her lips. She patted the empty stool next to her saying, "Sit. We will become very good friends."

Desperate for something to say, Noah motioned toward the main house. "What happened to your roommate? I haven't seen him for some time."

She emitted a low snort. "Oh, don't worry about Leland. He's gone—for good this time."

"I didn't know him well, but he seemed like a nice fellow."

"Leland is a gentleman." She proceeded to caress Noah's arm. "Too much of a gentleman for me. I prefer a younger man, a more exciting man. Are you exciting, Noah?"

Noah gave a short laugh, as if he was in on the joke. "Sorry, I'm just a stodgy lawyer. Very unimaginative, I'm afraid."

She reached up and patted his cheek. "I can help you with that," she said.

"Please," she said, "no more talk about Leland, he is ancient history. Eat your strudel."

Noah then munched the pastry and Frau Wirtz had beamed as he praised her effort. She patted his hand saying, "It is so good because it is made with winesap apples, real butter and love."

Noah had finished his coffee and stood. "This was a lovely surprise, Frau Wirtz, but I'm nearly late for an appointment." He scowled at his watch and rushed away returning momentarily wearing his overcoat and pulling on leather gloves.

Reluctantly, Frau Wirtz slid from the stool, moving with him. At the door she turned and tilted her head, lips pursed and eyes closed in anticipation.

"Frau Wirtz," he said, trying desperately to conceal his revulsion. "I'm overwhelmed with the possibilities ahead of us." He patted her arm. "Please, give me some time."

Obviously pleased, she replied, "Of course, dear boy. Don't be frightened, you will find me a gentle lover."

Noah finished his Google search of Doctor Musk and turned his attention to a more diligent review of the Road Warrior website; focusing specifically on the pages of Jason's photos.

He was so intent on the task at hand that a soft rapping on his door was his first inkling of Frau Wirtz's return. "It's me dear boy."

"Ah, shit," Noah grumbled. Still not prepared to alienate his landlady he headed for the door. He was relieved to find that she was empty-handed and fully clad in a beige pants suit.

She made no attempt to enter and Noah forced a smile.

"Frau Wirtz, good morning. I'm on the phone. Long distance," he added, expecting this would be a reference that she understood.

She dismissed his words with a wave of her hand. "Dear boy, you never called and I grew concerned. At night, when you park your car behind the garage I cannot know if you are home and I worry. You never turn on your lights, always with those little candles."

She squeezed his arm and batted artificially long eyelashes. "I am relieved that you are well. Why don't I cook you a nice meal tonight? Only the two of us. I am just returned from the market with a nice *schnitzel*."

"That sounds lovely, but I won't be home until quite late."

She formed her lips into a pout and patted his cheek. "Until next time, *liebling*."

Noah closed the door behind her and breathed a sigh as her footsteps moved toward the stairway.

Returning to the laptop, he searched the Internet for any scraps of information pertaining to Jason Jefferson's family. It was a long shot, but perhaps some family rift was instrumental in his death. At one o'clock after a fruitless search, he logged off and dialed Jen's cell.

"This is Jen."

"It's Noah. Can you talk?"

"I'm just leaving the building for lunch, headed for the Inner Harbor."

"Where are you going to eat?"

"I'll decide when I get there. What are you up to?"

"I'm trying to find a place to hide out tonight."

"Who are you hiding from?"

"My landlady."

"Behind in your rent?"

"Not yet. My immediate problem is that she invited me over for dinner."

"What's wrong with a home-cooked meal?"

"She's trying to get in my pants."

Jen laughed. "Really? I can't imagine any woman having trouble with that."

"I'm serious. She shows up at my door at all hours and talks about a future together. It's scary."

"Sounds to me like a solution to your rent problem."

"What? Oh, God no. I'd rather live in my car."

"Well...if it will help..."

"Yes?"

"The library is open until 9."

"Not funny."

Noah heard a muffled voice over her phone, then Jen saying, "Hello, Billy."

"Who is that?"

"It's Pratt Street Billy. This is pretty much his corner."

"I hope you pay attention to your surroundings when you're walking around town."

"Thanks, but not to worry. I'm a single woman who is reminded every day how dangerous this city is. No chance I'll forget."

Noah sighed. "Since you are not going to make this easy for me, I'll be blunt. Can I see you tonight?"

Jen hesitated before saying, "I wish I could say yes, but I have plans."

"A date, I guess."

"If that bothers you then, please do something about it. You were out of my life for months, and then, by your own admission, you only called me to talk to a detective you thought I was living with. I was an afterthought. If you want it to be more, you'll have to do better than that."

Noah hung up, feeling strangely heartened.

9

Noah took Jen's blithe suggestion to heart and spent much of that evening at the Catonsville library on Frederick Road. He browsed the selection of hard-cover books featuring accounts of World War II espionage, becoming especially drawn to two books describing intrigue in the British intelligence service, *Agent Zig Zag* and *Operation Mincemeat*. It interested him to learn that Sir Ian Fleming, creator of the fictional British spy James Bond, had played a major role in some of the real life exploits of the British secret war against the Nazis.

Next he spent time scouring several daily newspapers and struggling not to wonder what Jen was doing at that moment.

Noah concluded that he preferred gripping a newspaper in his hand while he read. Newsprint and ink, he reasoned, was like flesh and blood compared to staring into the sterile glow of a computer screen. The news seemed more vibrant to him when gleaned from the printed page.

The Baltimore Sun carried an obituary for Jason J. Jefferson, and Noah noted that the funeral had been held that morning mere blocks away down Frederick Road. Tomorrow he would pay his respects to the family.

Noah left the library just before 9 o'clock and drove out Frederick Road for one of Dimitri's signature Beef-Ke-Bob sandwiches and a bottle of Samuel Adams. He sat at the bar and watched a basketball game, which held no interest for him. But mostly he worked out the story he would tell to whoever answered the Jefferson's door tomorrow.

Shortly after 11:00 he deemed it safe to go home.

The next morning Noah spent time at the computer, tracking down the street number for Jason Jeffersons' family home. After changing into a business suit, he paused to glance out his front window before opening the door. His window looked down on Frau Wirtz's house just across the macadam driveway. No activity.

Last night, he had again parked behind the garage in an effort to evade his landlady. Was he going to have to do that every night? Hopefully she would find someone else to pursue, or grow weary of chasing him.

Once in his car, it was an easy ten-minute drive to the Jefferson's residence on Southmont Road in Catonsville. The house was a split-level with attached garage and shake siding. A five-year-old Honda sat on the concrete driveway, a newer Toyota Celica was parked at the curb. Noah studied the house for a minute and then, deciding he had nothing to lose, walked up the step and rang the bell.

The door was opened by a teen-age girl with shoulder-length straight brown hair. Eyes, red from crying, peered at him through thick glasses. She called out, "It's the police again, Mother."

The girl whirled and stalked off, giving Noah no opportunity to correct her mistaken impression. By the time an older woman appeared in the doorway, he decided he would only speak up if she demanded identification.

This woman, though older and heavier, held the same look as the girl: red-rimmed eyes behind identical glasses. She stepped around Noah and glanced up and down the street before motioning him inside.

"What must the neighbors think? Eighteen years we're on this street with never a call to the police. Eighteen years. This week we've had a damn parade, city and county."

She eyed him momentarily. "Which one are you?" Her challenge was immediately followed with a wave of her hand. "It don't matter. The city cops came like you, in a suit and everyday car;

the county comes up in their marked cars, 'cruisers,' I think you fellas call them. That right?"

What the hell is she talking about? The county wouldn't come here in connection with Jason's murder; they would go through the city.

"Yes, ma'am. They are called cruisers."

"Next time, call. I could've saved you a trip. We found nothing missing besides his computer." She shook her head. "What kind of person preys on folks while they're at a funeral? Our neighbor says there's scoundrels who go through the obituary notices and figure out when a family will be gone and come in bold as brass and rob their house. Awful people, just awful."

"Yes…"

"We come direct from the funeral to find we been broken into. The place was a mess yet all they took was Jason's laptop, it was sitting right next to his new TV, which they didn't take. And, they left a jar of quarters he kept on his desk. Go figure. I told this all to the young man yesterday."

She stopped speaking and looked away. "Jason." she murmured. "I just like to say his name." Her body shivered and then she turned back to Noah. "Anyway, the officer in the cruiser says they must have got scared off. Maybe the phone rang or somebody came to the door to deliver some flowers."

Gently, Noah said, "Was there any message on your machine?"

She thought a minute. "Not during that time, no. Everybody who wasn't at the service had already called."

"Did you receive flowers, or a note from a florist that they tried to deliver them?"

She studied for a moment. "Now that you mention it, no, no, nothing like that. What does that mean, detective?"

"It might mean nothing. And you are satisfied that nothing else was missing?"

She nodded.

"Well, thank you for your time. Your neighbors will certainly understand about the police activity."

Dabbing at her eyes with a dainty handkerchief, she offered a weak smile and closed the door behind him.

Noah had switched to a latte and was trying to decide whether to ask the barista for a refill or just leave, when Detective VoShaun Taylor rushed through the front door.

"Sorry I'm late, but I am lucky to make it at all. I can't stay long."

Noah stood. "Sit down while I get you a latte."

She glanced toward the line at the counter. "It has to be quick."

He returned shortly and set a latte in front of her.

Noah watched as she sipped at her drink and concluded that she was in no mood for seduction.

"What's up?" She asked.

"Did you know that the house where Jason Jefferson lived was burglarized during his funeral?"

She was clearly bemused. "I can barely recall who that is, why should I care about his house? Didn't he live in the county?"

Noah nodded. "I thought you would care because you have the lead."

"I'm sorry. I'm up to my ass working everybody else's cases, I can't even think about that boy." She glanced at her watch. "How is the burglary important?"

"Someone hit Jason's house while the family attended the funeral. Just a routine burglary as far as the county is concerned. No way for them to connect that address to a murder in the city. I think it is connected; the only thing taken was his laptop."

Noah sat back waiting for her reaction.

VoShaun shrugged. "I don't see it. Sounds like neighbor kids, knew they were all away. Something like that."

"Not kids. Kids wouldn't have left a big jar of quarters behind. Neither would some street bum, for that matter."

"Okay. But, if it is connected to our murder, how is some street bum or inner-city punk going to get out to Catonsville? Cab? Bus? Rent-a-car? And what would he want with the boy's computer? Easier to steal one in the city."

"Exactly."

"What…?"

"That is my point. If all he wanted was a computer, it would be easier to steal it in the city. Why go to the trouble of traveling, by whatever mode, to that particular address for the purpose of stealing this particular computer?"

"I give up."

"Because there is something in that particular computer that he wants, or whoever he is working for wants. At least they believe there is."

"How do we know that the computer was what they were looking for? Maybe it's all they happened to find."

Noah shook his head. "They passed up a new TV and who knows what else to get that computer."

Again, VoShaun glanced at her watch. "Okay, maybe there is something to what you say, but so what? The loo has made it clear that I'm not to 'waste my time' on this 'dog.' Even if I knew what to do next, there's no way I could do it. I really have to go."

"I see. Well, you might want to get the county's report, to complete your file. If anything else comes up, I'll call you."

VoShaun waved over her shoulder as the door closed behind her.

10

Corky Kilmark turned his back to the wind and stamped his feet in an effort to generate some warmth. His face stung and his fingers were numb. The day had quickly turned windy and raw, and the tattered sweater he wore was little insulation against the first real cold snap he had suffered during his short career as a panhandler. None of the street people he had seen today seemed worried about scaring off clients. All were better dressed than was he against the cold.

Earlier, Marvel happened by, cocooned in a threadbare purple cape fashioned from worn heavy drapery material. A veteran of the first Iraq war, Marvel left the service with the rank of master sergeant in the Army and returned to Baltimore, where he drifted into the life of a streeter.

After finding the cape on a rack in a local thrift store, he assumed the name of the hero in one of the tattered comic books that had accompanied his unit across the desert.

Marvel's approach routinely unnerved Corky. Dark eyes glared beneath a shaved head, a grizzled jaw set in a block of granite. Marvel spoke as if he were still bawling orders amid the din of a desert battlefield.

"Morning," Corky said.

"Where's your damn coat, private?"

"The cold surprised me."

"Don't be too proud to stop by the mission and pick one out. And don't lag back; the good ones go in a wink."

"Thanks. I'll do that."

"Ain't you the one they call Corkscrew?"

Corky nodded.

"I hear the police were around to see you about JCube."

"JCube?"

"The boy that was stabbed, street name was JCube. Likely due to him having three names that started with the letter J."

Jason must have reserved the name 'Road Warrior' for the Internet.

Corky said, "Oh. Right. I guess the cops will get around to most every streeter."

"I've not seen 'em yet. What'd they want to know?"

Corky hesitated. *What should I say? After all Marvel could be the killer.* Aloud he mustered a casual response. "They wanted to know if I had ever spoken to him, I said I had, a couple of times. Asked to see my cell phone. I showed it to them, that was it."

"Why'd they want to see your phone?"

Corky shrugged inwardly. *What the hell.* "Whoever killed JCube must have taken his cell phone. I hear it was real fancy. Could do everything but brew coffee."

"Damn shame," Marvel muttered. "Damn shame." A dark look crossed his face. "You in the war? Any of them?"

Corky quickly discarded a couple of lame excuses and merely shook his head.

"Lord knows there's been plenty of opportunities. Never mind. It don't matter. As for the boy, I don't know if he was one of us, but that don't matter either. The cops won't bother looking for the killer of a streeter, leaving the bastard free to kill some more of us. Or the cops will grab one of us to blame it on."

Marvel scowled. "Either way, it's up to us street people to do the job. We got to defend ourselves from killers *and* the damn police."

Corky waited, eventually realizing that Marvel expected him to speak up. He shrugged and glanced along the street. "What can we do?"

"Damnit private! There's plenty of good folks out here. I'm asking them to join up. We may be rabble but we got eyes and ears, most of us anyhow. We can listen, we can watch and we can ask questions. For one thing, we got a lot better chance than the cops of finding the boy's cell phone. We see someone talking on it; we follow him to where he coops," Marvel produced a filthy fist which he shook under Corky's nose, "and make him talk."

Corky thought of Doctor Musk. *Need to find out if he has a phone.*

He spoke up. "I'm all for catching him; you can count me in. But what if the killer isn't a streeter? Everybody walking down the street has a phone in his ear, how we going to find that particular one?"

"Do you think some suit did it? A stockbroker or lawyer strolls passed JCube, pulls a knife out of his brief case and stabs him?"

"No. No, I don't, but…"

"Me neither. It was some street bum—one of us. Not many streeters with a cell phone. He's out here—on the streets. It's our duty to find him. You ain't afraid, are ya?" Marvel challenged.

Corky shook his head emphatically.

Marvel's fist disappeared under his cape. "There is one thing," he said. "Suppose we find out something that the cops should know. Who's gonna tell them? Nobody out here'll talk to 'em if he don't have to. They ain't gonna listen to one of us anyways. We're not respectable enough."

"I guess we can worry about that if we ever got something to tell 'em."

Marvel nodded. "I'll be by in the next couple of days to see what you found out. If you hear something important, come find me."

"How am I going to know what is important?"

Marvel turned on his heel and stalked off.

With Marvel gone, Corky again felt the cold and went back to stomping his feet. Heavy snowflakes had begun to settle on the sidewalk, and a young girl stopped to deposit a quarter in his cup. She was out of ear shot before he could chatter "Bless you."

The streets were suddenly empty.

It's only November and I'm already freezing my ass off. I'll never make it to spring out here.

Corky stomped his feet and thought back over the eight months he had spent as a streeter. Coming out here, he had expected to be met with anger and outrage by street people who would feel threatened by another rival for the few dollars passersby grudgingly gave out each day. Some had been hostile, but, surprisingly, most of them were civil; a few even friendly. None threatened. His second day there, Wise Eddie happened along and engaged him in conversation.

"They call me Wise Eddie, he had said. "You look pretty well fed—must be new to the street."

Corky had nodded. "A recent turn of bad luck."

Eddie puffed out his chest. "I been out here eighteen years." Spoken as if he was proclaiming an Olympic record. "I'll learn you what you'll need to know to get by."

Corky mumbled, "Thank you…Mister Eddie."

Eddie's laugh revealed two rows of discolored teeth.

"Wise Eddie, no 'mister' needed. Now, first you got to learn who the players are."

That was when Corky learned that a "road warrior" was a young street person who kept on the move, spending a night or two on a strange sofa or floor, careful not to wear out his welcome in any one place.

Eddie had said, "A fella who begs for spare change is called a 'Spanger.' Used to be you'd see Squeegee men on every street corner. A Squeegee works stoplights, hopin' to get some change for wipin' off folks' windshields before the light changes. 'Course they pissed off the swells and got run off for their trouble. Swells feel threatened by us, don't you know."

Corky nodded.

"Then there's them like Mata Hairy, who believe they ain't panhandling or begging, and I guess they got a point. She pushes that shopping cart all over the city, collecting cans, bottles, newspapers— anything she can sell to the recycle. That's nature's way ain't it?"

"I guess…"

"Think about it. Streeters are natural scavengers, same as vultures. It's the job of both of 'em to keep the land rid of trash and disgusting stuff the swells don't want to have to look at. Yet them same swells will come along and kick us and the vulture birds to the curb without a second thought."

Eddie shook his head. "Anyhow, Mata Hairy's a strange fish in a whole sea of strange fish. For the longest time she pushed this old grocery cart from the A&P—I still call it by its real name, the A&P. Well, one day there she is coming down the street sporting a brand-new cart. One of them what has a seat for a baby."

He waited for Corky to nod understanding.

"I was on Howard Street talking to Pixie when Mata Hairy rolls up, beaming all over and dying for us to say something about her new wheels. Who could blame her? Shiny chrome with a polished black pushing handle. She'd hoofed it all the way up to Eager Street to Eddie's Market to claim it when no one was looking. No more A&P, no sir. Be the same as working folks trading in an old Ford Pinto for a brand-new Cadillac car.

"'Course we couldn't let it go easy, now could we? Pixie starts it off by pointing to the baby chair and real serious asking Mata if she's pregnant."

Wise Eddie made a face and shuddered. "The idea of what a man would need to do to get her with child makes a person sick. Anyhow, I chime in with, 'How much did they give you on a trade-in?' Well sir, Mata lets out a snarl and rams the cart into my shins—not gentle either. Then she pulls back and takes off down Howard Street." He laughed at the memory. "A real hit-and-run driver."

Wise Eddie was suddenly somber, staring somewhere above Corky's head. "What was I sayin'? It gone again."

"A story about Mata..."

"No, that ain't it. It was before that."

"You were talking about the different jobs..."

"Okay, okay. I got it back. I was tellin' about the different players out here. Some start out like Mata Hairy but they soon slip across the line into stealin.' First you're pickin' up stray cans and paper, then before you know it, your stripping brass and copper from empty houses. Take Iron Mike, he claims any kind of metal he gets his hands on. What part of it is stealin' and what ain't is beyond me.

"Then there's Greasy Pete. He has some kids working in restaurants who cop grease from the kitchens for him to sell." Eddie shrugged. "Again, is that actual stealin'? The restaurants is only goin' to toss it out."

Wise Eddie cleared his throat and peered into the paper cup in Corky's hand.

"It 'pears you got enough in there for a couple cups of coffee from that joint over yonder?"

Corky hesitated, uncertain of the right move. He felt sorry for this pitiful soul, but he envisioned Wise Eddie spreading the word that this new guy—this rookie—was an easy touch. The word would spread and he would be plagued by fellow-panhandlers.

"Come on. I'm tellin' you what you need to survive on the streets. You expect to get all these Life Lessons for nuthin'?"

When Corky hesitated again, Wise Eddie knew he had him. "Little milk and plenty of sugar. I'll wait here."

Wise Eddie was standing in the same spot when Corky returned with two cups of steaming coffee.

Eddie took the cup. "Much obliged. While you was gone I thought hard on what we was saying about." He grinned. "It's still with me, but we should get right back to it."

Corky nodded and slipped his cardboard sign—"Please Help"—over his head.

Eddie pointed at the sign with his coffee cup. "Jesus. Fer one thing, your sign there sucks. This is a cut-throat business, like hamburger joints sittin' side by side. With that sign, you're a White Castle going up against that red-haired girl from Wendy's or the Burger King."

Dismayed, Corky looked down at the piece of cardboard hanging from his neck.

"If you didn't know," Eddie added, "White Castle has been gone from Baltimore's streets for years. They fell by the wayside, and so will you."

Corky shrugged. "What should I do?"

"I'll give you a couple ideas; it's for you to decide what to do. For instance, there's a couple of fellas who will pick you up ever' morning and drive you out to a mall or big shopping center. At the end of the day they drive you back to where they picked you up."

"What's in it for them?"

"They get half of your take. And don't expect you can cheat 'em either. They'll shake you by the heels until every penny falls out. You got to be at the pick-up spot every morning at 7, and you have to wear what they tell you. It's like a uniform."

Corky shook his head. "Sounds too much like a job. Anything else?"

"A ninety-five," Eddie corrected and slurped his coffee. "You need to find what they call a 'high traffic' spot. Like the bottom of a freeway off-ramp where there's a stoplight to back up the cars. Or just about anywhere downtown when the Ravens or Orioles are playing."

"Seems like any panhandler worth the name will know to be there. All the good spots are going to be taken. What can I do?"

Eddie shrugged. "I can only get you started. Pointed in the right direction. You'll have to figure it out for yourself. Hey, if it was easy, everybody would be doing it."

"Well, thanks…"

"There's more. Some say it's better to tell them what you want."

Corky frowned.

"Your sign there could say, 'I need 43 more cents for a cup of coffee, or four more dollars for a bus ticket to Boston.'"

"People believe that?"

"They don't have to believe it. See, if you don't say nothing, they'll figure that you'll use their money for booze or drugs. This way it gives them something to feel better about where their money's going.

"There's a few regulars who take the bother to clean themselves up of a morning and hustle down to the aquarium or a museum. Any place where out-of-towners will show up. Say a family from Wisconsin is huddled on the sidewalk at the Pratt Street pavilion looking confused or lost. A streeter will slide in next to them and try to hear where it is they is looking to go. He can't seem too scruffy or he'll scare them off. Then he'll say something like, 'I couldn't help but hear that you are looking for the B&O Railroad Museum. It's not far, I'll be glad to show you. And he will. The swells, being grateful, will offer a few dollars which they expect he will refuse, but he don't.

"At least they got something for their money. If the place them rubes is going is too far off, he'll tell them the best he can. Those folks likely'll give up some change, but if they don't he ain't out nothin.'

"If he don't know the place they're going, he'll still give directions to somewhere, making sure to get them far enough away that he'll be gone if they come back angry.

"Another way is to give the swells a laugh, or at least a smile. One fella would come to his corner all scruffy-looking. His sign said, 'Need funds to find a rich wife.'" Eddie thought for a minute, "You know, I haven't seen him for a while—maybe it worked."

Corky started to speak up and Eddie snapped, "I ain't done. A sign I saw just last week, it was Lame Roger that had it. Roger's too lazy to stand up all day so he fakes being a crip. Sits on a thin old pillow on that cold sidewalk. Ever' day, all day. Don't know how he does it; it's got to give him the red ass. Anyhow, he sits there with a propped up sign that says, 'Need money for weapons to fight terrorists.' There's another fella asks for money to go kill bin Laden. Saw him just a few days ago. Guess no one told him that somebody beat him to it.

"Here's another thing. You got to have a good story ready. Most folks aren't interested in your life history, but there's the occasional old busybody with nothing better to do, will stand there clutching her money while she looks you over."

Eddie looked into his cup. "Sure as this coffee is cold she'll say, 'You poor boy, what happened to you?' You got to give her a sob story that'll pry that money from between those bony fingers. Folks like that seem to want to give a prize to the streeter who has suffered the most."

Eddie made a face and finished his cold coffee.

Corky said, "You want another…"

"Salvation!" Eddie shouted. "Salvation. Makes 'em feel good, like their two dollars is gonna be your salvation. So you need a story for them… Being a recovering drug addict is real popular…"

"No drugs. Never smoked grass—nothing."

Eddie viewed him with suspicion, and then shrugged. "Whatever. But that don't really matter now, does it? I been sayin' it's a story, it don't have to be the real thing. It's whatever you can get away with. Another one, popular right now, is you was laid off from a good job and can't find no work. And, as bad luck would have it, your three-year-old daughter needs expensive treatments or a operation. Now don't tell me you don't have no daughter. You'll get more from some if it's your sick old ma. Either one of them should do the trick."

Corky, guessing that Wise Eddie was finished was about to speak when the other man blurted out, "Now listen up. This here is the most important thing I got for ya. Don't never tell no other streeter where you are cooping at night. No streeter worth the name will ask 'cause he won't tell you where his coop is. Anyone you would tell will figure you for easy prey so he'll come around and rob your stash while you sleep."

Corky, stung with guilt about where he slept, said nothing.

Corky shook off his memory of Wise Eddie and realized that while he was daydreaming about the start of his eight-month odyssey as a panhandler, the snow was still falling and the wind was sharper. His ears ached with the cold and he could only think of the warmth and smells of Peace and a Cup of Joe. His feet were wooden, and as he considered whether he could make it the few blocks on foot Wise Eddie turned the corner, heading toward him.

Layers of sweaters were visible under Eddie's oversized hunting coat, once a vibrant buffalo plaid check. Corky rubbed his ears and envied the black leather cap with faux fur earflaps tied securely beneath Eddie's chin.

"Surprised to find you out here today. You won't do no business on a day like this."

"I was just leaving, headed to Cup of Joe. Walk along and we'll get a cup."

Eddie shook his head. "I got to find Marvel. You seen him?"

"He was here about twenty minutes ago. Headed toward Charles Street."

"He say anything about what we're doing?"

"Told me he was going to find out who knifed that boy and asked if I wanted to help."

Wise Eddie waited.

"I told him I doubted we could find the killer, but I would do what I could."

Eddie nodded. "You got the time?"

Corky checked his cell phone. "It's almost 3."

"You're turning blue, you better get inside. I'm heading over to the BeeHive, Marvel's got a waitress there who usually slips him a coffee and a stale roll about this time of day."

Wise Eddie disappeared into the swirling snow.

11

Noah rolled the wineglass in his hand, admiring the deep rich red of the cabernet as it swirled around the bottom. He took another sip and nodded, content with his choice. He was seated on a futon across an area rug from where Jen worked in the kitchen.

"Have you tried the wine?" he asked.

"Yes. It has a beautiful color."

"Does that mean that it looks better than it tastes?"

"No, it's fine. I'm not big on wine."

"It will improve with food." He scanned the room. A maple drop-leaf table with four matching chairs crowded the room just to the left of the futon. Beyond, a dim hallway led to the likely one bedroom and bath at the back.

"One bedroom?"

"It has a two-bedroom floor plan, but the spare room is filled with books. I use it as a half-assed office."

Noah patted the futon. "I guess this makes into a bed—when you have a sleepover."

Jen, at the sink, turned and glanced over her shoulder. "Let's not get ahead of ourselves."

"That's why I mentioned the futon. I wasn't kidding when I said I was afraid to go home. Frau Blucher waved to me when I drove out this morning. I know she has something planned."

"Frau Blucher? I thought your landlady's name was, Wirtz."

"That was before I got to know her. She's scary. A real flesh-and-blood Frau Blucher."

Jen shrugged. "I don't…"

"Mel Brooks' *Young Frankenstein*. Gene Wilder was Frankenstein's grandson but he insisted on being called, *Fraunkensteen*. Cloris Leachman was a great Frau Blucher?"

"Sorry, I didn't see it. I was probably trying to survive law school."

"Law school? You weren't born when it came out."

"No wonder I missed it."

"Looks like I have my work cut out for me." Noah lifted the wine bottle from the end table and poured himself half a glass. He raised his glass and sniffed the air.

"It smells like you can cook."

Jen laughed. "I can cook spaghetti, toss a salad and buy garlic bread."

"Then I hope that's what we are having."

"You're about to find out," Jen said. "Come and get the salads while I dish up the plates."

They sat at the table and ate in hungry silence before Noah stopped to dab the meat sauce from his mouth. "You did not lie, counselor, you *can* cook spaghetti. Though this is much daintier than the spaghetti I'm used to."

"It's angel hair pasta. Much thinner than old-fashioned spaghetti." Jen sipped her wine and said, "VoShaun told me that you have spoken."

"Yes. A couple of times. And, since you brought it up, I have to say I'm a little distressed."

Jen reached for more bread. "I'm sorry. I thought I told you she was green. It's her…"

"That doesn't bother me. In fact, it's better. A veteran wouldn't have given give me five minutes."

"What is it that 'distresses' you?"

"She's…well, she's hot."

"And you prefer uggos?"

Noah laid down his fork and lifted his wineglass. "I'll admit it. I was hoping you might be interested in me…"

"What does one have to do with the other?"

Noah drank some wine before saying, "Unless it was a test, you know—tempting me; I can't imagine you putting us together. And, if it was a test, I must confess, I failed, counselor. I was definitely tempted."

Jen stood and reached for his plate. "I see a long evening; we have a lot to discuss. Unless you call me 'counselor' again, in which case we have nothing to discuss. There's plenty of pasta—and no dessert. If you are still hungry?"

Noah nodded. "Since I promise not to call you…that word again, I had better get fortified." He made a rectangle with this thumbs and forefingers indicating the portion size.

While Jen refilled their plates, Noah said, "I'm sorry if I hit a nerve with that word. I didn't mean anything by it; after all, I too am one of those. At least I once was."

Jen set the plates on the table and brushed his hand as she sat down. "You have nothing to be sorry for. I'm having difficulty dealing with the whole Drew episode…"

"Maybe I should…"

She shook her head. "Please don't say that you should leave. Maybe it's the wine," she said. "But I want to talk about it. I believe I really *need* to talk about it."

"Go ahead." He smiled, "I'm too stuffed to escape now anyway."

"Good. You must promise that you won't repeat this to anyone."

"…Okay."

"I mean it, Noah. You can tell no one."

"I promise. What you tell me will be treated like confession." It occurred to Noah to ask for a five-dollar retainer; instead he touched the collar of his shirt. "Father Cassidy."

Jen picked at her food while searching for the words to tell her story. She sighed and then began. "Mostly, I'm ashamed to admit that I stayed with him as long as I did. I went off on you about 'counselor' because Drew called me that when he was being nasty, which was frequent toward the end. We were fighting almost nonstop; he delighted in making 'counselor' sound like a dirty word.

"I know he resented my education, and that as an assistant state's attorney, a woman had the power to find fault with cases he brought for prosecution. We never had a case together, but we might as well have. I endured his fury when another assistant insisted that he go back and do it right. It was bad enough when he had been scolded by a male assistant; if he was dealing with a female it was much worse. It usually ended with him knocking me around the apartment."

Neither of them raised a fork, and the food grew cold on their plates.

Jen sipped at her wine. "You probably want to ask what a girl like me was doing in a place like that."

"Only if you think I should know."

She sighed deeply. "I've made my share of mistakes, but Drew was my worst. I ignored everything my mother ever told me about men and went for superficial. Drew scores a ten on superficial. You've seen him; even with a thin head of hair he is good looking, and charming, which he turns on and off as it suits his purpose. Eventually, I learned to my chagrin that all of his feelings are operated by remote control as necessary for his amusement. I'm not a psychoanalyst but I believe Detective Jordan is a sociopath."

She waited for a response. When Noah shrugged, indicating that he had no way to know, she added, "I'm serious. I Googled the word and at the start of a long list of traits it says that a person doesn't have to exhibit all of them to be a sociopathic personality. He scored a ten on damn near every one. It's a scary list, but the line, 'Ultimate goal is the creation of a willing victim,' frightened me the most, and that's when I decided I had to bail."

Noah, stirred by a swirl of feelings, reached out to caress her cheek. Jen covered his hand with hers and began to cry. "This is a hell of a way to start. I have you over for dinner and a sob story." "I…"

"She took his hand away from her face and held it tightly in both of hers. "I have two reasons for telling you this now. I'm going to be edgy for awhile and it's going to take time before I can come to trust a man again. If that is going to be a deal-breaker—and I wouldn't blame you a bit—it will save us both a lot of heartache. Second, you have a right to know that Drew is mean and vindictive. If you decide to stick around, you'll need to be careful."

Noah put his other hand on top of hers and smiled. "A date with you is certainly not boring."

Jen laughed and withdrew one hand to dab at her eyes with a napkin from the table. "Does that mean you are up for another one?"

He nodded. "I need some excitement in my life. Seriously, has he done anything? Threaten, or try to frighten you?"

"At first, there were some phone calls. Nothing was said, just breathing. Once it sounded like a bar in the background. I know it was him. It hasn't happened since I changed to an unlisted number."

"Not that he couldn't get the number if he wanted to," Noah observed.

"True. But if he did that he would be stalking me. He couldn't say that he had mistakenly dialed his old number. I'm probably being paranoid. Hopefully he has found someone else to be his willing victim and has forgotten all about me."

Jen looked at the plates of cold pasta. "Weren't we supposed to eat these?"

Noah stood and gathered up the dishes. "It will be great heated up. Food, like love, is often better the second time."

Jen replied, "I never waste anything. Just set those on the sink and when I get back from the other room, I'll address your concern about VoShaun."

Noah paused. "VoShaun?" Oh, what I said about you introducing me to such a hot woman. That was pretty silly."

Jen had disappeared down the hall. "There's something you should know about her," she called.

She returned with fresh makeup, having erased any evidence of tears. Noah, seated on the futon, was draining the wine bottle into his glass. "In view of your indifference to wine, I took the liberty of emptying the bottle. Can't have sour wine sitting around the house. Draws gnats."

Jen grabbed her wineglass from the table. "That's kind of you. Let me help." She walked over and emptied her wine into his glass.

"I hope it doesn't bother you to drink my dregs. Now I am free to fix myself a vodka and tonic."

"'Drink my dregs.' Good name for a neighborhood bar."

Jen quickly fixed her drink and seated herself at the other end of the futon. She drew her feet up, watching Noah as she sipped her drink. "Tell me what you think of VoShaun—Detective Taylor," she said.

"I'm glad I took the rest of the wine. That's a leading question. Can I take the Fifth?"

"It's been my experience that only guilty parties exercise their Fifth Amendment rights. Are you guilty of something?"

"I plead guilty to finding her attractive. And, frankly, I thought there was a little something from her, as well.

"As for her job, I think she wants to do the right thing but is stifled by her lieutenant. I've learned a couple of things about the killing and passed them along to her, but she as much as said nothing will be done. She is too green to be able to work around the brass who, by the way, seem singularly uninterested in finding out who killed the boy."

"What does VoShaun say about that?"

"About the lack of enthusiasm up the ladder?"

Jen nodded.

"If she thinks some funny business is going on, she's smart enough not to say anything to me. Follows the party line, more shootings and homicides than they can deal with. Even though it is not one, Homicide is treating Jason's killing like a B.O.B. case. It stays at the bottom of the pile."

"B.O.B.?

"Bum on bum."

"B.O.B. I don't think I've heard that one. Besides I thought the victim was a college student."

"That's true but city homicide is doing the minimum. They're acting like it was a B.O.B."

Jen sipped from her highball glass.

"Did I miss anything?" Noah asked.

"About VoShaun?"

He nodded.

"Before, you assumed that if I cared about you, I would never have let you meet her. Am I right?"

Noah knew when he was being set up. He had mousetrapped too many witnesses on cross examination not to see it coming. Still he answered, "Yes."

"And, you admitted to finding her attractive."

"Asked and answered."

"And, you said you believe she was attracted to you."

"That is hearsay and if you continue this line of questioning, I will invoke the C-word again."

Jen couldn't help but laugh. "In answer to your own question, yes, you missed something. I attribute it to the male ego. VoShaun is gay."

Noah, speechless, stared at her. If she now saw VoShaun as a rival what a clever way to put a stop to anything before it started. She could be pretty certain that he would not ask the detective if it was true. *Any truth to this story I hear about you being a lesbian, detective?*

"Whoa! That came out of left field, very deep left field." He waited but Jen gave nothing away.

"Can I ask is this based on hearsay or direct evidence?"

"I know it's hard to accept, but I would not repeat such a thing on mere rumor. I have the best evidence—her confession."

Noah shook his head slowly. "I don't doubt your word, but I can't understand how I missed the signs."

"Don't feel bad, I didn't see them either. Nobody is supposed to see them."

Jen sighed. "I'm afraid I'm going to have to ask you, once again, to take a vow of extreme silence on this."

Noah felt along his shirt collar. "I feel like I'm taking confession. I should have worn my ecclesiastical shirt."

"I'm sorry, I shouldn't…"

"No. I was just making a bad joke. This murder case may not go anywhere, but if it does I want to know all about her." He reached over and squeezed her hand. "Please…"

"I'm sorry to be dropping all of this on you in one night, but I believe I can trust you and there has been no one else I can talk to."

He reached out and gave her hand another squeeze. "I can handle it."

Jen hesitated only a moment. "VoShaun and I worked a couple of cases together and became—good friends. Things were rough at home so I was looking for any reason not to come here. She and I started lingering after work, usually over a couple of drinks. One night, after I'd made it clear that Drew and I were over, she asked me if I had ever experimented. I assumed she was talking about some form of kinky sex with Drew, but she wasn't.

"Once I understood, I declined as gently as possible, afraid I had lost a friend. She apologized, saying she didn't find me 'all that attractive,' she was just very lonely. As an apology it left a lot to be desired. Anyway, she went on to explain her dilemma, which is quite evident if you think about it. She is a black woman in a detective bureau dominated by men. Mostly white men. That's two strikes against her which she can do nothing about; she's trying to avoid a third."

"By pretending to be something she isn't?"

"It's instinctive in gays. It's something they have lived with for centuries. She's had these feelings since her early teens. Even then she knew it was something to be hidden if she expected to survive."

"Survival? Isn't that a little melodramatic?"

"That's easily said by those of us who don't have to live it."

"*Touche*. Sorry. But, society's views are changing."

"We're talking about the Baltimore City Homicide Bureau. Hardly a reflection of society as a whole.

"VoShaun told me that she worked hard to learn the art of flirting with men, without taking it too far."

"It must be a problem for her," Noah replied. "Working with all that testosterone every day. Some of them are going to have trouble taking 'no' for an answer. I've heard of hot women in such a situation who solve the problem by *pretending* to be gay. Never one who pretended not to be."

Jen nodded. "She mentioned that but it wouldn't work for her, not in that environment. She is stuck with playing it straight, so to speak."

Noah laughed "Sounds like the plot from *Victor Victoria*."

"Another movie?"

"Not just a movie, a film classic. For future reference, I only quote classic films. In *Victor Victoria,* Julie Andrews plays a struggling singer who figures she can do better posing as a man who is in turn, a female impersonator."

"Sounds confusing."

"It gets confusing when she starts falling for a night club owner played by James Garner."

"I'm not sure, but I think I see a similarity. I'm curious, you aren't that much older than I am, so how come you know so much about old movies."

Noah wagged a finger.

Jen smiled. "Sorry. So much about—*classic* movies?"

"Well…"

Jen gave the palm-forward stop signal. "Wait. Let's save that for next time."

Noah nodded, pleased to hear that she was considering a "next time." "As you wish." They were both tired so he resisted announcing that those words were a quote from a more recent movie, *The Princess Bride.*

Jen said, "Returning to VoShaun's dilemma…"

Noah thrust his right hand out at arm's length and swept it across his front. "'VoShaun's Dilemma.' Sounds like a great book or movie title. 'Return to VoShaun's Dilemma' will have to be the sequel. "

"Will you let me finish? It's getting late and I need to get you on direct examination."

Noah submitted with a sigh.

Jen continued, "Thank you. VoShaun has two answers for men who hit on her, depending on the circumstance. One is a question,

'Aren't you married?' And the other, a statement—'I don't date co-workers. No exceptions!'"

Noah threw up his hands. "Okay. Clearly, I missed it. I must compliment her the next time…"

"Don't you dare say a word, not a word. If you do…"

"Just kidding. She'll never hear it from me. Now, what's this about getting me on direct examination?"

"You can't expect me to do all the talking. I'd like to know more concerning the 'nothing' murder you needed to meet with VoShaun about. And, I want to hear more on this 'sabbatical' you claim to be on. The word around the office is that you come from old money so maybe real work is just not your thang?"

Noah studied her momentarily before saying, "All right. Fair is fair. But, you have to be sworn to silence on both topics."

Jen raised her right hand. "So help me, God."

Noah kicked off his loafers. "I hope you don't mind, but I'm more comfortable sans shoes."

Jen laughed. "That's nice, no holes in your socks," she said as her own shoes fell to the rug. "Enough foreplay, let's hear from you."

"Okay. First, about my sabbatical," He mimicked the air quotes she had made around the word 'sabbatical.' "I'm thinking about writing a book."

He waited for Jen's reaction. Finally, she said, "I guess you're not kidding, are you?"

"No. That reaction is why I haven't talked about it. People don't know whether to laugh, or be embarrassed for me."

"I'm sorry, I don't read that much. But don't you need an agent or publisher? I've heard of writers who have been turned down…"

"Rejected."

She nodded. "Yes, rejected—hundreds of times. Couldn't it could take years to be published even if you were accepted?"

"Five years ago, yes, but not today. Now, I am guaranteed publication, sight unseen. No agent. No publisher."

"Really? How?"

"E-books."

Jen was puzzled.

Noah responded, "You don't have an e-reader? Kindle or a Nook?"

"Not yet. I've seen them, but between case files and law books I have no time for pleasure reading. Someday…"

"Fortunately, lots of folks are buying them. E-books are already outselling hardcovers."

"So?"

"So, when my book is completed all I need to do is upload it to Amazon and/or Barnes & Noble, and I'm a published author."

"It doesn't matter what you've written about or how well you wrote it?"

"Doesn't matter. They will only turn it down…"

"Reject it."

"Yes, thank you—reject it—for objectionable content. Otherwise it will be listed for sale."

"What have you chosen to write about? Is it fiction?"

"Good question. I haven't decided. It is an account of an actual incident. Do you remember a few years ago, an assistant U.S. Attorney from Maryland was found dead over the state line in Pennsylvania?"

Jen nodded. "Quite unusual circumstances, as I recall."

"Indeed. They still haven't officially ruled it a suicide, homicide or some bizarre accident. A friend of mine, Jack Douglas, was an AUSA here when this happened. We've talked about it over drinks and he has an intriguing theory of the case. I've been doing some research."

"And?"

"It's too early to be certain, but I think he might have it right. I am undecided on how to write it; as a novel or non-fiction. There are pros and cons for both."

Noah swallowed the rest of his wine and sat back.

Jen waited. "Well?" she said.

"Well what? That's it for now."

"What's your friend's theory?"

"Let's save that for next time."

Jen folded her arms. "Don't be so sure there will be a—'next time.'"

"The Douglas theory is designed to leave you wanting more. Ensuring that there will be a 'next time.'"

"All right, only because that is ancient history. But you're not getting out of here without telling me your theory on the B.O.B. case."

"There is not much to tell. I'm not at all convinced Jason's killing was a random act. There's at least as much—evidence is the wrong word—as much basis for my theory as there is to support the cops' B.O.B. position."

"But the B.O.B. theory is better for them. It's much easier to deal with."

Noah nodded.

"Try me. Let's see if I, as a prosecutor, see merit to your theory."

"All right. But, please keep in mind that a lot of it is old-fashioned gut feelings. Since the police are kissing it off anyway, what can it hurt?

"Let's start there. From the get-go, the cops labeled it a B.O.B. killing because that's what it looked like. Within hours, they learn that their victim is not a streeter and they conduct a few interviews, but VoShaun's lieutenant still treats it like a nothing case."

Jen held up a hand. "Do you know that the cops' B.O.B. theory originates with her loo and not someone higher up the chain?"

"Good point. No, I guess we don't. Wonder what VoShaun would say about that? Do you have a pen and some paper? I want to make notes."

When she left the room, Noah mentally aligned the facts of the case to bring some order to his jumbled thoughts.

Jen returned and stood over him, holding a ballpoint pen and a legal pad. "Would you like me to take the notes?" she asked.

He gave her a quick look and decided she was not being snide. "No thanks," he said, taking the writing materials from her. "It's better for me if I do it. A habit from prepping cases."

While Noah jotted some notes, Jen fixed another vodka and tonic. "Would you like one?"

"Thanks, no," he answered. "They say 'never mix the grape and the grain.' I learned the wisdom of that adage the hard way."

Jen settled on the futon and sipped her drink.

"First," he said, "we have the fact that Jason had money on him. Only a few dollars, still, if this was a B.O.B., why didn't the killer take it?"

"Someone happened by and spooked the killer," Jen offered.

"Certainly a possibility. If so, then there is a witness out there. Why aren't the police trying to find him, or her?"

She nodded her agreement.

Noah made a note. "In any event, there could be a witness. A student nurse looking out a window; an intern coming out of the building.

"Jason had been posting random photos on his site. The pictures, with one exception, seemed harmless enough, but there may be more there than meets the eye." He scribbled as he spoke. "Most likely he took the photos with his cell phone and forwarded them directly to his laptop at home. I want to spend some more time going over the pics that made it to his blog. And Jason made vague threats about exposing some unmentioned city corruption. Again, it sounds like braggadocio, but if you bother to accept that his killing might not be a B.O.B. then anything is possible.

"There is also his website—the Road Warrior. Again, it may not mean anything, but someone had offered to meet with him and failed to show…"

"Why would that be significant?"

"Keep in mind that nobody out there knew the Road Warrior's identity. The emailer sounded anxious, like he had some real dirt. The next week Jason posts a note saying he's sorry the guy didn't show and offers to meet the following week. It's an old cloak and dagger trick. You want to know what someone looks like, you offer to meet them. That person has no way of knowing you, so you hang around the meeting site to see who shows up. And then you know who you need to kill."

"What movie is that from? Never mind."

Noah grinned and jotted a few additional lines.

Jen said, "I don't know. That's a little…"

"According to VoShaun, the cops didn't even know about the Road Warrior website. It was a class project for a course Jason was taking at BCCC Catonsville. VoShaun spoke to Jason's professor on the phone, but, according to him, the website was not mentioned. If you are still not convinced the *pièce-de résistance* is Jason's home was burglarized while the family was attending his funeral."

"Could be a coincidence. There are burglars who prey on …"

Noah finished her sentence. "…homes where they know the residents are all at a funeral service. It's a hell of a coincidence."

When Jen started to interrupt he prevailed by adding, "When you factor in that on that date there were twenty-four funerals published in *The Baltimore Sun* and Jason's house was the only one burgled."

"You thought to check on that?"

"I did," Noah said, adding more notes, "Just as significant is the fact that the only thing of value taken by the burglars was Jason's laptop. His computer could establish that he was in fact killed at the site of a second meeting, or at least identify the email address from which the message was sent. We need to get a look at his email."

"You think that's why someone stole his laptop?"

"To remove the emails, yes. These are all legitimate leads that should be covered, but who's going to do it? Not the cops."

Jen raised her glass in mock salute. "Bravo. You have me convinced. So what happens next?"

12

It had been after 1 when Noah yawned and suggested that it was time for him to leave. He was not dismayed when Jen offered no argument. At that hour they were both drained, and he knew that any attempt at love-making would end in frustration for both of them. And there was the reality that, at least for the present, he would rather sleep in his own bed.

She had returned his short goodnight kiss and locked the door behind him.

Noah sighed as he entered Peace and a Cup of Joe. Wondering what Jen's actions might portend for their future would have to wait. Corky Kilmark was seated at a small window table sipping coffee. He nodded a greeting and, within minutes, Noah was sitting across the table, a steaming cup of coffee in hand.

"I wasn't sure you'd come," Corky said.

"Why not? Coffee with a client."

"That's the thing; I don't think the cops are interested in me anymore—so I guess I won't need a lawyer. Am I right?"

"What a shame. There goes that big fee I was counting on."

Corky smiled. "You earned all of it."

"The whole five dollars?"

"What can I say? I'm a big spender."

Noah studied the man's face. Corky had not asked him here to say "thanks" and "goodbye."

Noah said, "If not a client, how about—coffee with a friend, then?"

"Friends. I like the idea that we could be friends."

Noah saluted with his cup. "Why not? A slot for one more friend just opened up in my world. How about yours?"

Corky dropped his eyes to the table top, his face coloring. "It's funny, the things that cross your mind when you spend hours alone on a street corner. Still, it has been awhile since I thought about this—I don't have any real friends. Not one."

Noah opened his mouth to speak, but Corky was saying, "Oh, I got neighbors, and they're okay—and a brother-in-law—but nobody I could say, 'He's a friend of mine.'"

"Does that bother you?"

Corky shrugged. "Not sure. I guess if it did I would go out and get me one or two. When you think about it, they're all around and a good one doesn't cost anything. Anyhow, I wanted to see if you would be willing to work some more on the killing of that boy. If you say no, I'd still like us to be friends."

Noah considered the proposal before saying, "Tell me what you want me to do and I'll decide if we're going to be colleagues, or friends."

Corky spent the better part of an hour describing the street people of his acquaintance, and detailing his conversations about Jason's killing with Wise Eddie, Captain Marvel and some of the others. He left the table once to refill their cups while Noah scribbled in his spiral notebook.

Corky returned and continued his story.

"You said yourself that the cops aren't going to do jack, so that doesn't leave Marvel much choice. Granted, we don't have any idea what we're going to do, still we got to try. I know you think there's more to it than just a random street killing. But suppose that's just what it is. A killer who gets off on slicing up street people just because they are there. He doesn't have to be a genius to figure out that once he gets away from the scene, the cops won't be busting their hump looking for him."

Noah nodded.

"Or what if the killer is another streeter?" Corky added. "I could just stay home, but street people—the real street people—don't have that option. Marvel has slipped his chain, but his heart is good and he needs help on this."

"I'm with you so far, but it's still not clear what you want from me."

"I told you that Marvel has appointed himself the leader of this 'investigation.' If you can call it that. Here's the problem, if we do come up with something; Marvel doesn't trust cops and refuses to talk to them."

"So what is the point? You think he plans some frontier justice. Find the guy and hang him from a street light?"

"I doubt he's thought that far ahead. That's tomorrow's problem, to be dealt with another day. Let's be honest, Marvel is right, the cops are not going to take seriously anything they hear from street people. It's just as likely they'll lock up any streeter who goes to them."

Corky waited, and hearing no disagreement said, "So, I was thinking—how about if he tells me what he hears and I can pass it on to you. Would you take it to the cops? It's not likely we'll come up with anything, still…"

Noah laughed. "Sorry, it's not funny but it is ironic. I have been talking to a detective about the case and she has sort of agreed to let me do some follow up, providing I keep her filled in, and now you and your friends want me in the middle. Essentially I'd be working for two clients looking for a killer and not getting paid for it. I'd have to be nuts."

"I'll try and get you some more money. It won't be much—still."

Noah waved that thought away and continued. "The idea is intriguing. It's not clear where the boundary lines are as to where I can go, or what I can do without getting jammed up. The good news is we are private citizens, not restricted by department policy and court decisions that can frustrate the police. That can also be the bad news. If I go to them with something solid, the first thing they'll ask me is, 'Where did you get this?' If my answer is, 'Sorry, I can't say,' it goes in their round file or, depending on the cop I'm talking to, I wind up in jail for obstructing a police investigation. The more solid the information is, the harder they'll come down on me. If it is obvious crap, they'll show me the door; if it looks good they'll try and sweat the source out of me. That's one reason PIs avoid working on active police cases."

As an afterthought he added, "And I can't go to VoShaun. Her lieutenant wants this to be over with; he's not going to let her follow up on any leads."

After a moment's silence Corky mused, "It can be damn hard to do the right thing."

"It almost always is. Now, let me tell you what I have been doing before I give you an answer. First, though, I'm invoking client-attorney privilege."

Corky frowned and Noah added, "Its attorney-client privilege in reverse. You can't repeat what I'm about to tell you."

Corky raised his right hand and then sat back and listened while Noah sketched out his discussions with VoShaun, his visit to Jason's professor and the burglary at Jason's home.

When Noah finished he looked at his empty cup and stood. "When I get back I'll tell you what the Internet had on Doctor Musk," he said, taking both cups and heading to the urn for refills.

Corky nodded his thanks as Noah handed a re-filled cup across the table.

"What about Musk?" he asked.

"I found a couple of Ellis Musks on the web and only one who is listed as a physician in Baltimore. I'm certain I have the right guy."

Noah flipped open his note pad and read aloud. "Ellis Musk was born in 1963. Graduated from Johns Hopkins medical school and interned at U of M and then had an OB/GYN practice in Towson. He was married with a couple of kids and a home in Dulaney Valley.

"There was a lot of stuff about his downfall. Essentially he got caught doing narcotics and at least one patient, apparently simultaneously." Noah smiled. "Sounds like sex, drugs and rock and roll."

Corky frowned and Noah flipped the page. "He's been in divorce court and criminal court where the judge ordered him into rehab. To sum up, he was living the dream and woke up in the meth line next to Wise Eddie. His domain suddenly shriveled from a big house in the country to a couple of rooms in a Baltimore flop house. He was a member of the esteemed Center Club, now reduced to peeing in a cup under supervision.

"It's no wonder he walks the streets looking pissed off. Who wouldn't?"

"Sounds like his life's an open book."

Noah nodded.

"So why'd he stab JCube?" Corky asked.

"Maybe he didn't."

"What about Jason's picture of this Doctor Musk bearing down on him?"

"It doesn't mean much. A defense attorney would say that he looks pissed off because he was running to catch a bus, and missed it. And the buildings in the background look more like Howard Street downtown than Penn Street where Jason was killed. On the other hand Musk would likely be familiar with Penn Street amid all of the U of M medical buildings."

Both men paused to drink some coffee and stare intently at the table top.

Noah looked up first, saying, "Then there's the burglary at Jason's. Musk doesn't seem right for that."

"You're thinking the burglary is connected."

Noah nodded.

"If you're right, then this was not just a random street killing."

Noah sat quietly while Corky stared out at the traffic crawling along Pratt Street.

Eventually the streeter had it straight in his mind. "You are probably used to this," he said, "but I'm not. I'm just trying to..."

Noah said, "It's certainly nothing to be ashamed of if you—"

"Whoa. I'm not going to cut and run, if that's what you are about to say. I am thinking that it's only right that I warn Marvel and the others what they might be getting in for—"

"—Of course—"

"But you said I couldn't repeat any of this under that client-attorney privilege thing. How can I warn them, if I can't tell them about the burglary at Jason's house? And they would feel a lot better if they knew you were out doing something and not just sitting around waiting to hear from us."

Noah was thoughtful for a couple of minutes, before saying, "You are right, of course. They need to be told of the dangers. You can tell them the person you are in contact with will be doing whatever he can to help. Don't tell them about me being a former assistant state's attorney. And, for God's sakes, don't say anything about a detective giving me the okay to snoop around."

After a moment Noah added, "You can tell them you heard about the burglary, just don't dwell on it. Keep in mind what we are saying here is mostly guesswork. No need to make too much out of it, but mention that it could be dangerous for anyone who asks around about the killing. How's that?"

Corky nodded. "That should work. And don't worry, I won't tell them anything else unless you have okayed it first."

"Good."

"I don't suppose you have something in mind."

Noah indicated the notebook lying on the table. "I've jotted down some thoughts—not what you could call a real plan, yet. First off, I can treat this like a case that the police might bring to a prosecutor. Look for holes where the case is weak and needs more investigation."

Noah wagged a finger between the two of them. "The problem is we have severely limited resources for such an undertaking. Are you familiar with Sherlock Holmes stories?"

Corky beamed. "Of course. Back when we could afford Netflix, I watched 'em all."

"Well—"

Corky broke in, "Rathbone or Brett? Who was the best Holmes, Jeremy Brett or Basil Rathbone?"

"Brett," Noah replied without hesitation. "I was going to say that Sherlock Holmes had his Baker Street Irregulars, street urchins he used to gather intelligence on London's streets; we have Marvel and his streeters on the streets of Baltimore."

Corky nodded enthusiastically.

Noah made notes as he spoke. "The streeters can watch and listen and report back. If we want somebody watched, who better than street people? They are practically invisible—nobody pays them any mind."

He paused, his pen hovering over the notebook and then scribbled again. "I would like to see a timeline of Jason's final days—a week at least."

"How do we do that?"

"Our Irregulars will need to talk to every street person; somebody had to see him around town. Where and when did they see him, to the best of their recollection? Who was he with, what did they talk about? That kind of thing. You have spreadsheet software on your computer, right?"

Corky nodded.

"Put everything Marvel tells you on a spreadsheet. Maybe we'll identify a person or place of interest. Someone who doesn't want it known that he was meeting up with the Road Warrior."

"It would help if we had a picture of him to show around."

"We do!"

"On the website, am I right?"

"Exactly. I'll make copies and you can ask Marvel to hand them out. Oh—you know what that means—"

"I'm not sure…"

"Somebody out there took Jason's picture for the blog with Jason's own phone. We should try and find out who took it and what that person can tell us about the Road Warrior?"

13

The driver of the battered white Chevrolet Cobalt had no trouble finding a parking place. A row of crumbling three-story brick houses stretched along this block of Harlem Street. All were long-abandoned and boarded shut, a few showed siding of scorched brick from random fires.

His was the only car in sight, but that fact did not worry him. A vehicle displaying the Baltimore City crest on each door was easily explained. It was the job of the city housing department to inspect the thousands of abandoned homes spread across the city. Tony, his boss, had assured him there would be no trouble about their furtive visits to the house on Harlem Street.

The driver walked around to the passenger's side, pausing to gaze up and down the street. He would have been surprised to see any movement. Opening the car door, he hefted a case of Yuengling lager long-necks from the seat and headed across the front yard. He skirted the end-of-row house and headed for the back door.

Up the back steps, he paused at the doorway, covered by a piece of one-inch unpainted plywood decorated with swirls of graffiti. The driver set the Yuenglings down and took another look around before tugging at the plywood. The hinged sheet easily swung open, allowing him and his cargo quick entry. Inside, he sat the case on a table and pulled the door shut.

"Tone? It's me," he called. "I got the beer."

"I'm here, Vern, and thirsty as hell."

At 30, Vernon Watkins was 5 years his boss's junior. His family had left the mountains of West Virginia years before when his father, Ralph Watkins, found work in the Bethlehem Steel Mill at Sparrows

Point on Baltimore's outskirts. By the mid-nineties the mill and shipyard, which together had once employed thousands of men, was struggling to survive.

As a teen-ager, Vernon listened intently to his father's endless anecdotes about goings on at "The Point." One evening Vernon interrupted a story by declaring that he "Could not wait" to begin work there. Ralph stared at the boy for a long moment before saying, "Get that out of yer head right now. That place is dying. No future there."

Vernon heard no more stories about the steel mill and he knew better than to think about working there.

Vernon maneuvered down the narrow hallway, setting the beer on a small table in the middle of a room that had once been the kitchen. He pulled two bottles from the case, crossed the hall into the open game room and handed one to Tony DeRosa.

"It's about time. They cold?"

Vernon snorted. "Jesus. You think I would hand the boss a warm beer?"

Tony stood, twisted the top off and posed. "These inspections are making me thirsty," he parodied.

"Then drink your beer."

Tony took a step forward, posed again and repeated, "These inspections are making me thirsty."

"I get it, Tone. You told the office you're out for the day on your regular Friday inspections, when all we're really gonna be doing is drinking beer and playing poker."

Tony tried the pose once again. "You don't get it! Kramer from *Seinfeld?* Remember, the one where he was gonna be in a movie and drove them all nuts rehearsing his one line? 'These pretzels are making me thirsty.'"

Vernon shrugged.

Tony gestured to the fifty-two-inch flat-screen TV mounted on the far wall. "Jesus, you idiot, we just watched it, a couple of days ago."

"Oh, right. The thing is Tone, you don't look nothing like Kramer." Vernon waved the bottle of beer over his head. "He's tall, with all that hair. And you're—"

"I'm what?" He challenged.

"You're not."

Tony DeRosa had been employed by the Housing Authority of Baltimore City just short of fourteen years. To say he had worked for the city for that period would be inaccurate. After a short stint in the maintenance section he resolved that a job requiring actual labor was not for him; not when the other kind was so easily attainable.

Tony kept his eyes open and grabbed a slot in the housing department's Code Enforcement Division. He intended to bide his time, waiting for his shot while doing the least work needed to get by.

As a housing inspector, opportunities to accept cash gifts for favorable reports were abundant. And Tony rebuffed them all. Over the years, several building contractors had been caught up in the bribery investigations periodically conducted by the area office of the United State's Attorney.

Federal prosecutors cast a wide net, invariably scooping up a few building inspectors among the contractors and elected officials. Unfortunately for the small fish in these schemes, the feds kept everything they caught. Starting on the lowest rung of the ladder they offered you a plea deal—flip on your pals and testify against the bigger fish or do time.

At that point, someone unfailingly turned into a rat, taking everyone down with him.

Tony DeRosa wasn't no rat.

Tony knew a couple of cops who got caught with their hand in the pocket of a local bookmaker a few years back. They only did a few months in federal prison, yet both were different men when they came out.

Tony was not morally opposed to taking "easy money." It was his view that all the smart guys did it; anybody who actually worked forty hours a week was a schmuck. But taking bribes figured to be a losing proposition; it set you up to be taken down by one of those rats. For the few bucks you get, you figure to spend some time in jail, lose your pension and your family hates you. Who needs that?

Tony had been patient. Over the years, he watched and waited and plotted. Four years ago, he was offered a supervisory position. "More money for even less work," he had said. "What's not to like?"

His next step was to weed out the undesirables in his crew. In Tony's world undesirables were anyone he deemed too honest or too smart. Either was a likely threat to his scheming.

Nine months ago Tony maneuvered to have Vernon Watkins assigned to his shift. He then watched the new man for a time before approaching him one warm spring afternoon.

"Come on and take a ride with me." Tony had invited.

"Sure, boss. Where to?"

"I'll drive. You relax. Take a nap if you like."

Dutifully Vernon climbed into the passenger seat of the city car and Tony headed west on Lombard Street. Too wary to doze, Vernon stared out the windshield as they threaded their way through blighted neighborhoods.

Tony took one hand from the steering wheel and waved it at the street. "Ain't this terrible," he said. "There's only three houses with anybody in them on this whole block. They're probably home to more rats than people. All the rest boarded up. Abandoned."

Puzzled, Vernon figured that some response was expected. Tony's comment must have something to do with their work— housing inspections. Hoping he had it right, Vernon said, "The city has them listed as 'abandoned,' but some of them got bums living in them. You want we should start doing something about it?"

Tony turned a corner and stopped in the middle of a narrow street. At this end, the row homes had been displaced by vacant lots strewn with chunks of foundation, old tires and shards of smashed bottles. At the other end a few empty houses continued to decay.

Tony allowed the car to roll along the street. "Homeless bums are not our problem. Besides, this is too far from downtown for your average street bum. Might stumble across a family trying to survive in one of these dumps, but again, not our concern."

The Cobalt rolled through the intersection and into the next block.

Midway in the block, the car drifted to the right curb and Tony switched off the engine.

Vernon glanced along the desolate street swallowing hard. "What are we stoppin' here for, boss?"

Tony pointed through the back window. "This block is as deserted as that one, and the next one up ahead is the same."

"Why do we care?"

Tony laughed. "You look nervous. No tellin' what you was thinking. You'll have a good laugh when I tell you what's going on."

Vernon managed a weak smile. "That's just what I need."

"Today we just seen a small sample of all the boarded-up places in this town. You know how many empty places there are in this city?"

"No idea."

"More than fourteen thousand. Fourteen thousand! What do you think of that?"

"That's a lot, huh?"

"Damn right that's a lot. A lot of empty buildings going to waste. So I got to thinking, 'Why not put a couple of them to good use?'"

"You thinking we should rehab them? For the homeless? Oh, right. You said they're not our problem."

Tony smirked. "You got half of it. We're going to rehab a couple of places, but they're for us, not some bums. We got jobs. We work hard and get damn little for ourselves. This is a chance for the city to reward us for all we done for them."

Tony's voice sobered. "It's a once-in-a-lifetime opportunity, Vernon. I want you with me on this."

"Sounds good to me, boss. Whatever you say."

Tony pointed to the end-of-row house beyond Vernon's window.

"This one will be for us, my crew. I planned this out real good. Real careful. You don't know this, but I picked each of you guys with this in mind. I have watched you and I figured you're the guy to be my number two on this."

Vernon frowned. "I gotta say, that don't sound so good. Ain't number two—you know—when a little kid shits his pants?"

Tony roared with laughter. "I never thought of it like that. No, no. Being number two means you're in charge when I'm not around."

"Thanks, boss. Don't think I don't appreciate it, but what would I be in charge of?"

Tony nodded at the house. "We're gonna turn this into a snazzy party spot, just for us. You know how sometimes our Friday poker game gets interrupted by somebody dropping by the garage? We gotta scramble to hide everything?

"No more. We're getting new stuff and moving it out here, where nobody can find us. On one wall we'll put up a big flat-screen TV, we'll get us a real nice poker table, not that piece of crap we have to use now, and a new refrigerator. Whatever we want. Upstairs we'll have a couple of bunk beds on one floor and my office on the top floor. We'll get binoculars to watch for snoopers."

Vernon was overwhelmed.

"I know," Tony gushed. "Spies got what they call 'safe houses.' You seen them on TV, right?"

Vernon nodded.

"This'll be our safe house." He put a finger to his lips. "Very hush-hush. No one but us can know."

"I like it boss, it's just, well, who's gonna pay for all this stuff? I don't think the boys—"

"Stop worrying. I got the whole thing figured out real good. As for the money, the city's going to foot the bill. They just won't know it."

Vernon was silent, fretting about what he was being dragged into.

Tony added, "This is not an idea that just popped into my head. I spent months scouring the whole city for the right spot. This is it. No one ever comes around here. No reason to. Those City Hall assholes'll never find out about it. If someone should see a city car parked here, so what? We're just doing our job. There's a couple of garages still standing across the alley in back. We'll stash any extra cars in there during the poker game."

Vernon nodded slowly, without exhibiting any of the enthusiasm Tony had expected.

"Trust me on this, its fool-proof. It's been years since the city sprung for a decent raise. They owe us." Tony took a breath. "And here is the best part—" he paused waiting for the other man's admiring gaze. "—this is only the start. The other thing we're gonna do will make us both rich."

Now he had Vernon's attention.

"Rich?"

"Rich. But that's for another time. For now we'll call it 'the other thing.' Just remember you're gonna have to do some of the heavy lifting if you want a big payday."

Vernon stared. "What's that mean—heavy lifting?"

Tony grinned.

Tony DeRosa had indeed planned well when he chose this house. At the rear of the third floor, a door opened onto a tiny railed balcony that offered an unobstructed view of the sky to the southwest. This was vital if they were to have a suitable satellite signal for the fifty-two-inch high-definition TV to be anchored on a first floor wall. The small residential satellite they would install on the balcony was obscured from street view. Electricity to the property was courtesy of a bootleg hookup that pirated power from the Baltimore Gas and Electric Company.

In the weeks following that car ride, Vernon came to learn what his boss had meant by "heavy lifting." He exalted with the thrill of helping Tony deceive their bosses regarding Vernon's work day. Soon his gusto for the project equaled Tony's and he had listened intently when Tony described "the other thing."

Tony drained his beer and motioned Vernon for another.

As he passed it across, Vernon said, "Any luck with the password on that laptop?"

Tony shook his head. "My nephew is a genius with those things, but he hasn't been able to crack it."

"What did you tell him, Tone?"

"That it belongs to a guy worked for me and left without telling me his password. Smart kid, he comes right back with 'the city must have tech support, how come you don't give it to one of them?' I wanted to slap him upside his head, but I don't. I laugh and say that the dipshit has got some stuff on there he shouldn't. Then I give him a wink, 'You know what I mean.' "

"Good thinkin,' Tone."

Tony guzzled some beer, which he followed directly with a long belch. "No it wasn't," he said. "Kid is thinking porn, which is what I wanted him to believe. He gets this shit-eating grin and says, 'I'm all over this.'

"You see my problem. I can't have him seeing the Road Warrior website stuff so I told him there was secret city files which would get us all in a lot of trouble if they figured out he had seen them."

"They can do that?"

"Damn straight. The machine keeps a record every time anybody opens a file."

Vernon shook his head. "The things those machines can do," he said. "It's like they got brains."

Tony nodded. "They're smarter than some guys I know. Anyhow, I don't think it matters. I doubt he can crack the password. I gave him the kid's street address, Zip code and the names of all the relatives that was in the newspaper. Leonard didn't see no pet at the house. If the kid had a girl friend we don't know her name. If the password was something with his birthday, we could be screwed."

Vernon frowned.

"I had to give the nephew a phony birthday. You know older to match a guy who's supposed to work for me. I kept the same month and day, just changed the year."

"I gotcha."

Tony held up a finger. "One more thing. My guy on the cops is slow getting the names on those license tags you got from that house."

Vernon shook his head. "He's probably being careful so it don't come back to bite him in the ass."

"He should be more worried about a kick in the ass from my size twelves. One of them cars might be the kid's girlfriend. That might give us what we need to figure out his password."

"Maybe you should go easy on him, he might get pissed off."

"He's the one should watch it. I know for a fact, he needs the money I'm giving him."

"Who is he, Tone? I should know since you made me number two and all."

"No way," Tony snorted. "The deal is between him and me. If he thinks that anyone else knows what he's doing the deals over."

"What can he do about it?"

"I don't want to find out. It's working just fine the way it is."

There was a noise at the back door and Tony rubbed his hands gleefully. "We'll finish this later," he said. "I hear the guys. You know Bobby bluffs a lot. Watch for me to go 'all in' on his ass and see if he shits himself."

14

The day before, Noah had found a note in his mailbox inviting him to "dinner and a show" at Frau Wirtz's house that evening. He had scrawled "Sorry, busy" below her request and left it in her mail box on his way out. This morning, as he drove away, Noah had spied Frau Wirtz in his rear-view mirror, waving frantically as he turned onto Wetheredsville Road. While watching her, he narrowly missed hitting a white car bearing City of Baltimore door decals parked a few houses along the narrow street.

As Noah neared Franklintown Road, his cell phone began playing Abba's "Mama Mia." With his right hand, Noah dug into the cup holder for the phone while keeping his eyes on the road and steering with the other hand.

I have to get one of those hands-free devices, he thought.

He glanced in the rear-view mirror for the presence of a police car before putting the phone to his ear. "Noah Cassidy."

"Mister Cassidy, this is Arnold Martin—Jason's professor."

"Yes, sir. What can I do for you?"

"Are you still interested in his murder?

...If not, I apologize for the call."

"I am still very much interested."

"This may be nothing, but I will feel better if somebody else knows about it."

Noah stopped at a red light and shifted the phone to his left hand. "Go ahead, sir."

"Jason's killing has bothered me a great deal. I can't help feeling somehow responsible..."

If Martin was waiting for Noah to reassure him, he was disappointed.

It wasn't Noah's place to let him off the hook. Besides, the professor's guilt was motivating this call.

Martin continued, "I heard about the burglary and that all they took was his laptop…"

"Yes."

"I guess—I don't think it was a coincidence. Is that foolish of me? The police don't seem interested."

"Not at all."

"I called them to ask about the memory stick for Jason's computer. I wound up speaking to a lieutenant. He was polite, but very uninterested. Impatient to get me off the phone. Anyhow, do you know if the thieves got Jason's thumbdrive?"

"His thumbdrive?"

"Yes. It's an external memory stick."

"I know what it is," Noah said, "I'm trying to grasp the significance."

"Maybe there is none, but it seems to me if they were so desperate to get his laptop that they'd break into the house, they must be afraid there's something on it that could hurt them. Does that make sense?"

Way to go professor!

"It makes damn good sense."

Mainly because you agree with me.

"Jason was fanatical about backing up everything on a memory-stick. If his killers don't have the stick, I think somebody should take a look at what is on it."

Noah's mind was a boil with the possibilities presented by the professor's idea. It may well be the technological equivalent of yesteryear's 'smoking gun.'

A smoking stick?

Noah, already knowing the answer, asked the question anyway. "You don't think the police are going to follow up on this?"

"Very doubtful."

He must have spoken to VoShaun's lieutenant. It would be interesting to see if this potential case-breaking lead gets passed down to the lead detective.

"Do you know Jason's parents?"

"I've met them a couple of times," Professor Martin replied. "I think they would know who I am. Why? What do you want me to do?"

"Go with me to see if they have the stick. If so, ask if they will give it up. Without alarming them."

"Why would they be alarmed?"

"If the killers think of this, they may return for it. Jason's family could be in harm's way."

"I ...see what you mean. I can't really go today..."

Noah, nearing the entrance to the parking garage on West Pratt Street, pulled to the curb. "I can't make it either. I've got to meet someone. ... How about tomorrow afternoon, about 5:30. Somebody should be home there."

"That's doable."

Noah was seated with a cup of coffee when Corky arrived at Peace and a Cup of Joe. He was hard to miss, clad in a sleeved camouflage blanket of faded pink.

Noah started to rise, "I would have gotten you a cup," he said, "but it would get cold quick on a day like this."

Corky waved him back in his chair. "Sorry I'm late, I'll get it."

Back at the table Corky shivered as he stirred cream and sugar into his coffee. "You are right about the cold." He jabbed a finger at the frayed blanket which covered him from shoulders to below the knees. "This still isn't enough in the wind."

"Pink camo? Where in hell did you find that?"

"Army surplus store. I had to get something, I was freezing out there. I went looking to get a fatigue jacket or the like. They had row after row of regular camo jackets and it dawned on me that nearly every street person you see is wearing camo this time of year. Then I spot a bin of these blankets that they were closing out..."

"I can see why."

Corky pointed to his head. "But I'm thinking, see. On the street you need something that stands out, so that customers are drawn to you instead of your competition. Like McDonald's Golden Arches, you can spot this thing blocks away. I spent a couple of days trying to get it ratty-looking. You know, for the street."

"It also makes you a good target. Until this is over, I suggest you get an old fatigue jacket so you look like everybody else out there."

Noah brought him up to date on what had transpired since they last spoke. He finished up by asking, "Do you know what a computer memory stick is?"

Corky nodded and held the thumb and forefinger of his right hand about two inches apart.

"That's it. Jason's college instructor, Professor Martin, says that Jason backed up all of his work on a stick, so there may be some critical information for us."

"How are you going to get it?"

"VoShaun mentioned a memory stick in the list of property the cops turned over to Jason's mother. Martin and I are going to visit Jason's folks to see if they still have it."

"What if they won't give it up?'

Noah shrugged. "We'll see."

Corky said, "Yesterday, I heard about a street person called Deacon. Apparently Marvel is the leader of all the street people on this side of Broadway. If I'm right, this Deacon is the same thing for street people east of Broadway."

"Street people have their own gangs?" Noah asked. "With these two—like gang leaders?"

Corky was thoughtful before saying, "More like tribes, with tribal chiefs, I think. I thought you should know."

Noah shrugged. "Whatever. In any case, we should talk to him."

"He's in East Baltimore, what's he going to know about a street corner stabbing on this side of town?"

"Maybe nothing," Noah said. "But we won't know until we ask him. The least we can do is alert this Deacon and his 'tribe' to protect themselves."

15

Barbara Peterson answered the door and recognized Noah as the "policeman" who had stopped by a couple of days before.

It was in situations like this that Noah was thankful he bothered with seemingly minor details. In reading Jason's obituary, he noted that the boy's mother was remarried and her surname was now Peterson. Had he not read the obituary he likely would have called her Mrs. Jefferson, a mistake a police detective assigned to the case would not be apt to make.

"Mrs. Peterson," Noah said, "I believe you know Professor Martin, from Jason's school. May we come in? We just have a couple of questions."

"Nothing you folks can do will bring Jason back; still, I'm comforted to see that the police are still working on it."

Noah ignored Martin's questioning look.

She led them into the living room and directed the two men to a slip-covered sofa while she occupied a Boston rocker. "Of course we'll do anything to help; but, my husband will be home soon, expecting his supper."

"We will try to be brief," Noah said. "A question has come up about your son's computer. Do you know what a memory stick is? They are also called thumb drives."

Barbara shook her head. "That's all beyond me. Beats me where Jason gets—got it from."

"It's a small device, about the size of a nail clipper, which fits into the side of a computer. Professor Martin mentioned how diligent Jason was copying all of his work to one of those sticks. We hope to find his work with the street people on such a drive. Would you mind looking for it in his room?"

She looked to Martin, seemingly for assurance that such an intrusion was really necessary.

The professor nodded. "It could be quite important," he said.

Jason's mother sighed and heaved herself out of the rocker. After a couple of steps, she stopped and glanced back at the two men. "I 'spect you two better come along, as I have no idea what it is you want."

Inside Jason's room, his mother motioned toward the student desk along one wall. "Help yourself," she said. "Just don't be all day about it."

On the ride to the house, the two men had agreed that the professor should search Jason's desk, the most likely place to find the memory stick, while Noah looked over the rest of the room.

Noah preferred that, if the question arose, Jason's mother would tell the police she gave the stick to Jason's professor rather than to a phantom police detective. Granted, it was a fine line, but it would look better if Noah was forced to defend himself against charges of interfering with a murder investigation. An impersonation charge was easily explained by the confusion of a distraught family. At least that would be Noah's story.

Jason's bedroom was tiny, offering scarcely any place other than the desk to search. One twin bed sat next to the desk, leaving very little room for any other furniture. Between the bed and the wall, two-six-foot long two by eight planks resting on cinder blocks formed a crude bookcase, both shelves of which overflowed with hardcover books and magazines on sociology, social science and, strangely Noah thought—astrology. He wondered if Jason was clever enough to hide the stick inside one of the books.

A clothes closet with folding doors occupied most of the far wall. The doors were closed and Noah was mulling the propriety of asking to search through the dead boy's clothes when Martin stepped away from the desk.

"There are two sticks in this drawer." He looked to Jason's mother. "Do you mind if I pick them up?"

Barbara shrugged. "That's why you're in here, isn't it?" she said.

Martin held the memory sticks in one palm for her to see. "I hope you'll consent to let us take these with us," he said.

"Both of them?"

"There's no way to tell which one might be important."

"They are so small, there can't be much on them."

"On the contrary," Professor Martin said, "These amazing little sticks can hold volumes of data."

"Well, I never." She was thoughtful for a time and Martin started to speak but caught Noah's eye and both men were quiet.

Finally Barbara said, "I'm afraid I don't understand. What could he have put on those little things?"

Noah nodded and Martin spoke. "We have no way of knowing, but I'm hoping to find some of Jason's papers on his study of the street people."

Silently, Martin asked forgiveness for the lie he was about to tell. "I would like to review his work in the event there is something that would merit submission to a professional journal."

"Oh, that would be wonderful. A tribute to Jason's work…"

"Please understand," Martin interjected, "Even if we find something worthy of submission, there is no guarantee that it will be published."

"All the same I'll be relieved to have them out of the house. My husband says he believes the thieves who stole Jason's computer were the same ones who killed him." She shuddered. "The thought is frightening, and we have said nothing to my daughter, Isabel."

Barbara looked from one man to the other in anticipation, when they did not reply, her eyes stayed on Noah. "With these sticks out of the house there is no reason for those awful men to come back."

Martin pretended to closely study the memory sticks in his hand. Noah nodded, seeing nothing to be gained by pointing out the flaw in her logic.

At the Peterson's front door both men thanked her again.

As they descended the porch steps Professor Martin handed both of the sticks to Noah.

A white car with the City of Baltimore seal on the door passed slowly along the street in front of them.

It did not occur to Noah to question the presence of a City of Baltimore car in a Baltimore County neighborhood during the work day.

16

Vernon parked in the alley behind "the party house," then climbed the steel steps and disappeared through the back door.

Tony, waiting in the TV room, grabbed a beer from the refrigerator and handed it across the pool table.

"Man, do I need this," Vernon said and drank deeply from the bottle.

"Following people is a lot harder than it looks on TV. I gotta hand it to cops who can do that."

Tony opened a beer for himself and dropped into an oversized La-Z-Boy recliner. When the chair was delivered, he had exhilarated in the rich buttery soft leather and immediately proclaimed it his personal domain. It seemed to empower him, making him feel like royalty ascending the throne. Even when he was not present, no one was allowed to sit in what had become known to Vernon and the others as, "Tone's throne."

The chair, like the other furnishings in the party house, was purchased new with a city housing credit card. Tony had dismissed, with a shrug, Vernon's concerns about being caught.

"Don't worry about it. I got it covered," was his response.

Vernon came around the pool table and dropped into a cloth rocker. His chair, as he perceived it to be, was comfortable, but not as plush as Tony's recliner.

Now came the tough part, his report.

Vernon was anguished over being ordered to follow a former prosecutor. He failed to see the point and was perpetually frightened of being discovered. To say that he lacked enthusiasm for the job was a gross understatement.

Tony had exploded when he learned that one of the license tags Vernon had copied at the Jefferson kid's house belonged to a former assistant state's attorney.

"What the fuck is he doing there? Vern, I want you to follow him. See what he's up to."

Vernon, puzzled by the order, said, "Where's he going?"

"Jesus, Vern. If I knew where he was going you wouldn't have to follow him. We know he's a former prosecutor; he could be up to anything. I don't like surprises."

The truth was that Vernon was not very good at conducting a moving surveillance. The few days he trailed the man had, in general, been a failure. His one triumph was the time he managed to follow the car from the address in Dickeyville to Catonsville Community College. A fact which he proudly reported to Tony only to be assailed for not knowing who this Cassidy had met with at the school.

"Let's hear it," Tony commanded.

Vernon had to be careful. If he reported what really happened— that he was parked a few houses from the man's apartment when Cassidy drove out of his driveway and narrowly missed colliding with the city car while looking in his rearview mirror—he would be forced to admit that he had immediately lost Cassidy and it had taken the rest of the day to find him.

Vernon only knew of three places Cassidy might go and filled the day driving between them. As the hours passed he grew more frantic over Tony's anticipated reaction to his report of another failure.

It was on a final swing through the community college campus that he spotted the car. He could hardly believe his eyes as he watched a man getting in with Cassidy and drive away.

Tony was visibly agitated as he listened to Vernon. "He could be trouble for us. We gotta find out what he's up to."

"They was at the dead kid's house maybe ten minutes when here they come out the front door. They was coming down the walk when the other guy hands something to our boy."

Tony leaned forward. "What did the guy give him, for Christ's sake?"

Vernon shrank into his chair, averting his eyes from his boss's glare. "Geez, Tone, I couldn't tell—it was real small. Whatever it was, our boy stuffed it in his pocket right away."

Tony began chewing his lower lip and stared at the dark TV screen on the wall behind Vernon. "We know our boy quit the state's attorney, so he's nothing now. You think this other guy was a cop?"

Vernon made a face. "Dunno. But, he didn't look like no cop. Too…"

"Too what? Too what? Spit it out, for Christ's sake."

"Hey. Take it easy, Tone. I'm doin' the best I can, here."

"Yeah, yeah, okay. Get on with it. Too what?"

"He looked too much like a weenie to be a cop. You know what I mean?"

"How the hell would I know, I didn't see the bastard."

"Cops have a certain look they get from years of pushing people around. You can see it in their faces. This guy has never pushed nobody around. If I had to guess, I would say he's been pushed around some."

Vernon sat back and tried to coax the last drops of beer from his bottle, dreading another blast of his boss's anger.

Tony appeared impervious to his surroundings, saying nothing as he gazed at the ceiling.

A fidgety Vernon, finding the quiet unbearable blurted out, "Hey, Tone …You remember you told me you had some news. I guess it's bad, huh?"

Tony stirred, groped for his beer bottle and chugged the remainder before turning to the other man. "News? Oh, yeah. It's not good, but it's better that we know it than if we didn't?"

Vernon walked to the stainless steel refrigerator and pulled out two cold beers. After handing one to Tony he said, "I'm not sure what you are saying, but I guess you'll tell me, huh?"

"Look, I shouldn't have been so rough on you, you did good. It's just that I got a lot on my mind right now. You'll see, after I explain."

Vernon sat down and hoisted his bottle in salute. "I'm not worried. I know you got it covered, boss."

"Remember, we talked about Junior trying to hack into that kid's computer?"

"Junior?"

"Jesus. My nephew. I told you he was doing it."

"You never told me his name," Vernon grumbled.

Tony dismissed the excuse with a wave of the hand.

"Anyway," Tony continued, "he got into the kid's files. He got rid of what we needed him to." He made air quotes and added, "Deleted it."

Vernon brightened. "Well, that's good, ain't it, Tone?"

"It was. Until he noticed that those same files had been saved to something he called an 'external drive.'"

"You lost me."

Tony held a fist in the air, his thumb pointed skyward. "Junior showed me one. It's a piece of plastic about the size of your thumb." Tony shook his head. "It's hard to believe, but Junior says you can keep thousands of pages stored in that little stick."

Vernon, sensing that somehow this problem was going to be his fault, fidgeted in his seat. "What's that mean, Tone?"

Tony leaned forward waiting for Vernon to meet his gaze. "It means that we still got trouble. That email I sent to the kid is still out there. It means that this Cassidy is smarter than we figured. He's way ahead of us. Must have gone back to the kid's house and found that memory stick. If that was it, he can sink us. Anyhow, I asked Leonard did he see one of them sticks in the house. He says no."

Anxious to please his boss, Vernon offered, "I don't think we got anything to worry about, Tone. This guy is not a cop, and we been told he left the state's attorney's months ago. Maybe he is just a friend of the family and that's why I spotted him there the other day. Yeah, I bet that's it." Believing himself to be on a roll, Vernon added, "And it's for damn sure he doesn't know about—you know—our other place."

The empty beer bottle narrowly missed Vernon's head and smashed against the wall behind him. The second bottle, half-full, bounced off of his shoulder and rattled to the floor.

"Shut up! Just shut the fuck up! You're making me crazy. You should have shut up after you said—'I don't think.' That's your problem—you don't think."

Tony glared at an ashen Vernon, who rubbed his aching shoulder with one hand. "I gotta think," Tony snapped. "Since you're not doing nothing but causing trouble, get me a beer."

Vernon hesitated, reluctant to rearm his boss with another missile. But to refuse would re-ignite Tony's short fuse. A sullen Vernon crossed to the refrigerator and opened a bottle, which he set on the table next to his boss.

After several minutes, Tony stirred and drank some beer. He wiped his mouth and looked at Vernon still working his shoulder and whimpering softly.

Vernon kept at his injury in hopes of some sympathy, but Tony was in no mood to oblige him and turned his gaze back to the dark flat TV screen. He reached for the remote and clicked on "The View." Though both men hated the show, Tony increased the volume until the gabble of female voices filled the room. He shot Vernon a look daring him to utter a word of complaint.

Vernon was quiet and gave up rubbing his shoulder.

"Come on, boss," he eventually whined. "Turn that shit off, it's giving me a headache. You gonna tell me what's going on? How much trouble are we in?"

Tony hesitated over the remote button and then clicked the show off.

"Did you ever look at that kid's blog—'The Road Warrior'?"

"I don't know nothing about computers, I told you."

"You know how to...never mind. When I saw the pictures he was putting on the Internet, I knew it was only a matter of time until..."

"You mean pictures of this place, Tone?"

"That's bad enough but it's the other place that we gotta worry about. When Junior erased all of that stuff, I figured we was home free. Then he drops this fuckin' A-bomb about the memory stick thing."

"What are we gonna do?"

"We need to find out what this Cassidy knows. Better yet it would be real nice if somebody was to come forward and confess to killing the kid." Tony brushed his palms together. "Then—case closed. End of story."

Vernon was panicked. He did not understand what the boy's murder had to do with their troubles. Did the boss expect him to confess to the killing?

Tone knows what he's doing. Everything'll be fine.

"You know who killed that kid, Tone?"

Tony glared across at him. "I know somebody who can find us a candidate for the job."

17

Frau Wirtz sat in the shadows of her darkened living room. Across the driveway she was able to glimpse a portion of the second-floor balcony leading to Noah Cassidy's front door. Recently she had decided to become more aggressive in the love story playing out in her head: The Seduction of Noah Cassidy.

She imagined the two of them as the star-crossed lovers from the film classic *Casablanca*. She the lovely Ilsa Lund, he the dashing Rick Blaine.

Tonight, following a leisurely bath laced with fragrant petals, she donned a 1940s-style peignoir recently purchased online. She had waited impatiently for its arrival. An elegant gown of silk charmeuse-satin in a soft peach-glow shade with which she would consummate her fantasy.

The French lace trim set it apart from the other gowns she had viewed. Against her skin the feel of satiny soft undergarments heightened her fervor. She smoothed the gown over a thigh with a gentle stroke.

What man could resist this? She mused.

When Frau Wirtz had converted her carriage-house to rental apartments she rejected the contractor's suggestion that motion-sensitive floodlights be installed, to illuminate the paved area surrounding the apartments. She had already spent more money than she intended. Besides, the headlights of any car entering the driveway would be sufficient notice of an arrival.

She knew, from previous nights of spying, that Noah often parked behind the garage and then climbed the darkened stairs, slipping through his door before she was aware he had returned.

Now she gazed at the dim glow from the electric candle in his front window. An interruption of the tiny gleam would indicate that the present object of her affections was passing in front of the window to reach his front door. Tonight she would rush out and confront him, desperate that she not be denied.

When finally the light blinked, Frau Wirtz jumped up, her heart racing. She gathered her gown and rushed across the drive.

At the top of the stairs she heard his door click shut. When she reached the door, Frau Wirtz rapped firmly calling out, "Please open the door dear boy! I must see you."

She patted her coiffure and, after a moment, repeated her plea.

"I know you are in there and I will not be denied." In a sultry voice she added, "You will not be disappointed."

The door swung open and an aroused Frau Wirtz rushed into the gloom.

Noah Cassidy inserted his key and pushed. His door moved mere inches before meeting resistance. Puzzled, he withdrew the key and worked his head around the door. When his eyes became accustomed to the dim early morning light, he distinguished the inert form of Frau Wirtz sprawled across his rug.

It took a moment for the stunned former prosecutor to react. After squeezing his way into the room, he closed the door and clicked the wall switch, illuminating a desk lamp. It appeared that Frau Wirtz had come to his apartment wearing some sort of fluffy negligee, now soaked in her blood, the hem of which was pulled up around her waist.

She wasn't wearing panties and Noah averted his eyes as he knelt to check her pulse. Had she worn no undergarment when she came to the door, or had her killer taken them with him? A souvenir.

After confirming that she was indeed dead, he stood and quickly assessed the room. Immediately his eyes fell on the empty desk where his laptop sat yesterday morning when he left. It seemed that nothing else had been disturbed and he knew better than to look any further until the police arrived. Noah placed the call on his cell phone and stepped out on the balcony to wait.

It was obvious, to him, that she had been killed sometime the night before and he would be required to account for his whereabouts during those hours. He hesitated only a moment before touching 2, his speed-dial number for Jen's phone.

They spoke briefly, clicking off when he heard the first sirens coming down Forest Park Avenue. Shortly the city cruiser would be turning onto Wetheredsville Road.

In moments the siren ground to silence and the police car, lights flashing, turned into the driveway. Noah remained completely still as two uniformed officers clamored up the stairs, each with one hand gripping the handle of a holstered weapon.

Once the officers were satisfied that the apartment was secure, Noah was escorted to the sofa, where he watched as his home quickly filled with detectives and crime scene personnel.

The sight of a corpse would not normally make Noah queasy, but the presence of a deceased Frau Wirtz in his own living room had shaken him. After the coroner removed her body, Detective Jeff Baines approached the sofa and introduced himself.

"I'm Detective Baines, Baltimore City homicide. All right if I sit down? I need to ask you some questions."

Noah nodded. He was heartened by Baines' professional mien. The detective appeared fit and confident, a veteran officer in his mid-forties, and yet he seemed serious about his work. Noah knew several detectives who would arrive at a crime scene wearing their boredom and distain for the job for anyone to see. Such men were routinely clad in loud sport coats and wrinkled slacks—seemingly a uniform for the insolent.

Baines was an exception, sharply dressed in a dark suit, a shirt of pale yellow and a matching tie decorated with tiny blue anchors. Noah noticed shirt cuffs at the man's wrist. Many detectives wore short-sleeve wash-and-wear shirts, often the same one for succeeding days, summer or winter.

Baines sat and flipped through his notebook before looking up. *I got a lot of information in here, so don't think about lying to me,* was the intended message.

"Noah Cassidy. Seems though I should know that name."

"I spent a few years with the state's attorney in Baltimore City."

Baines nodded. "Good. You should know the drill. What happened here?"

Noah, with nothing to hide, knew it was wiser to volunteer everything, providing Baines no reason to give him further consideration as a suspect.

The detective took detailed notes as Noah recounted his activities of the previous day. Baines paused and gave Noah a brief glance upon hearing the name Jennifer Stambaugh. In his call to Jen, Noah had alerted her to expect a contact from homicide.

I hope Baines is not a particular friend of Jen's ex.

Noah nodded toward the small dining table. "And I noticed my laptop was gone from that table."

"Anything else?" Baines asked without looking up.

Noah shrugged. "I took a tour around the place with the uniforms. Doesn't seem to be anything else missing."

"Anything special on the laptop—anything worth killing over?" Baines asked as he flipped his notebook closed.

Noah thought of the research notes for his book, relieved that he had saved them to an external memory stick. It was then he realized that the memory stick was still plugged in to the laptop when he left this morning. Though troubled at losing his own research data, Noah was consoled by the thought; *it could well have been Jason's memory stick in the computer. Doubtless that was what they were after.*

He could think of no reason to mention the stick, so he told Baines what the detective was expecting to hear.

"Nothing I can think of."

18

"Noah Cassidy."

"This is Detective Taylor. We need to talk. How soon can you get to the Centerpointe Starbucks, on Eutaw Street?"

"About thirty minutes. In fact, I was just going to call you. Is this about—"

"Thirty," she repeated and hung up.

Noah was relieved to have somewhere else to be. As he closed the door behind him, he experienced a sudden anguish at the notion it would no longer be necessary to fend off Frau Wirtz's clumsy advances.

Seated at the Centerpointe Starbucks, Noah had a steaming latte waiting for Detective Taylor when she sat down. She blew through the vapor and nodded a thank you as she took her first sip.

She looked directly at Noah and said, "I thought you should know the investigation into Jason Jefferson's murder is closed."

Noah's mouth was agape for several seconds before he replied. "Based on what?"

"Earlier some uniforms locked up a drunk. Some street bum. For no reason anybody can think of, Masterson sends the squad idiot down to talk to him."

"You weren't involved in the questioning?" VoShaun shook her head. "By some mysterious coincidence, I was out on a bullshit interview with Detective Rollie Corbett when the bum, one Spike Jones, was brought in."

"But you are going to follow up."

She shook her head. "When I walked in to the squad, Detective Dickson was waving some papers which he said was Spike's confession. Crowing about how he had cleared my case for me."

Noah fidgeted with his coffee cup before asking, "Did you see anything wrong with the statement?"

VoShaun took a deep breath. "You won't believe this, but I never got so much as a glance at the cover sheet."

"Jesus!"

"I said, 'Let me have a look' and reached for it. Dickson sneers, 'Why don't you just say thank you, detective,' walks into Masterson's office and drops it on his desk. Well, I'm really burning—I'm right behind him and before I can pick it up Masterson grabs the file and shoves it into a desk drawer. Then he folds his hands and sits there grinning at me.

"Now I'm yelling, 'What's this bullshit? I'm the primary.' I stick my hand out, 'Let me see it.' I look over at Dickson. He's smirking and Masterson, with a shitty grin, says, 'Wrong tense, detective.' I yell right back at him, 'What the hell does that mean, wrong tense?' He says, 'You *were* the primary. The investigation has been closed for several minutes, so now—you're not. See? Past tense.'

"What could I do, I just stormed out, with them laughing behind me. I wish I had slammed his goddamn door and broken the glass like in that movie. But I couldn't think straight. And another thing, it was no coincidence that I happened to be out of the squad when this happened."

"Why do you say that?"

"It's early. I'm at my desk. Masterson appears in his doorway—again with that grin—pretending to look over the squad. Finally he says in that sing-songy voice he uses when he knows he's being shitty, 'Detective Taylor, I need you to go with Detective Corbett on an interview.'

"I'm sitting right next to Kelly, who is supposed to be Corbett's partner on the rare occasion when Corbett leaves the office, and I look like, 'What's wrong with him?' When I glance back, Masterson is back at his desk and Corbett's up at the board getting the keys to a unit. It's a done deal."

Noah thought a minute before asking, "What can you tell me about this Corbett? If it was rigged he would have to be in on it."

VoShaun drained the by-now tepid coffee and pondered her empty cup. "If it *was* rigged, and loo needed somebody to play that part, it would be Corbett, aka DA, as he is known around the squad. DA stands for 'Dumb Ass,' and that says it all. Dumb as he is, Corbett's got to be related to some politician to keep his job. His days are filled by hanging around the squad waiting to do Masterson's bidding. He runs errands. I mean picks up the man's dry cleaning, for God's sake. Fetches loo's coffee and drives him anywhere he needs to go. Since my lieutenant never appears at a crime scene, Corbett only drives him to lunch."

"What about the interview you went on with him? If Corbett doesn't work cases, what was the interview about?"

"We'll never know. Nobody was home when we got there, so we drove straight back to the squad." VoShaun hunched forward. "I may be green, but I know when something doesn't smell right. It took us about twenty minutes to get to the address—a rowhouse in Highlandtown. I was pissed, but I still wanted to do my job, so naturally I ask him to brief me on the case we're supposed to be working. He just laughs—real snotty like—and says he's got it covered. Tells me to sit back and enjoy the ride.

"At the house, he barely taps on the front door—when was the last time a cop merely tapped on somebody's door? He waits about five seconds, mutters 'nobody home,' and heads for the car. I say, 'Don't you want to try around back?' Over his shoulder he says, 'I'm leaving, you wanna walk back, it's fine with me.'"

"Do you remember the street address in Highlandtown?"

VoShaun nodded.

"You might want to check it in the Reverse Lookup and see who lives there."

"What would that tell me?"

Noah shrugged. "Maybe nothing, but if it turns out to be some cop's relative, then maybe something. If not, just tuck the name away for future reference."

"What do I do about the case?" She asked. "That wasn't right, what they did. Shouldn't I report this to someone up the line?"

Noah was careful with his response. "I applaud your keen sense of right and wrong and I agree the whole thing stinks. But whether they are corrupt or merely bozos in blue is impossible for you to determine. What exactly are you going to report? You were told to go on an interview and nobody was home? You didn't get the glory for clearing a nothing homicide?"

He waited and getting no reply, continued, "You want to do the right thing, but that's never easy and God knows I'm not going to make that decision for you. I'm guessing you want to stay on the job."

She nodded.

"Ever hear of Frank Serpico?"

VoShaun shrugged.

"Serpico was a New York City cop in the '70s who tried to blow the whistle on major corruption in his department and almost got killed by fellow cops for his trouble. How long do you think he lasted on the job?

"While you're mulling what to do, you might check him online. More apropos, also in the '70s a Baltimore City vice cop helped the FBI put away some of his corrupt pals. Wore the proverbial 'wire'; testified against them and then immediately left the department for parts unknown."

Sadly, VoShaun shook her head.

Noah continued, "It's doubtful that the NYPD or your department is less corrupt today because of what those two officers did. But that's really immaterial. Each man believed that it was something he had to do and, other than getting killed doing it, the consequences were pretty much irrelevant to them.

"If I were to give you advice it would be this; keep an unofficial record of everything that happens and keep it somewhere safe. Watch your six o'clock all the time and don't trust anybody. Wait and see how it plays out. A move now could be premature. Sometimes things have a way of working themselves out without your help."

VoShaun looked up sharply, her dark eyes flashing. "That seems awfully cavalier advice from someone who is no longer concerned with this case. I may be a rookie, but I'm smart enough to know when I'm getting wedged between a large rock and the highway. The reality is—you have no dog in this fight. For you, this is a lark, an adventure to kill time between gigs. Tomorrow, you could get an offer from a big law firm. The day after that," VoShaun waved a hand over the table, "This becomes a story to amuse your clients with over an expensive lunch.

"Meanwhile, this is VoShaun's life. I have worked too damn hard to get here."

She started to rise from her chair.

Noah, stung by her tone and her words, managed a quiet response. "I am sorry that you feel that way. However, I am in this case until the end and it would be in your best interest to let me bring you up to date. There have been some rather somber developments of which you are obviously unaware."

VoShaun sat down folded her arms and returned his gaze without a word.

"Do you know a Detective Jeff Baines?" He asked.

VoShaun shook her head. "Should I?"

"He is a city homicide detective. Blonde, near forty, good looking and very well dressed—for a cop. Looks like the cover of *GQ*."

"That's Hollywood! Remember, I'm new in homicide. One of my first mornings I saw him—a real pretty boy, almost glamorous." She gave Noah a look and added, "Anyhow, being eager, I was in early and he was going off the graveyard shift. I never heard his name—they just called him 'Hollywood.' "

Noah said, "He's been on the job long enough to be off of nights. Any idea why he's on that shift?"

"Nobody tells me anything directly, but from what I hear he had no choice. Masterson had him transferred to graveyard."

"Has to be a punishment. For what?"

VoShaun shook her head. "It wouldn't have to be much. The scuttlebutt is that Corbett, the lapdog, hated Hollywood for obvious reasons—better looking, smarter, you name it—and pushed to get him off the squad. Masterson rode Baines hard until he got an excuse to ship him to nights. How do you know him?"

Noah told her.

VoShaun stood and gathered up both cups. "I'm sorry about going off on you like that. When I get back with these tell me how I can help—preferably without getting fired."

When VoShaun returned, Noah told her of receiving a call from Professor Martin and their retrieval of Jason's memory stick. This he followed with a description of his finding of Frau Wirtz in his apartment earlier that morning.

VoShaun's eyebrows raised when Noah related that his computer, with a memory stick installed, was missing from his apartment. Finally he conveyed his assessment of the manner in which Detective "Hollywood" Baines conducted himself.

When Noah finished, VoShaun said, "Again, I'm sorry about before. I didn't know about your landlady. You think what happened at your apartment is connected with Jason's murder and the theft of *his* computer, don't you?"

Noah nodded. "Don't you?"

VoShaun angrily snapped a wooden stirring stick.

"It really doesn't matter what I think. Masterson is not going to okay my working on a closed case. Anything I do could easily be considered insubordination. Loos come and go and I'm determined to wait him out. I love this job and I intend to hang on long enough to become accepted as plain Detective Taylor, without any of the colorful adjectives."

Noah feared she would get up and stalk out in frustration; instead she stared straight ahead obviously waiting for his response.

He said, "Let me say up front that I couldn't agree with you more about being in a tight place. And, while I have no intention of being as cheeky about this as you suggest, I wouldn't ask you to let everything ride with only me rolling the dice. That's why I asked about Baines. Fortunately, he's working for a different lieutenant and I don't see him being pushed off of a case."

VoShaun nodded her understanding.

Encouraged, Noah went on. "I'm assuming Baines knows nothing about Jason's murder and the significance of the computer thefts. How could he? I felt I owed it to you to discuss it before saying anything to him. I propose that the three of us meet. I'd like to lay it out for him and if he doesn't agree that the two cases are connected, you won't hear from me again."

"It sounds good, but I don't know about approaching Baines with the idea. Masterson has me on a short leash."

Noah shook his head. "You don't have to say anything. Baines knows me as the complainant on his murder case. I'll say I need to talk to him about it and the three of us can meet."

"Set it up."

19

Overhead the sky was choked with furrowed rows of dirty gray clouds, reminding Noah of tilled earth in a farmer's vast field. It could mean one thing: snow. And soon.

He waited at the curb while a city bus rumbled passed. Across Pratt Street, Corky Kilmark was already seated at the window table inside Peace and a Cup of Joe.

Though Pratt Street is one-way eastbound, Noah, from force of habit, glanced both ways before stepping from the curb. Down the block to his left, he glimpsed the flashing turn signal of a small white car pulled carelessly to the far curb. He recalled having narrowly missed sideswiping a similar car as he drove from his apartment two days before. That car had borne the crest of Baltimore City on the driver's door. Maybe he was being paranoid, but he recalled seeing a similar car at other locations recently.

Passing Jason's house in Catonsville?

The car's present position made it impossible to identify any markings on the doors. It was probably nothing; still it was worth a look. It was a longshot, but if the car was following him, now was the ideal time to find out.

Noah regained the sidewalk, glanced at his watch and proceeded to stroll west along Pratt Street against traffic. He feigned interest in locating an address on his side of the street.

At the end of the block, South Fremont Street joined Pratt Street on the north side, just before Pratt crosses Martin Luther King Boulevard. At the corner of South Fremont, Noah halted to study a sign for Sail-Cloth Factory Luxury Rental Apartments prominently displayed on the second floor of a four-story corner building.

The building exhibited a façade of refurbished red brick with each window framed by ornate stone blocks. The entire ground floor was devoted to a gated tenant garage. Still gazing upward, Noah pretended to dial the telephone number displayed on the sign. When Corky answered, he said,

"Did you see me across the street?"

"Yeah. Where did you disappear to?"

"I'm down at the corner in front of the Sail-Cloth Factory apartments. I spotted a small white car idling at the curb in the next block. I'm pretty sure I've seen this same car at my house and a couple of other places. I may be paranoid, but I think he has been following me."

"I'm looking out the window and I don't see anything."

"He's farther down, toward town."

"What do we do now?"

"I want you to see if there is a company name on the car doors and get the tag number. You up for it?"

"Yeah... I guess ..."

"All right. Do just as I say and nothing more, you got that?"

"I'm ready."

"What you are going to do is—come out the door and turn to your right, keep talking on the phone as you walk by the car. Without being obvious recite the tag number to me and discretely check the doors for a name. Don't stop and don't look directly at the driver. Turn the next corner, circle the block and approach Joe's from the west. Go back inside and get a table away from the window."

"What if he's still there?"

"He'll follow me."

"What are you going to do?"

"I'm parked on a meter a block up on Penn Street, only a few feet from the murder scene. I'll stroll back to my car and drive off. I should be back in thirty minutes. If I can't shake him without being obvious, I'll call you."

Corky was silent momentarily before saying, "What the hell is going on?"

"I'm not sure, but this may be the break we need."

Noah drove into the center of the city and, after not seeing the white car for twenty minutes, called to tell Corky he was on his way back.

By the time Noah carried his coffee to the table, Corky was visibly distraught. One leg jounced, coffee sloshed in the cup he held. He nodded as Noah drew a chair close, his eyes never straying from the front door.

Corky said, "I guess he's gone?"

"At least for now."

Corky let his eyes rest on Noah. "Any chance this is not connected to that boy's murder? Maybe a pissed-off husband?"

Noah snorted. "None. They have made their second major blunder. "

"Second? What was the first one?"

"Killing my landlady in my apartment and thinking they could get away with it."

Corky shook his head. "Wait a minute. She was in your apartment, but you weren't? How does that work?"

"It's a long story. Just say—wrong time and place for her."

Corky stared across the table as Noah briefed him on the morning's developments.

"The decals you saw on the door fit the car that was parked near my place."

Corky understood the heightened danger implicit in Noah's words. He swallowed hard and, his voice nearly a whisper, said, "Whoa! You had me stroll past maybe a killer's car—and copy down his tag number? And, he's following us? Jesus."

"We have no proof that this car is connected to any killings. None. Besides, I'm the one he's following and, like I said, it's doubtful that they know about you."

Corky sagged in his chair, shaking his head. When he spoke his voice was tight. "How in hell is you being followed a good thing?"

Noah sensed that Corky was losing his nerve and needed a pep-talk. It was in Corky's best interest to see it through and help put these guys in jail, rather than going it alone on the hope that they did not know about him. Noah was going to need his help, and his instinct not to relate VoShaun's news that the case is closed seemed the right one.

"You did great. Getting this guy's tag is huge for us. We not only learned that somebody is following us, but after we run it we'll know who it is."

"Following *us*? You just said they didn't know about me."

Noah shook his head. "I said it was 'possible.'"

"You said, 'doubtful.'"

Noah wagged a finger. "But we have to plan like they know about you. Too risky to approach it any other way."

"I wouldn't think of leaving you out there on your own. My landlady's killing was horrible. Poor thing. Never would have dreamed she was in danger."

"I still don't see how her murder is a 'break' for us."

"It is *if* both killings are connected which, admittedly, is still a *big* if. The cops treated Jason's stabbing as 'bum on bum,' assigned it to a rookie and filed it away under 'Who Gives a Rat's Ass?' Frau Wirtz case is being handled by a seasoned detective who reports to a different lieutenant. The media has taken a ho-hum attitude toward Jason's stabbing but the grisly murder of a helpless widow in Dickeyville is news. You can imagine how the citizens of Dickeyville will be clamoring for action. It's not a crime the cops can afford to ignore—no way can they can kiss it off as a nothing killing."

Corky, deep in thought, raised his cup to his lips discovered the coffee was cold, returned it to the table. Eventually, he heaved a sigh and asked,

"What do we do now?"

"I take it you're signing up for the duration."

"Doesn't sound like I have a choice."

"Good! Now it gets interesting."

"You mean more dangerous, right?"

"It's always been risky, now we are going to do something about it." Noah patted his coat pocket. "Very soon we'll know who our shadow is. Then you and Marvel can set up a network of streeters to report on any sightings of this car. Particularly noting the time of day and location."

Through clenched jaws, Corky asked, "What else?"

Noah produced the two memory sticks from Jason's desk and held them out.

"You said you were a computer programmer, right?"

Corky nodded.

"That makes you a lot smarter about computers than I am. These are from Jason's desk. I might be holding the solution to both killings right here. I want you to hack into them and reveal the secret to me."

Corky studied the two small pieces of plastic.

Noah added, "My guess is this is what they were looking for at my place."

Corky's hand trembled as he took the two sticks from of Noah. "Didn't Jason and your landlady get killed for them?"

Noah reached across the table. "I'll find somebody else to do it," he flared.

Corky jerked his hand back and jammed both sticks into his pocket. "I said I was in for the duration, I'll do it. I'm just not used to people being killed around me. And now maybe this guy knows about me. I got a right to be jumpy."

Noah nodded. "Look at it this way—now we have the edge. He doesn't know that we are on to him, we can use that to our advantage.

"Any progress on finding that streeter 'tribal' chief, Deacon?"

Corky nodded. "In all the excitement, I forgot. That's why I called you. I was told that if you want to see Deacon, you have to meet a streeter named 'Riley, like in *The Life of Riley.*' I don't know what that means,"

Noah laughed. "If you are living '*The Life of Riley*,' you have it made. You're on Easy Street. Maybe this Riley believes that he's living the good life."

"Whatever. It's what I was told."

Noah said, "Anyhow, do you want me to pick you up here at, say—10 o'clock?

Corky shook his head.

"Don't worry. I'll make sure that car isn't tailing me, before I get here. I'll call you—.

"It's not that. I was told that Deacon won't come out if two of us are there. He's pretty paranoid and believes two strangers are a threat."

Noah hung his head. "Jesus. Okay, where do I meet this Riley?"

"Thames Street, Fells Point. This Riley'll be standing in front of a bar called The Cat's Eye, tomorrow morning 10 o'clock."

20

Noah was seated in the Starbucks on North Eutaw Street by ten minutes after 7, drinking his morning coffee. He had agreed to Detective Jeff Baines' suggestion of a 7:30 meeting. Early was good, he concluded, for it was unlikely his shadow would be in place at that hour.

He had driven out of Dickeyville at 6:30, scrutinizing the traffic as he left the village. His route meandered its way into downtown, and when he reached the Starbucks he was satisfied that no vehicle, of any color, had been following him.

Once inside Starbuck's he claimed a table with a view of the traffic converging at the intersection of Eutaw and Baltimore Streets. As he studied the street corner he spotted a Police Department security camera perched near the top of a street light stanchion.

Interesting.

He made a note to follow up.

Within minutes, Detective Baines came through the door and Noah was at once reminded why Baines co-workers had dubbed him "Hollywood." He had worked all night and yet, somehow, managed to look like he had just stepped from a magazine cover.

"Good morning, detective. Guard the table and I'll get your coffee."

Baines waved him back in his chair. "Sit still, I'm particular about the construction of my morning brew."

Noah scrutinized the street, hoping for a few minutes with Baines before VoShaun arrived, necessitating a premature explanation of her presence.

Baines was talking as he took his seat. "Thanks again for

agreeing to meet this early. When you work nights it is assumed that you will accommodate your schedule to the day people. Court appearances, admin meetings, lineups, coroner's inquests—all conducted in daylight. But then you would appreciate that, having spent some time with the state's attorney."

Before Noah could speak, Baines added, "That reminds me, if you are still seeing Jennifer Stambaugh, you need to keep on your guard. It's no secret that her ex, Drew Jordan is pissed about it and is looking to make trouble for both of you."

"He said something to you?"

"He suggested—insisted really—that I charge you with the murder of your landlady. Naturally I told him that I had confirmed your alibi of having been at Stambaugh's all night. He went nuts."

After a moment, Noah shrugged. "Thanks for the heads-up but right now I want to focus on the two murders."

"Two murders?

"Mrs. Wirtz and a young college student named Jason Jefferson."

Baines' face was blank.

"Do you know a homicide detective named VoShaun Taylor?" Noah asked.

"Who doesn't? A rookie, she's black and hot."

"She has the Jefferson case and is on her way over here. I believe the murders are connected and I want you both to hear what I have to say. If we work the cases together, I see no reason why you can't clear both killings."

Baines studied Noah, drank some coffee and set the cup in front of him. "I don't recall that we had any cases together when you were in the state's attorney's office."

Noah nodded his agreement.

"But, from everything I can find out, you were a tough prosecutor. You didn't bring any bullshit to the game. That's the only reason I'm here. You should know—that only goes so far.

"I'm just as sure you have done your due diligence on me, so you are aware that I have a history with James Masterson, Detective Taylor's lieutenant. I'm sure as hell not saying anything in front of a rookie, who's probably scared to death of him and will run right back and spill everything that gets said here. He leaned backed and finished with, "I must be nuts to even be here."

Noah hunched over his coffee cup. "I understand, and I appreciate that. My 'due diligence' on you is that you are a hard worker who's smart and, above all, a standup guy. Think about it for a minute—there's a damn good reason we are meeting here instead of at the squad. I'm concerned about Masterson and so is Taylor. You'll hear why, as we proceed.

"This is not the first time Detective Taylor and I have met, 'off site' if you will. Just hear what we have to say before you jump to any conclusions. And, I am telling you right now, she may be a rookie, but she has stones as big any cop in that building."

"Thank you, Noah. That's the nicest thing anyone has said about me –that didn't include my tits—in a long time."

Both men scrambled to their feet.

VoShaun Taylor, a cup of steaming coffee in one hand extended the other to Baines. "Detective Baines, I'm VoShaun Taylor. Nice to meet you. I've heard a lot."

Noah grabbed a chair from an adjoining table and held it for her as they sat down. He began by saying, "Since I called this meeting, let me start. Either of you can say anything you are comfortable with, or nothing at all."

He looked from VoShaun to Baines and added, "For the record, I'm not wired. Are either of you?"

Baines shook his head and looked at VoShaun who said, "Don't either of you get any ideas about patting me down. You'll have to take my word for it."

Noah smiled. Indicating Baines, he said, "I want to bring him up to date on Jason's killing and then we'll talk about Frau Wirtz."

VoShaun's nodded.

At the outset, Noah announced that, in the interest of full disclosure, Baines should be aware that he represented someone of marginal "interest" in Jason's killing. Baines accepted the lawyer's declaration that his 'client' was not a factor in the Wirtz investigation and motioned Noah to continue.

In his account of the case, Noah stressed his theory on the significance of the Road Warrior website; ergo the theft of the computers in both killings was crucial. Then he asked VoShaun to recount for Baines the circumstances of a streeter's problematic confession to Jason's murder and the precipitate closing of the investigation by Masterson. At the end of her narrative, Baines muttered, "That sonofabitch."

Noah waited, but when Baines added nothing, he launched into a brief history of the investigation into the killing of Frau Wirtz, for VoShaun's benefit.

That done, he looked at Baines. "Anything I missed?"

Baines turned up empty palms. "I wish I had something new to add," he said, "but I'm coming up dry."

Noah collected the three empty cups and stood. "Well, I have something. Let me get refills and I'll be back with 'the rest of the story.' Feel free to talk among yourselves."

While at the counter, Noah noticed the two detectives talking intently and speculated on whether that augured well for the future of what he had come to regard as *his* investigation.

Noah returned and distributed the cups. "Anything either of you want to say before I finish up?"

Baines spoke for both detectives with a shake of his head.

Noah produced a scrap of paper with the license number and description of the white sedan and described the emblem on the car's doors. "It's evident that he has been following me. Unfortunately I have no idea for how long."

A look passed between the two detectives and Noah added, "I made certain that he wasn't with me this morning."

Next Noah spoke of Professor Martin's concern that Jason's memory stick may contain important data and of their subsequent visit to Jason's home.

Baines looked at VoShaun. "Do you have the stick?"

She shook her head. "*Moi*? What would I do with it? My case is closed."

Baines turned to Noah. "Where is it?"

"I have a computer geek looking at it."

Before Baines could protest, Noah explained. "Masterson didn't leave us many options." He made a hand motion to include all three seated at the table. "The Jefferson case is closed and I gave it to him before things took this turn."

Noah experienced a twinge of anxiety over the thought of what Baines would say if he knew that his 'computer geek' was the phony panhandler who was also Noah's client.

"He can be trusted," Noah added.

Detective Baines dismissed any concern with a shrug. He spent a moment processing this information before pointing to the paper in Noah's hand. "If—and it's a big if—these mopes were watching Jefferson's house waiting to get their hands on that stick—that could be where they picked you up.

"They run your tag and decide to see what your story is. Are you a mourner, or a threat to them? They are desperate for that memory stick and decide to see if you might have it."

Baines sat back and proclaimed, "That's the only way this makes any sense. The reason for the burglary Frau—Mrs. Wirtz interrupted."

Noah nodded and Baines took the paper bearing the license number from him. "I'll run it, but it's a fleet car. We won't get an individual name."

VoShaun spoke up. "At least it'll give us a department, right?"

Baines nodded. "Normally we would stake out this vehicle and put a tail on whoever drives it. You got any description of the driver?"

Noah shrugged. "A white male. That's it."

Baines frowned. "If we're real lucky, the car could be assigned to one person. But if the guy is connected and gets the word that we ran the tag he'll merely sign out a different car and we could spend days following some poor schmuck making a lunch run."

Noah considered mentioning his plan to mobilize the street people to aid in catching Jason's killer, and decided against it. The idea sounded wobbly even to him, but if there was a better way to proceed he couldn't see it. For the present he needed to retain whatever credibility his status as a former savvy prosecutor would buy.

He said, "Let's hope the city tag leads somewhere."

Baines waved the paper with the license of a city fleet car. "Maybe we'll get lucky and figure out who drives this car; then we can plan some strategy."

Baines looked from VoShaun to Noah and waggled a finger indicating a connection between the two detectives.

"We want to make sure that we are all agreed as to how this is going to work. Thanks to Masterson and his band of fools, I'm the only one at this table who can officially work on these murders."

He locked his gaze on Noah. "I don't know what you have in mind, but if whatever it is suddenly turns to doo doo, it is going to splash all over my beautiful suit."

Noah waited for him to finish.

"In that case there is no 'us.' You are on your own. Get it?"

Noah nodded his understanding.

"I don't want to know it." Baines added, jerking a thumb at VoShaun. "And neither does she."

21

Noah turned left onto Thames Street and followed the venerable streetcar rails embedded in the stone roadway. He passed the city-owned building which had served as the detective bureau in the TV series, *Homicide: Life on the Street*.

On his right, across an inlet, a tugboat bobbed on lapping waves at the end of Ann Street. To his left stretched a long block of historically preserved buildings. Wedged among the facades of restored red brick stood the Cat's Eye Pub, an Irish bar with a bright teal exterior.

He parked facing the harbor and carefully scrutinized the road behind him as he got out of the car.

Noah had no doubt that a lone figure, seemingly anchored to the sidewalk in front of the pub, was Riley, his contact.

As he negotiated the uneven cobblestone street, it occurred to him that while street people dressed in various ensembles of cast-off clothing, they were still as distinctive from everyone else as if they all wore the same uniform.

Jammed atop Riley's head was a soiled deerstalker cap, earflaps untied and dangling. Both hands were concealed in the pockets of a double-breasted gray mohair top coat. The coat, a women's style from thirty years before, was at least one size smaller than the man's heft required. No one would mistake him for anything other than a street person.

The man regarded Noah with suspicion as he approached. Both men kept their hands jammed in their pockets.

"Mister Riley?"

"Huh?"

"I'm here to see Deacon."

Riley tilted his head. "Where's our presents?"

"What kind of presents? Nothing was said about presents."

There was movement in Riley's coat pockets as his hands balled into fists.

"Oh boy! Oh boy! I'm in trouble. I'm in big trouble now. Deacon wants presents. I said real plain, you was to bring presents."

Noah gauged the length of Riley's arms and moved to the side in hope of being out of range of a meaty fist.

"Just take it easy," he said. "I'll get his presents; you tell me what he wants."

The man looked around vacantly before pulling a scrap of wrinkled paper from his coat pocket. He thrust it at Noah.

Riley commenced bouncing from one foot to the other, muttering unintelligibly.

Noah managed to keep him in focus while trying to make sense of the block letters printed in pencil across the paper.

"Does this say fags?"

"Oh boy! Oh boy! Lucky Strikes."

"Okay, cigarettes. Relax. We'll get them. What's this?" Noah ran his finger along the paper. "Books?"

Riley pulled a hand from his pocket and jabbed a finger at the paper. "Booze—Jim Beam," he growled.

Once in Noah's car, Riley directed him the few blocks to Patterson Park. They made a quick stop at a liquor store, where Noah purchased the required "presents" for Deacon along with a Hershey chocolate bar which he handed to Riley.

"Presents!" Riley cried, immediately tearing away the candy's wrapper.

They left the car on South Linwood Avenue, and Riley led the way into the park. As they crossed an empty tennis court, Noah wondered if the absence of a net at midcourt was due to the fact that it had been safely stored for the winter, cut into pieces by vandals or simply stolen outright.

And he was beginning to wonder where he was being led. Did this fellow Deacon really exist, or were the "gifts" he bought intended for Riley and one or two of his pals?

Through a smattering of bare trees appeared the cement decking of the park's swimming pool, drained for the winter, and just beyond a shuttered pool house. It had not escaped Noah's notice that Riley puffed-up when addressed as "mister." "Mister Riley, hold up!" he yelled.

Riley halted and glanced over his shoulder.

Noah, speaking in a voice loud enough to be heard in the pool house called out, "I want to know where we are headed."

Riley pointed to the pool house. "Deacon be there."

"In that pool house?"

Riley jerked a quick nod.

"Have him walk around the pool to this side. I know what he looks like," Noah bluffed. "If he doesn't show, or I see anybody else," I'm leaving and taking these presents with me."

"Oh boy! Oh boy! I'm in big trouble now."

Noah turned around and placed a foot on the tennis court. Behind him a voice shouted, "Hang on—I'm Deacon. I'm coming over."

Noah turned to see a tall black man outfitted in military camouflage heading toward him. The man glanced at Riley. "It's all right, man. You're not in any trouble—you did good."

Noah had difficulty gauging the streeter's age. Large brown eyes probed him over a heavy beard that was more white than gray. A floppy black hat, which Noah recognized as an army surplus boonie cap, was tied under the man's chin, concealing his hair. Lean and trim, his cadenced gait was still fit to march across a military parade grounds.

Living on the street must agree with him.

Deacon halted a few feet in front of Noah and eyed the plastic bag he carried. "Who might you be?"

"Noah Cassidy. I was told that you might help me with a problem."

Deacon raised his head slightly to better study the stranger. "What kind of problem?"

"A young fellow was killed on the street a few days ago. You might have heard something."

Deacon snorted. "You a poleece?"

Noah was careful to hold the man's gaze as he answered. "No, I'm not."

"I know the law—you can't say that you are not a poleece if you are one." Not waiting for a response he said, "What is it you want then?"

Noah motioned to a faded wooden picnic table just behind Deacon. He held up the bag and said, "How about we move over there so I can set these presents down."

Deacon reached out a hand. "I can hold 'em for you."

Noah shook his head. "When we get to know one another some better."

Deacon turned and started toward the table. To Riley, he said, "You stand down. I'm okay."

At the table, they sat across from one another. Deacon was clearly disappointed when the bag of gifts disappeared from his sight on the bench next to Noah.

"Where'd this killing happen?" Deacon asked.

"On the other side of town. By University Hospital."

"Over there's not my concern. If you not a poleece what concern be it of yours?"

"I'm an attorney. I was a prosecutor, but I quit there a few months ago. Right now I'm trying to help out a friend. He's a streeter, like you."

"Poleece got him?"

"Not yet. I mean to keep it that way."

Deacon stretched his frame across the table in an effort to get a look inside the gift bag. "You got any fags in there? I wouldn't be near so tense if I was to light up while you keep on talkin.'"

Noah brought out a fresh pack of Lucky Strikes and slid it across the table.

Deacon signaled Riley over as he tore open the package. "You go ahead on with your story," he said to Noah. "I'll be all right now."

Riley gleefully accepted two cigarettes and stood by while Deacon lit one for each of them. Then, puffing contentedly, he wandered back to his post.

Noah hurried through a bare-bones account of Jason's murder. He omitted any reference to Corky, and Deacon bristled upon hearing that Marvel was also involved.

"Marvel be a fool."

Noah shrugged. "I need a lot of help and I don't have many choices."

Deacon lit a second cigarette on the stub of the first before grinding the stub into the table. He drew deeply and watched Noah through the smoke. "I guess you would like for me to ask around among my folks."

"Like I said, I need help."

Deacon studied the glowing end of his cigarette. "What's Marvel getting' for his services?"

"Payment never came up. He hates the idea of a streeter being killed. Maybe the killer is going to kill more streeters, like you or Mister Riley there."

"Marvel be doing anything for you so far?"

"We're still getting organized. It was just a couple of days ago that he came forward to help," Noah said, stressing the words "came forward."

"One thing for damn sure, Marvel didn't tell you about me. We don't get along." Deacon peered over the table again. "This talking makes a person dry. You got some Jim in there?"

"We're almost finished. Then we'll have a drink."

"Hurry right along then."

Noah said, "Maybe you can help me understand something."

Deacon licked his lips and waited.

"I'm told that the street people on this side of Broadway are sort of one tribe, one clan, with you being their chief and those on the other side of Broadway are of a different tribe. Marvel being *their* chief. Do I have that right?"

"What would make a person ask such a question?"

"I need to know if I'm wasting my time—" Noah held up the plastic bag— "and these gifts on you. I want to know that you can deliver what you promise."

"That's easy—I ain't promised you nothing."

Noah gripped the bag and tensed as if to stand. "You going to help me or not?"

Deacon waved him to keep his seat saying, "The folks over here look to me for advice. They'll do what I ask of them. I've survived out here longer that any of them, longer than some of 'em been alive. I guess they figure that counts for something."

Deacon pointed to the low-slung cinder block building at the edge of the cement pool deck. "That's where me and Riley squat during the cold months when nobody comes around. It's the only building I will go into."

"Why is that?"

Deacon held out his lighted cigarette. "The damn politicians got it so a person can't smoke these in no building, but his own house. And that probably won't be for long. Anyhow, a while back I tried to go into the courthouse to visit a friend of mine going to be on trial for some damn fool thing."

Deacon cocked his head. "Cops grabbed him watering some of the bushes in that park in front of City Hall. Hell who ain't done that? Anyways, you know how just as you come through the courthouse door, they make you empty your pockets and step right through a electric archway?"

Noah managed to keep from smiling as he nodded.

"I had me a brand-new pack of Pall Malls which I was slow to produce. Soon as I dropped them into that little tray one of them guards grabs 'em up saying, 'There's no smoking in this building. I'm confiscating this pack for being contraband.'

"Well sir, I yelled 'You're a damn thief' and made a grab for the pack. This guard hustles me off to the side and still holding tight to my arm says I was guilty of 'possession with intent' and if I didn't get the hell out, he would lock me up. So I went. Outside, on the

steps, I turned around and shook my fist yellin' 'The hell with all of you!' And that's the last time I was in one of their buildings." Deacon glared at the memory. "You blame me?"

Noah placed the bag of gifts in front of Deacon and said, "I believe that calls for a drink."

Riley was at the table before the bottle cap was off. He and Deacon each took a generous pull of whiskey, then Deacon, smacking his lips, held the bottle out to Noah, who shook his head.

"Thanks, but I brought that for you. I'll have mine later."

Deacon held the bottle a little higher.

Okay, this is a test. Am I an uppity white boy, too good to drink with the likes of him?

Noah accepted the bottle and resisting the urge to wipe it off, slugged down enough, he reckoned, to pass the test. He returned the bottle to Deacon and asked, "Where do you go when the pool opens?"

Deacon chuckled. "I know of a small sloop that, come the warm weather, ties up down at the end of Ann Street. The owners are a nice couple who only use it on weekends, and not every one of them. I figure as long as I'm out by noon Friday, there'll be no trouble."

"They know you're living there during the week?"

"Mebbe, mebbe not. I'm real tidy."

Noah glanced at Riley.

Deacon said, "Oh, the sloop isn't big enough for the both of us. He's got his own summer place."

To Riley's obvious dismay, Deacon capped the bottle, which disappeared inside his fatigue pants. Then he lit a cigarette and leveled a look at Noah. "If this client of yours is a streeter, how's he payin' you?"

"I'm doing this pro bono—that means for free."

Deacon exhaled a cloud of smoke and waved a hand. "Let's say I believe you. Then what's in it for me?"

When Noah hesitated, Deacon added, "I don't require much. A present here and there; a few bucks so's I can do my Christmas shopping."

"Listen to yourself. 'What's in it for me?' I can give you some self-respect. It's up to you how much that is worth."

Noah let the words sink in before adding, "Somebody has killed a streeter in cold blood, stabbed him out on the street in the middle of the day. Okay, it happened in Marvel's territory, but I need your help to catch the killer before he kills one of your tribe. If you are a real leader then act like one and help me to protect your people by getting this killer off of the street.

"How long has it been since you felt like you did something worthwhile? I don't mean snitching somebody out for a few bucks, or a get-out-of-jail-free card, I mean doing something that might benefit someone else? Can you even remember back that far?"

Deacon ground his cigarette butt into the table, grabbed the whiskey bottle and unscrewed the cap. He tilted his head back and a dismayed Riley stood helpless as the Jim Beam disappeared. Deacon wiped his mouth with a sleeve and held the empty bottle out for Riley. "Recycle," he declared.

To Noah he said, "No extra sugar with your coffee, is there? At least a fella knows where he stands with you. If we was to throw in, what is it you would expect us to do?"

Noah dug into his coat pocket and produced a pre-paid cell phone, which he placed on the table in front of Deacon.

"Another present for you. Ever used one?"

Deacon stared at the phone, his head shaking slowly. Intrigued, Riley moved closer, peering over the big man's shoulder. "Now that's what I'm talking about," he muttered.

"It's what is known as 'pre-paid,'" Noah explained. "When the minutes are used, you just throw it away."

The phone had been cheap enough, but Noah had no intention of paying for additional minutes that Deacon or Marvin might rack up.

As Deacon cautiously caressed the phone with a big hand, Noah wondered if the cops had bothered to determine whether Jason's cell phone was still active. As a prosecutor he had seen instances where they had overlooked other steps just as basic. Given VoShaun's inexperience and Masterson's lack of concern—

I'll give Baines a call when I leave here.

Gazing at the phone, Deacon muttered, "I got nobody to call — but it's still mine all the same, right?"

Noah smiled. "I counted on you having no one else to call. This is a business phone," he motioned between Deacon and himself. "Only for our business." Noah reached for the phone, but Deacon tightened his grip, refusing to give it up.

Noah extended an open palm. "It's yours; I'm not taking it back. But I need to show you how to use it."

Grudgingly, Deacon released *his* phone into the open hand.

Noah said, "I've programmed my number into the system. When you need to call me, just flip open this top piece and hit the number 2."

This Noah did—waited a few seconds—and from a pocket produced his own cell phone sounding its current ringtone—Abba's "Take A Chance On Me."

He closed both instruments and placed Deacon's phone in the man's eager hand. Next, Noah flipped his phone open punched the number 9 and held it to his ear. The phone in Deacon's hand suddenly shook as it rang. Startled, he almost dropped it but quickly recovered and looked across the table. Noah nodded and Deacon opened the cover with care placing the phone to his ear.

Through the phone he heard Noah's voice, "This is just a test— we can't waste minutes."

Deacon mimicked the other man's actions and closed his phone.

"You got it now?"

"I think so—"

"You must only call me if it's important. This is the only phone you are going to get."

Deacon nodded and held the phone up in one hand. "Did Marvel get one of these?"

Noah shook his head.

Deacon nodded, smiling. "A minute ago, you said that when we use all the minutes on here, we would throw it away. Just so you know, I ain't never lettin' this go. One other thing—how was it that phone of yours played music and mine rang just like any old telephone would?"

Noah chuckled. "You have a song in mind for your phone?"

"I used to hear Mister Ray Charles. It's been a long time, though."

"Any song in particular? Just in case I can do something for you."

Deacon studied for a minute then smiled broadly. "There's "Sweet Georgia Brown," but everybody loves that one. The one that would fit me better is, "Hit the Road, Jack." What do you think?"

"I'll see what I can do."

Noah spent twenty minutes explaining his plan of action, stressing that streeters were to watch, listen and report. They were to take no action of any kind.

Noah, satisfied that Deacon would not let him down, stood to leave and shook hands with both men.

"Be sure and tell that fool Marvel I got a phone," Deacon called after him.

22

While Jen dished out the Indian carryout from Lexington Market, Noah uncorked an inexpensive bottle of a fruity Argentine Malbec, filled two wine glasses and carried them to the table.

Jen had agreed to try this wine after he explained the difference in taste from the drier cabernet that had accompanied their Italian meal.

When they were both seated, Noah raised his glass; she quickly mimicked the gesture.

Noah said, "May the roof above us never fall in, and may we never fall out," then sipped from his glass.

Aloud, Jen slowly parsed his words. "May... we... never... fall... out. I wonder are you really that clever?"

Noah sat his glass down and picked up his fork. "Clever? Me? Hardly ever. What do you mean?"

"That phrase could be construed as having more than one meaning. A bifurcated statement, in legalese."

"How so?"

"It could be a reference to our future, without actually incriminating yourself. Or, it could be nothing more than a pleasant toast."

"You give me too much credit."

She shrugged. "Do I? That's for another time. Tell me, what do you think of the food?"

"They're generous with the spices," he said reaching for a plastic bottle of water. "I can distinguish two separate flavors, but am not sure what they are."

She pointed to his plate with her fork. "That's Tandoori chicken and that's lamb curry. I find it's more fun to share two entrees—

particularly with ethnic food. Now, while I eat catch me up on 'the case.'"

Noah, grateful for an excuse to ignore the spicy food on his plate, responded, "A lot has happened in a couple of days, so I'm not certain what you already know. Did I tell you about meeting with Detectives Taylor and Baines?"

Jen laughed. "Hollywood Baines?—no."

"Something about him I should know?"

Before she responded, Noah added, "I read him as being a good cop. Smart and a hard worker. I need to know if I've got it wrong."

"You've got him right. He's too full of himself for my tastes, but he is good at his job."

"Are Baines and your ex tight?"

She gave him a questioning look and said, "They were, but something happened between them near the end of our time together."

"What was it?"

She shrugged. "I have no idea. Drew didn't talk about it, and frankly I never cared enough to ask."

Noah decided not to mention Baines's remarks about Detective Drew Jordan's rage and his zeal to have Noah charged with his landlady's murder.

Noah began with a narrative of the mysterious white car which followed him. "I was careful not to lead him here—drove around for at least a half-hour and parked a block over. All the same, you should be alert for it. I'll write down the tag number before I leave."

She was clearly amused by his account of his meeting with Riley and Deacon at Deacon's "winter quarters" in Patterson Park.

"What gave you the idea to buy this man a cell phone? How do you know he won't trade it for a bottle of booze?"

"You didn't see how proud he was of that thing. He'll protect it as if it was the nuclear football."

Jen sipped some wine. "It sounds like you are assembling quite a force of misfits—Mister Holmes."

Noah laughed. "Sherlock Holmes' Baker Street Irregulars. I gather you are a reader of Sir Arthur Conan Doyle's work?"

"It has been a while, but yes, I pored through his books, growing up. He was the world's first great private eye."

"He identified himself as a 'consulting detective.'" Noah launched into an atrocious English accent. "I say old girl, your analogy is spot-on."

Dropping the accent he continued, "The Baker Street Irregulars were ubiquitous urchins on the streets of London; quite invisible, much like my—Baltimore street people."

Jen watched his face as she spoke, "I don't know. I can see this coming up and biting you on the ass—big time."

"Don't think I haven't thought of that, but I don't have many options. Except for Baines, the police are a no-show on this case, and he's barely hanging on. The first time something goes wrong, he will jump ship."

He poked absently at the cold food on his plate. "A good lawyer would have these 'irregulars' sign a Hold Harmless agreement." He managed a faint smile. "I'm certain it was much simpler back in Holmes' day. But, I have to go where my gut takes me."

Jen watched him push his food around his plate. "Your food is probably cold. Let me fix you something else."

Noah dropped his fork, grasped the wine bottle and filled both of their glasses. "The dinner is fine," he said. "It's just that I'm not very hungry."

"Who would have thought you would be such a poor liar? And you a lawyer, with all that practice. You know the saying—'to practice law is to practice lying.'"

Noah held up one hand. "Spare me the lawyer jokes. As for dinner: the next time you want a variety of the hot stuff, get two different dishes for yourself and bring me a Reuben from Mary Mervis and we'll both be happy."

Jen lifted her glass and they drank to that notion. Then she said, "Does it bother you to go back to your apartment—after what happened?"

"Sure. How could it not? Besides being wary every time I open the door, I can't step inside without visualizing—her—lying there."

"Have you thought about moving?"

"Not really. With all that's going on, there's been no time. Besides, I was very lucky to get it. People would kill for that apartment."

Jen reacted and he shook his head. "Jesus," he grunted," that was a stupid thing to say. I'm sorry. But—"

She laid a reassuring hand on his arm.

He added, "I don't know who her heirs are or what they will do with the place. I may be forced to move, like it or not."

She sighed. "I don't like the idea of you going back to that place, especially late at night."

Jen watched his face carefully as she said, "Would you consider moving in here?"

When Noah didn't answer, she quickly added, "It doesn't have to be permanent if you don't want it to be. You told me that somebody is following you, and you believe they are involved in two killings. Doesn't that worry you?"

He nodded. "Of course. And that's one reason I can't move in here. Quite the opposite, I should keep away from you for the duration, but I'm too selfish. I have convinced myself that, if I'm cautious and stay alert, I can come here without endangering you."

"I—I"

"Let me finish. Whoever it is expects to find me at my apartment. If they can't, they'll look for me and I don't want them zeroing in on this place. I appreciate your concern, but it's not a good enough reason to take such a big step. If we were leading a normal life, you would not think of making such a move so early in a relationship. Would you?"

Jen shook her head. "No, I suppose not."

Gently Noah said, "I want us to have every chance to succeed."

Tears welled in Jen's eyes. "My father and mother had a wonderful marriage," she said. "Every night at bedtime, he would get out of his chair, walk over to her and say softly, almost in a whisper, 'Thank you for another wonderful day' and kiss her goodnight. Even if they'd had a tiff earlier, he was adamant about ending the day with affection. I want that kind of relationship for myself."

Later, as Noah headed to his car, he scanned the street on the lookout for a white city-owned car or an unmarked detective unit.

23

Noah closed his new laptop when Detective Baines, holding a fresh cup of coffee, slid into the chair across from him. He marveled at Baines' natty appearance after working the graveyard shift on the grimy city streets.

"I was engrossed in my new toy and didn't notice you come in," Noah said.

Baines failed to stifle a yawn, covering it with one hand. "I appreciate you meeting me this early. It was a tough night, and I had court yesterday."

Noah nodded. He planned that his business with the detective would be quickly handled and Baines would be gone before Corky showed up at Peace and a Cup of Joe. "You said you had something," Noah said.

"You seen any more of the white car?" Baines asked as he handed a scrap of folded paper across the table. "It wasn't around this morning. I can't figure what they expect to learn from following me."

Noah scanned Baines' note on the white car. It was assigned to Baltimore Housing.

"Can we narrow it down?"

"The vehicle is assigned to Housing's Code Enforcement Division—housing inspectors. That's the best I can do without tripping a warning buzzer for them."

Noah studied the note. "The car must come to an office." He glanced up. "We'll sit on the place until it shows up."

Baines pursed his lips. "It's not that simple. Code Enforcement has five area offices and staff members rarely appear at their assigned office. Mostly they take their cars home and go directly into the field. Besides, who's going to conduct the surveillance? I'm working nights; no way I can work days, too. VoShaun is out, and don't you even think about it. "

Noah smiled.

"What…"

Noah raised one hand in a "stop" signal. "I thought you didn't want to know—"

Baines stretched and yawned. "You're right. I'm going home and I want to be able to get some sleep. I'm guessing you're not talking to Detective Taylor about this."

Noah nodded.

Baines glanced around the small room. "Nice place. Next time, your treat."

Noah was back on his new laptop when Corky Kilmark walked through the front door and edged into the short queue at the counter.

Noah finished reading his email as Corky placed his coffee and a cruller wrapped in a paper napkin on the table.

Corky said, "There's something to be said for being a bum. The hours are good and no boss to answer to—except the one at home. Be real tough to go behind a desk when this is over."

"Nobody wants to go to an office if they don't have to," Noah replied. "And I think being a successful bum only works if you have a wife with a decent job."

Corky sloshed the breakfast roll in his coffee. "I was thinking," he said, "we catch this killer we could be famous. Maybe we should think of hooking up to do private eye work. 'Cassidy and Kilmark Investigations.' How does that sound? Be our own boss."

Noah shook his head, "Let's see how this works out. I really don't see us becoming famous unless we get killed."

"Not funny."

"Moving on," Noah said. "Did you get that cell phone to Marvel?"

Corky grabbed a napkin, wiped his chin and then reached into a coat pocket, producing the phone which he placed on the table between them.

"What happened? Don't tell me he doesn't want to use it."

Corky shook his head. "He heard that you made a personal presentation of a phone to Deacon. Whether you like it or not, you are the Big Kahuna and he is insulted that you sent me, another bum, to give him this one."

"Jesus. How did he even know about that? And who cares anyway?"

"Jungle drums."

"What?"

"Jungle drums. These guys are rival chieftains, at least in their own minds. Deacon pumped himself up by spreading the word about his visit from 'the Great White Father.' He looks like the favored son while Marvel eats shit."

"That's why he asked me," Noah grumbled.

Corky frowned.

"When I left Deacon, he asked me if Marvel had been given a phone and I told him no. Besides being the truth, I calculated that it would pump him up to be the first to get one. Did it ever. I can see now I was screwed either way. If I lied and said Marvel got one, likely Deacon would have been insulted that he wasn't first. Dealing with these guys is going to be a real pain in my ass. Unfortunately we're going to need both of them and their 'tribes.'"

Noah produced the slip of paper he had received from Detective Baines.

After studying it Corky smiled. "It was following us, now we can follow *it*. Am I right?"

"It's not that easy. We've got to find *it* first. Baines says there is no single time and place that *it* will show up. That's where the tribes come in. We'll have to convince them to fan out over the city until they find it."

Corky picked up the cell phone and worked it between his fingers. "Is this the same model you gave Deacon?"

"Yes. Thank God. That's all we need is for them to compare phones."

"True, but that's not why I asked. This model has a camera. Did you show Deacon how to take pictures?"

Noah nodded. "I just hope he doesn't use all the memory taking pictures of himself and Riley." Noah secured his laptop.

"Let's go see what Marvel thinks of me today."

Marvel waited at the Lexington Street entrance to the "world famous" Lexington Market, named for the Revolutionary War battle. He drew his cape close for warmth while bouncing to and fro on the balls of his feet.

He glared at Noah by way of a greeting.

"Marvel," Corky offered, "this is Noah, the man I was telling you about."

Noah nodded.

Marvel flared, "I figured you forget all about me. What with you being real tight with that no-account Deacon."

Noah opened the glass door and motioned the other two men through ahead of him. "Why're you standing out here in the cold? Let's get inside."

Inside the door Marvel motioned to a printed sign posted on the wall—*No Loitering*. "That's meant for us. There's no chance the likes of me is going to spend any money at their fancy stands." He nodded toward a food kiosk as they passed. "Quick as a wink they'd have the cops come and chase me out." He looked at Corky. "Streeters get used to the cold."

Marvel stopped and scanned Noah up and down. "You ain't foolin' nobody, if you is trying to pass for a streeter. It ain't just the clothes—you don't have the look. You been living too good."

Without waiting for a response, Marvel eyed the food stalls around them. "I believe I was told we was gonna eat."

"Whatever you like."

Marvel's arm appeared from beneath his cape and he pointed a ragged sleeve at one of the stalls. "My mouth has been waterin' for a Faidely's crab cake, ever since Corkscrew here told me we was comin' up to the market. One of them cakes will help make up for you giving that Deacon a telephone. Say, you didn't give him a crab cake, did ya?"

Noah shook his head. "Now why don't you and Corkscrew, settle yourselves at one of those tables while I get the food."

"And some boardwalk fries," Marvel called after him.

While Marvel savored his crab cake and fries Noah explained how the man and his "tribe" could help in the investigation of Jason Jefferson's murder.

When Marvel finished Noah handed him a stack of paper napkins from the counter and waited while the streeter wiped the grease of the fried potatoes from his hands.

Next Noah passed a stack of photos across the table.

"These are from the boy's Road Warrior website. In that stack is a closeup of Jason and a couple of shots with a white car in the background. It looks to be in an area of abandoned homes. It's important. A white Chevrolet; a Baltimore City car with a city seal on the doors.

"Pick some folks who will not let you down and have them show these to everyone they can. Did they see Jason on the streets? When and where did they see him? Was anyone with him? Have they seen anything unusual in the last few weeks? That kind of thing."

Noah tapped a picture of the city car. "Have everybody you got scouring the city looking for this car. Especially in neighborhoods like those where the car is parked in the picture. You folks know these streets; maybe you'll be able to tell from the background where they were taken."

Marvel held the picture inches from his nose. "Hmm. Real hard to tell. There's lots of us out here who don't see real good. 'Sides they's a bunch of these cars all over town. How's a body know which is the right one?"

"The license number of our car is on the back."

Marvel turned the picture over, grunted, and returned it to the pile on the table. "Corkscrew here tells me you agreed to talk to them poleece for us. Like you was my lawyer."

Noah nodded.

"Can't pay you nothing, you know."

Noah produced a cell phone, wrapped it in a paper napkin and held it out to Marvel.

"Before you ask, it is the same phone I gave to Deacon. It just happens that I saw him before I saw you. We're not picking favorites. We need both of you."

Again, Marvel wiped his hands before reverently cradling the device in his hands.

Next, Noah patiently explained the camera and telephone features of the instrument. As he had done with Deacon, Noah cautioned about the limited minutes available, stressing that the phone was not a toy and could only be used for urgent matters regarding the investigation.

"You spot that car, call me right away and wait there. I'll come a running."

Marvel handled the phone with tenderness, as if holding fragile crystal in his hand. Softly, he said, "I can't recollect the last time somebody needed my help and trusted me to do something important. I won't let you down, Mister Noah."

24

The headlights of Noah's car swept across an unmarked detective unit parked in the driveway to his apartment. The maroon Crown Victoria sat idling as it obstructed access to the stairway leading to his front door.

The police car's lone occupant emerged and motioned Noah to turn off the ignition and get out of the car. The figure stepped into the glow of his own headlights confirming Noah's suspicion.

Speaking across the top of his car he said, "Detective Jordan, how can I help you?"

A chill breeze whipped at the few remaining strands of brown hair on Jordan's head, requiring him to keep one hand busy in a perpetual smoothing motion. "I have something to say." He jerked his head toward the stairway. "Let's go inside."

"We can't have much to say to each other. Let's do it out here."

Jordan cursed under his breath and strode toward Noah, who used his driver's door as a shield.

"Unless you're here to arrest me, that is close enough."

Jordan added two more insolent steps before stopping.

"I'm not here to arrest you—this time. You may have others fooled, Cassidy, but you're not fooling me. That story about you leaving the state's attorney because of politics is a load of crap. You're dirty and we both know it. Baines doesn't believe me—yet."

He's definitely been drinking.

Jordan reached under his sport coat and for an instant Noah expected to see the muzzle of a pistol aimed at him. Instead, the policeman produced a set of chrome handcuffs, which he thrust at Noah.

"But," he spat, "I'll dig around until I get what I need to come back and hook you up."

He hung the cuffs on his belt and turned to leave. "Consider this a not-very-friendly warning. If you're smart you'll get the hell out of town before I come back for you."

Despite his resolve to be firm Noah, found himself shaking as he sought to insert his key in the lock to his front door.

Once inside the apartment, he relocked the door, sat his laptop on the table and pulled a bottle of Jack Daniels Black Label whiskey from beneath the kitchen counter. Having no patience for a glass or ice, he slugged from the bottle, wiped his lips and slugged again.

Jesus, if that guy was any crazier... He could shoot me and drag my body across the road into Leakin Park, *where I would be lying until a neighbor's dog came by and lifted his leg on me.*

Just as he shrugged off his topcoat Abba rang in his pocket. He answered and Corky hesitated before saying, "You all right? You don't sound so hot."

Noah covered the mouthpiece and inhaled deeply. "I just walked in my front door. Can't run up those steps like I used to. What's up?"

"I broke the code!"

"What?"

"I got into the files on the kid's thumb drive!"

"Great work!"

"That's what I thought. I got a neighbor who works at Fort Meade—you know..." he finished by whispering, "N...S...A. I'm going to check with him to see if they're hiring code breakers."

Having no interest in another discussion involving Corky's pipe dreams, Noah replied, "Why not?"

"You want to come over and see? I can explain it better in person."

Noah was loath to go out on the roads tonight.

I wouldn't be surprised if Jordan was lurking about waiting to tail me over to Jen's. The least that happens is he calls a black-and-white for a DUI and I spend the night in the drunk tank.

"I can't tonight."

"Oh. A hot date, am I right?"

Noah endeavored to keep the irritation from his voice. "What did you find?"

"It's hard to tell. I figured you would want to look at it."

"Bring it with you tomorrow. Same time, same station."

"You mean…?"

"Don't say it. Just acknowledge that you know where I will be waiting."

"Yeah. Sure, I know. You don't think…"

"We'll talk about it then."

They were huddled over a corner table in the front window at Peace and a Cup of Joe. Steam wafted up from the cups of coffee between them.

Corky said, "Do you really think they are listening to our calls?"

"Doubtful. Still, it doesn't cost us anything to err on the side of caution. It occurred to me last night when you mentioned that your neighbor works for NSA."

Corky stiffened and glanced around the small room. "Whoa! You saying that they could have the N—"

"No. But it doesn't require a super secret spy agency to listen in on local calls."

Both men hovered over the computer screen. "Do your magic," Noah said.

When the machine was running, Corky plugged in a thumb drive, located Jason's email and entered the password.

"What are we looking for?" he asked.

Noah, engrossed in the screen mumbled, "I'm not sure."

A moment later he said, "This looks like it," his voice animated. "'Romeo,me (3).'"

Noah took over from Corky and opened the first of the three messages reading softly.

"'Romeo917@hotmail.com.
Road Warrior

You are doing a great job! I can help. Meet me on the steps of the Enoch Pratt library at 10 o'clock next Wed.

You won't be sorry.

Romeo 917.

This entry was linked to two responses from Road Warrior. The first was sent later the same day: "I'll be there. Thanks RW."

Road Warrior sent his final message the following Wednesday at 5:39 p.m.

"Romeo, I waited until 11:30. What happened to you? Let's get together. Road Warrior"

Noah closed out the email and opened the first of three photo files. Filling the screen were about sixty pictures taken at numerous locations around the city of Baltimore.

After a cursory review, Noah minimized the page and opened the second file. The computer screen was deluged with more photos. As with the previous file, the pictures depicted desolate city blocks strewn with decaying abandoned buildings. In other photos, acres of vacant lots were overgrown with weeds and littered with discarded mattresses, automobile tires and the foundations of decapitated homes.

For the most part, the desolation and neglect were the focal point of the pictures, with random vehicles or pedestrians visible in the background.

However, in one or two it was readily apparent that the vehicle or people were the focal point.

Noah glanced up to see Corky watching him intently.

"You thinking the same thing?" Corky asked.

"No additional pictures of our Doctor Musk."

"What do you think that means?"

"It doesn't change anything."

Both men watched the screen as Noah scrolled rapidly through the other pictures. He closed out the file, shut off his computer and said, "I didn't notice anything that looked like a smoking gun."

Corky's disappointment was evident and Noah smiled. "You did a hell of a job, cracking this, and I have no doubt there is something in here that will bring them down. I've got a full day so I won't get back to it until tonight—at home. Let's meet here tomorrow, same time, and I'll give you a full report."

That evening as Noah turned off of North Forest Park Avenue, he thought of parking on Wetheredsville Road and stealthily approach his apartment on foot. He was in no mood for more surprises.

Instead, he drove past his driveway about a half-mile, stopping before a barrier beyond which the road shriveled into Gwynns Falls Trail and enters the 1200-acre wilderness that is Leakin Park.

A roadside sign banned entry into the park "From Dusk to Dawn," and city poles topped with vapor street lights continued alongside the road up to the barrier. Noah took notice of the fact that the last two lights were unlit, enveloping that stretch of road into a murky darkness. The car's headlights did little to belay the unease induced by his spectral surroundings.

He flashed his high beams and swept the surrounding trees as he maneuvered the car around and headed back to his apartment. He saw no one lurking and observed no white cars parked along the road; still the road here was gloomy and eerily silent with trees and underbrush pushing up to the narrow road.

Even more ominous to Noah was his recollection of scanning an Internet blog which listed more than sixty bodies recovered in the neighboring Leakin Park over the years. Several of them had been located secreted in thickets of honeysuckle along this very stretch of Wetheredsville Road.

In his own driveway, Noah parked a couple of steps from the wooden stairway leading to his apartment. He collected his laptop and an unread *Baltimore Sun* and started for the stairs, when he hesitated and looked across the driveway to the darkness of Frau Wirtz's house.

I wonder what will become of this place. I don't know of any relatives; she never spoke of children.

169

Starting up the stairs, it occurred to him that he could not recall the last time he had seen the couple who lived below him.

That's a bummer. Who's going to call for help when our killers come for me?

Since the killing of Frau Wirtz, it had become Noah's habit to secure a small piece of Scotch tape between his front door and the top of the door frame each morning as he left. It was a gimmick designed to alert the returning resident to the possibility of intruders. He had seen it used with success in a number of spy movies.

The flaw in this early warning system was Noah's inability to remember to check the tape before pushing the door open.

It was no different tonight. "Shit," he muttered as the door swung in. He reached around the door frame and found the light switch. With the light on, he eyed the area and determined, as best he could, that no one lurked inside.

He sat the laptop on the desk and, feeling somewhat foolish, quickly checked the bedroom and bath, brandishing a rolled up newspaper for protection.

The Sunday Sun would be a more formidable weapon, but I couldn't roll it up. I'd drop it on his foot and run like hell.

Satisfied that he was alone, Noah locked the front door, uncapped a cold bottle of Blue Moon and, sans the orange slice garnish, settled in to unlock the mysteries Jason had recorded on his external drive.

Gut feelings about a criminal case were not the exclusive province of homicide detectives; prosecutors came to the job similarly equipped. While Noah was certain that the email address Romeo917 would yield results, it did not qualify as a *gut feeling* since it was, to him, a known quantity and not speculative. It was merely a matter of determining how Romeo917 might best serve their case.

No, his gut was telling him there was something additional in Jason's files. Something that had escaped his cursory look.

For the next ninety minutes Noah scrutinized each file page, paying particular attention to the candid pictures of various city streets.The last photo file contained only fifteen snapshots, all of them familiar. They were familiar, he realized, because he had just seen them in the previous folders.

Apparently Jason had culled them from the other folders with the expectation of using them in an upcoming edition of the Road Warrior blog.

Several were close-ups of vacant rowhouses, their doors and windows boarded over with sheets of plywood. In a couple of instances the plywood was missing, revealing open doorways and shattered windows. In one such picture, Noah could make out grey smoke curling above the roof. If the structure had a chimney it wasn't visible from this angle. It made sense that squatters would burn anything combustible for instant heat, indifferent to the consequences.

It was the last two photos that jolted Noah upright. His hands trembled as he maneuvered the mouse to enlarge the frames.

The first shot had been taken directly across the street from its subjects. In the foreground, a white sedan with the crest of Baltimore City was parked in front of a seemingly abandoned house. A man escorted two children up the front steps, their backs to the camera.

It was the second shot that had Noah's heart racing. It was a close-up of the same white car with the local government license plate clearly visible. Indeed, it was the same car that was stalking him.

What were they doing in that house? Something so terrible that it got Jason killed?

Without a street name or house number how could he hope to find this particular derelict house among the thousands throughout the city? Quickly deflated, he spent many more minutes in close examination of the two photos.

Suddenly, his gut feeling was proven correct. Staring at the screen, he leaped from his chair, pumping his fist yelling, "We are coming for you bastards."

25

Vernon, clipboard in hand and pencil poised, approached the party house on foot. Two days before Tony, in a fit of rage, had issued strict rules for anyone visiting the place. Any deviation from these rules would result in the offender's banishment.

Cars were to be parked on an adjacent street, at minimum one block away. The garage across the alley was for Tony's use only. All others had to approach the house as Vernon was now doing, wearing a hard hat and carrying a clipboard.

Vernon, and the rest of Tony's crew, thought it funny that their reality had become so twisted; city employees were now required to pretend to be working during their actual workday.

"I don't know," Ronnie, one of the regulars, had whispered to Vernon, "It's been so long since I did a day's work, I think I forgot how to fake it."

During his rant, Tony had said, "Listen up. Any of you bastards screw this up for us, I'll have your ass." He slapped a hand on top of the yellow hard hat on his head. "You see any asshole on the street and he ain't wearing one of these, walk on past the house and call me pronto. I don't care if he looks like a damn street bum—especially if he looks like a street bum, stay away until you get my okay."

Eyes flashing, Tony included Vernon in the withering glare he directed at the gathering. "Got it?" Then he turned and stalked away, leaving Vernon confused and deeply injured.

Why was the boss turning on him? He had been in from the start, since Tone drove him out here and revealed his secret plan.

Back then it was just me and him, nobody else. Now he treats me same as the rest of the guys, like a piece of crap.

Only last week the boss was cracking jokes about how they had created their own Vegas joint under everybody's nose and none of the city big shots had a clue.

Now he acts like he's scared of something. Real scared. I never seen Tone scared of anything. What the hell could it be? Jesus, he's got me scared, too.

Vernon had waited in vain for Tony to get him aside and tell him what was going on. After all, Vernon was still the only one Tony trusted to visit the other place—the movie studio. Except for Leonard—that asshole.

Over his clipboard, Vernon scanned the street. With no one in view, he strode around the side of the house and up the back stairs. Just inside the door he stopped, the low murmur of voices reaching his ears.

One voice, he quickly identified as that of the boss, the other one he could not place.

Peering into the room Vernon glimpsed the back of a man's head seated in the chair across from Tony. Vernon's chair.

No one but the hated Leonard sported a flaxen ponytail hanging well below his shoulder blades. The finely groomed hair was gathered and held by four thick black bands, spaced precisely equidistant the length of the display.

Looks like the mane on a palomino horse. He must spend most of the day playing with his damn hair.

Vernon first met Leonard about six weeks before when Tony instructed him to pick up "a new man, Leonard" at the Star motel on Pulaski Highway and drive him to a meeting at the Oasis Club, one of a handful of strip clubs remaining on Baltimore's infamous "Block." The boss had made it clear that Vernon was not to accompany his passenger into the club, so he had monotonously circled the 400 block of Baltimore Street for forty minutes.

When Leonard reappeared he slid into the front seat and Vernon, desperate to make conversation, had asked, "How are the broads in that place?"

Leonard's response was a fierce glare. He snarled while putting a match to a cigarette clenched between his teeth. A heavy silence saturated the car on the return ride to the motel.

Another time they drove to that kid's house in Catonsville. A heavy snow was falling when Vernon picked-up Leonard. Once in the car, Leonard scowled from the passenger's seat while painstakingly brushing the snow from his hairdo.

Well, asshole, if you don't want to get your pretty hair all wet, put on a goddamn hat like everybody else.

Vernon had pulled into traffic, unnerved by the look he was getting from his passenger. They drove the few miles to Catonsville in a fierce silence.

At Leonard's direction, Vernon parked a block from the house. Leonard, a hand on the door handle, shifted in his seat and glowered at Vernon.

"Be here when I come back, dipshit," he threatened, "or—," he drew a finger across his throat in a slitting motion. With that, Leonard was out of the car disappearing around the corner, leaving Vernon quaking in silence.

Vernon had been staring through the windshield when Leonard reappeared carrying a laptop computer under one arm and munching on a Butter Finger candy bar.

You know damn well he stole that candy bar. He couldn't bother to steal one for me? Me and Tone are going to have a come to Jesus meeting about this asshole.

Vernon had yet to find the nerve to voice a complaint.

Vernon's most unsettling experience with Leonard had been just a few nights ago. Tony ordered him to drive Leonard to that lawyer's apartment in Dickeyville.

I gotta park and wait in the dark on that old road with them spooky woods all around? I ain't too proud to admit that is a scary place in the dark. And for what! Just to steal a cheap-ass computer.

Driving this guy around during work is bad enough, but being ordered to come back in the night and spend several hours with the asshole is asking too much. And forget about a thank you from this Leonard guy or from Tone for that matter. And I never told them about the hell I got at home for going out at night.

That night, Vernon had told his wife only that Tony needed him to do something. The real yelling came when he stumbled over telling her what exactly it was he would be doing. No way was he going to admit to her that he had to go out to drive some guy around. Anyhow, she would never buy that.

Tone orders me to carry this guy to this place and that place, but he don't tell me what's going on. And, this asshole won't say squat. He don't even say 'hi,' much less talk about what we're doin.' Shit, he could be around the corner murderin' somebody and I wouldn't know it. At least not until the cops show up.

Now, Tony waved him into the room. "Grab one of those folding chairs and sit in on this."

Leonard, whose principal forms of communication were grunts and nods, ignored Vernon's presence.

Vernon was aware that Tony had furtively added Leonard's name to the city's payroll a while back. When questioned about it, Tony had snapped, "Mind your own goddamn business."

Now the bastard plops his ass down in my chair and Tone tells me I gotta sit on a foldup.

Leonard wore a full biker mustache which framed lips cast in a permanent snarl, and a black earring in the shape of a swastika gleamed from the lobe of his left ear. He habitually wore a black leather biker vest revealing a profusion of tattoos sheathing his left arm.

Vernon would not even venture a guess as to the man's age. He could be forty-five or sixty-five, but of one thing there was no doubt: Leonard was mean and hard.

Vernon unfolded a chair and sat between the two men.

Tone gives this guy whatever he wants. No question. I been with Tone from the start and I don't count for nothing.

Tony was saying, "Leonard here is a business consultant from—"

Leonard turned and fixed Tony with a withering look.

"—from out of town. As you know, he's been helping us with some ...business problems."

Vernon nodded, suddenly very concerned—was he one of the problems? He had a vivid picture of how a guy like Leonard handled problems, recalling the terror that seized him when Leonard glared directly at him and drew a finger across his throat.

Jesus, did Tone get me out here so this bastard can cut my throat? No. No. Tone wouldn't do that. Would he? He's been acting real odd. What if he had no choice? That would be another story.

Tony, beer bottle in hand, pointed to the refrigerator. "Grab a beer," he said.

Instinctively Vernon knew he needed to keep his wits about him. At least until he could figure out if he was in any trouble. And Leonard was not drinking. Though his throat was parched, Vernon replied, "I'm good. Thanks, Tone."

"Leonard here doesn't drink. Usually I don't trust a man who won't take a drink, but I trust him. Now I got to worry—should I trust you?"

"Hey, Tone, come on. Don't kid like that. Okay?"

Vernon ventured a glance at Leonard. "I've been with you from the start," he said.

Tony laughed. "I'm just havin' some fun with you."

Quickly, his laugh faded. "All right let's talk some business," he said.

Tony laid a red file folder on the chair arm and opened it. He selected some photographs and passed them to Vernon. "You recognize any of these?"

As Vernon poured over the pictures, Leonard gazed at the wall, disinterested.

Has Tone already showed them to this asshole, or does he just not give a crap?

Vernon tried to pick out one photo; his hands trembled so he was forced to grip it with both hands.

Tony leaned forward. "You see something?" He asked.

Vernon felt both sets of eyes on him. "This here one looks like me from the back—walking up to the other place. This is my car parked in front of the place." He looked up, "Did you take them, Tone?"

Tony slowly shook his head. "Come on, Vernon. Think! I didn't take them, but somebody did."

Panic was taking hold. "What's going on, Tone?"

"I'm not sure," Tony answered. "But we need to find out and real quick. That's why I called this meeting."

Vernon's mind churned. *Maybe they think I took the pictures. No, I was in one of them. Maybe they think I brought somebody out there and it was him who took them.*

Very much alarmed, Vernon directed his plea at Tony. "I don't know who it was took these if that's the problem. Jesus Christ, Tone, I would never do that. You gotta believe me."

Tony drank some beer and, after a quick glance at Leonard, said, "Take it easy. We know that you didn't do nothing wrong. We got a problem and we need to figure out how to solve it."

Leonard smirked, "Oh, you got a problem all right."

Vernon shuddered as he dried his palms on his khaki trousers. His throat so parched his question was barely audible. "Tone, where did you get these from?"

"They come off that dead bum's computer. Only he wasn't no bum. He coulda been an undercover cop, or a reporter. Something like that. Looks like he took these pictures with a cell phone camera."

Tony glanced at Leonard. "We think he was getting ready to blow the whistle on us at the time of his unfortunate demise."

Vernon frowned.

Leonard, his jaws working silently, repeated a slitting motion across his throat.

"When he got killed," Tony explained.

Vernon clasped his hands in an attempt to stem their quaking. His stomach fell and unable to swallow he stepped to the refrigerator, pulled the tab on a Coke and drank deeply.

With his back to the others he said, "So what's the problem? The kid's not going to say anything and we got the pictures."

Tony heaved a sigh and held up the red folder. "The problem is Genius, that all these pictures and stuff he wrote about he also saved on a little thing called an 'external drive,' which was not with the kid's computer when you and Leonard drove to his house. We know the cops don't have it, so we figure that Cassidy guy has it. But the drive wasn't on *his* computer, either."

Tony paused to let his words sink in before adding, "We can't wait around while he puts this together or we'll be watching TV through bars."

Vernon's fear, which had eased, returned in waves and he struggled for breath. When able to speak, he said, "Don't say that, Tone. You're scarin' the hell out of me."

He glanced around the room. "Couldn't we just sell off this stuff—the TVs, soda machine, pool table—all that, and just pay 'em back?"

Behind Vernon's back, Leonard rolled his eyes.

"Jesus," Tony swore. "This place is not the problem." He snatched up the photo of Vernon walking up the sidewalk toward the house they called "the other place."

"This picture is of the other place, where we've got that family of bums stashed. Where we're making the movies."

Vernon slumped into his chair. He and Tony were silent, and clearly Leonard had no intention of speaking.

I wonder, Vernon thought, *if this guy, Leonard, is not talking because he's afraid the cops might have a bug in here. Or, God forbid, he thinks I'm wearing a wire.*

Tony stirred and gave him a hard look.

Jesus, can he read my mind?

Vernon, unnerved by Tony's scrutiny, strained for a way to show his concern for their collective security.

"I still don't see the problem, Tone? You said that we was just making those movies for some of your friends." He looked at each man and shrugged. "Like you always say, 'Who's gonna give a big rat's ass about that?'"

"Things have changed," was Tony's response.

Vernon waved the picture at Tony. "You mean because the kid that took these got killed, don't you?"

Leonard sneered. "Jesus Christ, is this guy for real?"

Vernon, fear in his eyes, looked to Tony for protection. "What'd I do, Tone?"

Tony held up both hands. "Let's take it easy, boys," he scolded. "We got to stay cool here."

He picked up the photo of the city car assigned to Vernon and pointed to the license plate. "We got to figure they have seen this picture so you can't use it no more to follow that lawyer."

Vernon nodded.

Leonard's gaze swung to Tony, "You got a lot of them little white cars, don't you? They all look alike."

"Big fleet. Only car you might see more around town is from gas and electric."

Leonard returned his gaze to Vernon. "Who's gonna know if you swapped the tags on this bozo's car with a different car in the fleet?"

A smile creased Tony's face. "I like it." He leaned forward, "I like it a lot. It would be a sort of early warning system. If the guy driving the car with those plates gets rousted, we'll know they're getting close."

Laughing he said, "Better that poor sap than you, right Vern?"

Vernon, struggling with the vision of himself in handcuffs, managed a weak grin.

By the time Vernon left the party house, he was deeply troubled. Leonard's mere presence was frightening.

The boss didn't say nothing when the scumbag called me a bozo.
I ain't no damn bozo.

And there was no doubt in Vernon's mind that the two of them were still sitting in the game room, making fun of him after sending him out to do the dirty work. They might be scheming so that he will be the only one who goes to jail. The bozo.

Tony had issued specific instructions. Vernon was to immediately drive to the city yard, park in an empty spot next to an identical city car and switch license tags between the cars. "And don't screw it up," he had said and laughed.

Leonard's accompanying laugh was empty, mirthless.

It occurred to Vernon to wonder—did Tony really think so little of him, or was he afraid to cross this guy?

Driving across town to the yard, Vernon reflected back, struggling to identify just when Tony's grand scheme had gone wrong.

At the start—*What was that, only five months ago?*—Tony had scoffed when Vernon questioned what they were doing.

"Relax. Nobody gives rat's ass what a couple of guys in Housing do. We're nobodies."

He had jerked a thumb skyward. "Them people up there got bigger things to worry about than the few bucks we're skimming off. Besides, I'm the boss and I say my guys have earned a bonus. That's what the party house is—a bonus."

Another time Tony had given a malevolent laugh and said, "You know, Vern, the city is spending big dough to get these dumps rehabbed. We're helping them out by rehabbing this one for free. Well, mostly free."

Soon after the renovation of the party house was complete, Tony had whispered his get-rich scheme to Vernon. "We're gonna rehab another hovel and turn it into a movie studio for porn."

"In the first place," Tony had said, "Nobody's ever going to know what's going on. There's thousands of these dumps—nobody can find us if they hunt for a million years. And you heard how the state is begging movie people to come to Maryland to shoot their movies. Giving them millions in tax breaks and incentives."

Vernon had nodded his awareness.

"Well, we'll have a movie studio right here in the city and it won't cost them millions. Nowhere near it. In fact, I think we should get some kind of award for taking the initiative on this one."

Once Tony had chosen his men and told them which address to work on, Vernon had headed up the crew. They installed new plumbing, hooked directly into the city's water system, and siphoned electric power from the nearest transformer. Outside, the building maintained the façade of an abandoned row home, while the interior glistened with newly painted walls and rugs scattered over patterned tile floors.

The day Tony arrived to inspect his movie studio; he insisted that Vernon take him to the bedroom first. "That's where all the action's gonna be," he chortled.

Vernon had led him down the carpeted hall and opened the bedroom door. Tony was awed by the spectacle.

A king-size bed occupied the center of the room, adorned with plush pillows and a quilt in competing shades of purple. A matching area rug covered most of the floor. The walls had been painted a soft lilac at the instruction of the film crew.

After a final look around the room, Tony turned to Vernon. "You tell them street bums that this room is off limits to them. If one of them lays his filthy skin on that bed he's dead. They're not to set foot in here, even when their kids are filming. Especially not then."

"Sure, boss."

Now, everything had changed. Tony was talking about early warning systems and being grilled by the cops. Thinking back, Vernon recalled that Tony's mood changed around the time Leonard showed up.

"A consultant from…out of town," Tony had called him.

I didn't like that guy from Day One. He looks like a killer, and I'm getting scared maybe he's the one killed that boy. That means I'm driving a killer around town.

Vernon, still blocks from the city yard, swerved to the curb, trembling with fear.

Jesus Tone, what are you doing to me?

26

Noah Cassidy and Corky Kilmark were seated at the window table they had come to think of as their own at Peace and a Cup of Joe. Two foam cups of hot coffee between them.

Noah, his cell phone to his ear, scowled. "Deacon's not answering."

"It's probably ringing in a pawn shop on East Monument Street," Corky said, and blew on his coffee.

"He loved that phone; if it's in a pawn shop somebody killed him to get it."

"What now?"

Noah folded his phone and set it on the table. "I'll try him again in a few minutes. If he doesn't answer, I suppose I'll have to go to the east side and hunt him down."

Corky stared out the window. "Look at those clouds. It's getting ready to come down out there. At least you'll be in a car; I got to tromp around the streets on foot looking for Marvel." He brightened. "You could drive me around until we spot him and then drop me off."

Noah picked up his phone and pushed redial. "It's ringing again—still no answer. I'll try again in a minute; meanwhile here's something to think about."

He leaned forward and, lowering his voice, said, "Now that we have an email address for Romeo, we could send him an email with a follow up request for a meet. Or, we could publish another edition of the Road Warrior. That should confuse them."

"You're thinking maybe they'll panic, figuring they didn't get the real Road Warrior."

"Or that there is more than one. Lure them into another meeting."

Corky shook his head. "One problem with that. What if they figure they know who it is and kill him, too? How does that help us; to get some innocent streeter killed?"

"You're right. We can't risk that."

"As for the email; wouldn't that tip them off that for sure we are on to them?"

Noah eyed Corky with new respect. "Right now," he said, "we have the edge because they don't know we are on to the housing department car." He smiled and saluted the other man with his coffee cup, "Pretty good for a Pontiac salesman."

Corky sat with a smug look as Noah again punched Deacon's number into his phone. Almost immediately, he slapped his phone closed and stood up. "I've got to find him," he said. "I'm afraid you're on your own."

Corky nodded.

Noah pressed a plastic lid on his coffee cup. "Come on, I'll drop you downtown," he said heading for the door.

After letting Corky out near the Inner Harbor, Noah drove east, heavy snowflakes settling onto his windshield.

Just my luck! This snow will drive all the streeters under cover.

Noah amped up the defroster. *At least I'm not walking around in it.*

Riley was absent from his station in front of the Cat's Eye, and there was no one on the street to ask the whereabouts of Deacon, or Riley.

Frustrated, Noah pulled to the curb and took out his cell phone and jabbed a finger on Deacon's direct dial number. On the second ring he heard Deacon's voice. "Who's there?"

"It's Noah Cassidy, Deacon, I need to see you."

"I'm in my winter quarters, come on over."

Noah parked on South Linwood and was shrouded in snow by the time he reached the Patterson Park pool house. He peered into the shadows beyond the open door. "You there, Deacon? It's Noah."

A flickering candle appeared in the far corner. "Come on ahead to this light. Stay close to the wall so you don't bang into nothing."

Noah hesitated, giving consideration to the wisdom of disappearing into the gloom facing him. He couldn't very well ask Deacon to join him out in the snow.

"Just you and Riley in here?"

"No."

"Who else is back there?"

"It's just me—Riley ain't here. Hurry up now, and close that door. This here candle won't last much longer—and you're letting the cold air in. I can feel it clear back to here."

Noah felt his way along the wall toward the candle.

It would be a big help if they had put a couple of windows in this place.

He strayed from the wall and kicked a stack of folding chairs.

"I hear you bumping up against them chairs. You're doing fine."

In a moment, Noah was standing next to Deacon's ominous form, relieved to find that it was just the two of them.

Deacon swung the candle, motioning Noah to one of two chairs. After he was seated, Deacon settled into the other one and extinguished the flame.

Though they sat separated by mere inches, Noah was barely able to make out Deacon's hulk in the gloom.

"Next time we'll do this at your place," Deacon said.

Clouds of breath appeared as Noah spoke, "I tried to call you several times and got no answer. Where were you?"

Deacon snorted and Noah reckoned that the tribal chief must be shaking his head.

"Took me some minutes to figure out that Ray Charles was singing to me from my own pants. 'Course then I knew it was you—nobody else got the number—and you would call back.

"See, if I don't say nothing you'll let it ring out and I can hear my song "Hit the Road, Jack." How'd it get on there? I know you never got hold of my phone?"

Noah had forgotten that he had downloaded the ringtone directly and laughed. "It's magic. I forgot that I did it, so it never occurred to me that you would be listening to Ray."

"You probably afraid I had hocked it or traded it for a bottle of Jim. It's like them bumper stickers say about guns—'the only way you'll get this here phone is to pry it out of my cold dead hand.' By the way you never told me what my number is."

"You don't need to be getting calls from anyone but me. You can't be wasting the minutes."

"But, ain't I right—time only starts when I say 'hello.'"

"Yes, but—"

"See, I ain't gonna say 'hello.' Somebody calls and I just let it play out; it's the only way I get to hear Ray."

"Okay, okay. I'm not going to give you the number of your phone, but I will call you more often, so you can hear Ray."

Noah gestured with one hand for emphasis, before realizing that it could not be seen. He quickly lowered it,

"When I call, I'll let it ring so you can hear Ray. When it rings again you need to answer."

Deacon agreed and Noah asked him to relight the candle as he produced a map and photos.

Wish to hell I had thought to bring a flashlight. Better yet, I'll get him one of those LED lanterns. A housewarming gift.

They huddled over the photos while Noah explained what he expected from Deacon's streeters.

"Don't take any chances; use only those you can trust to keep quiet about this."

Before Deacon could reply, Noah added, "It wouldn't take much for one of them to figure he might be able to sell what he knows."

"These are my folks. They won't do me thataway."

"Let's hope not. And, if you find what we're looking for, call me immediately."

Deacon stood and held the candle, preparing to lead Noah to the door. "You didn't bring ole Deacon no gifts this time."

He held up his cell phone, "I let you slide on account of this. Next time bring smokes."

27

"Sachs Goetz Bennett and Bell, good morning."

"Good morning. Noah Cassidy calling for Jack Douglas."

"Hold, please."

Noah watched his new laptop boot up as he waited.

Douglas came on the line, chuckling. "You looking for work? Maybe decided to return to the practice of law?"

"The day your name is included on the marquee, I'll give it more thought."

"You could starve before then. What's up?"

"A lot has happened since we talked. For one thing, my computer was stolen, my research on our book gone with it. I have no idea when I will be able to get back to it."

"I'm guessing you left your car unlocked while you were in the Pussy Cat Club?"

"I wish it were that simple. A burglar got into my place while I was gone. My landlady got nosy and I found her dead on my living room floor when I came home."

"Oh, shit! I'm sorry. It never fails—whenever I try to be clever, it bites me in the ass."

"How's your dance card?"

"Full. But, I've got to eat lunch; can you make it to Burke's by1?"

Noah walked through Burke's front door, skirted the line at the cash register and proceeded up the steps to a small dining room.

Not seeing Jack Douglas at one of the tiny tables jammed into the room, he retraced his steps to the larger dining area. This room was a narrow dusky rectangle, a couple of business men were eating at the mirrored bar stretching the length of the wall to his right. Booths of faux leather lined the opposite wall. Noah strolled the line of booths, glancing into each as he passed. Satisfied that he had arrived ahead of his friend, he claimed the last booth at the back of the room.

A plump middle-aged waitress, dyed blonde hair piled high, took his order for a Diet Coke and left two menus on the table.

Noah was taking his first sip of Coke when Douglas appeared, hung up his overcoat and slid in across the table, rubbing his hands.

"It's like January out there," the lawyer said and picked up a menu. "I'm tight on time, so without further ado…"

Jack Douglas belonged in a courtroom. Noah couldn't envision him anywhere else. It was not just his appearance: the dark hair, styled and worn long over the collar of an expensive suit, or the rimless John Lennon glasses. The poise and self-confidence which emanated from his presence was equally notable. Moving smoothly about the courtroom during final argument, it was evident that Jack Douglas never expected to lose a case, and he rarely did. Noah reluctantly admitted, if only to himself, that he would never be the advocate that Jack Douglas was.

Each man ordered a cheeseburger with a side of Burke's famed onion rings, and then Noah commenced his narrative, starting with the stabbing of Jason Jefferson.

Upon hearing that Noah had taken on a faux street bum as a client, Douglas raised an eyebrow but made no comment.

Douglas smiled as Noah recounted how he had finessed being mistaken for a police detective by Jason's sister and mother.

When Noah described coming home to find his landlady's body, Douglas stopped chewing. "Both her and the boy stabbed," he observed. "Same guy."

"That's the theory I'm working on."

Noah ended his account with the revelation that he had been followed by a car that Detective Baines traced back to the city housing authority.

He said, "It's pretty clear that the computers were the target in both burglaries. I haven't heard that the same knife was used on both victims, but come on; it's not just a coincidence. Any more than me being followed is not tied to both crimes. Ergo, the killings and the burglaries are connected to someone in the housing authority. Of that I'm certain, but what I can't figure out is: What are they involved in that's worth killing two people to keep secret? Drugs? A stable of girls? What?"

"Murder for hire?" Jack Douglas offered and then wiped his mouth and dropped the paper napkin onto his plate. He checked his cell phone. "I've got a few minutes yet. Why don't I talk while you eat?"

Noah hated eating hot food which had grown cold. He grabbed up his burger, pleased to find it still warm.

"I'll take that as a yes," Douglas said. He leaned his elbows on the table and began, "Was forensics able to identify the murder weapon in either case?"

Noah nodded as he chewed. He swallowed and said, "The weapon that killed Jason is a Stag Hunter sheath knife with a 5-inch blade and a gut hook. It makes a nasty, and distinctive, wound. Haven't heard from my landlady's autopsy."

"We can be pretty certain that the boy, Jason, was set up, because of the no-show from the email asking him to meet."

Noah nodded. "Most likely he was killed because of something he saw or heard that they didn't want posted on his website. We are thinking that it was no random street crime— a planned hit."

"Agreed. It's highly doubtful your landlady knew anything about their business. Yet she gets killed by the same guy. Why?"

Noah swallowed some of his Coke. "Why? Because she finds him inside my apartment."

"Think about it. You prosecuted more than a few burglars, how many of them carried around a hunting knife with a gut hook?"

"None."

"Your apartment was dark, right?"

"I had a couple of small electric candles glowing in the windows. So basically, yes."

Douglas leaned forward, speaking in earnest. "So, it's very likely she couldn't see his face, couldn't identify him. He could have easily shoved her down and ran out, or knocked her out if he wasn't finished with his search. But he carries this barbarous weapon, which he uses to kill her when there was no real need."

"What are you thinking?"

"He is a professional who enjoys his work."

"A hit man hired by someone in the city housing agency," Noah mused. "I wonder if he's on the city's payroll."

Jack Douglas smiled. "That's an excellent question. It would be no problem for someone in management to put a ghost on the payroll. It is done all the time with brother-in-laws, anyone with a surname that is different from the manager.

"We also have you being shadowed by a city car from housing. Probably some low-level slug following orders. It sounds to me like you are looking for a management type in the Baltimore City Housing Agency."

"It's thin but definitely worth considering."

Douglas held out his hand. "Ten bucks says I'm right."

"How about a steak dinner?"

"The Prime Rib or Ruth's Chris. No Texas Road House."

"If we get enough to prove that, I'll be thrilled to spring for the Prime Rib."

Douglas rubbed his hands together vigorously. "Now we are talking. I take it you got nothing from surveillance cameras."

"No cameras where he was stabbed."

"What about the others?"

Noah tilted his head and frowned. "What do you mean—'the others'?"

"You said there were several photos the victim had taken around the city."

"Yes."

"And one in particular that someone took of him on Cathedral Street at the Enoch Pratt library."

"Again, yes."

"Recently, I was involved in a litigation in which the city's security cameras were material. I learned that the Baltimore Police

Department monitors over five hundred such cameras, and most of them are on the streets of downtown.

"If I was prosecuting this case for the U.S. Attorney, I'd have a herd of FBI agents poring over the victim's pictures to try and identify a location and a time frame for them. Then I'd have them see which of those locations matched up with an existing security camera. And then—ta-da—I'd have these agents reviewing security photos for that time frame to see if any small white cars with the city seal, or anyone of interest appears. And, I'd have my agents pay particular attention to anyone skulking in the background, maybe following our victim. Skulkers by definition look suspicious."

Noah dropped his head. "I'm slipping. I took some of the photos off of Jason's website and passed them out to some folks to search for the locations in those pictures. But, I didn't think about the security cameras."

"You got soft. Too much time spent playing rock and roll music on the radio."

Douglas stood up, dropped some cash on the table and shrugged into his coat. "Who you got pounding the pavement for you?"

"Street people."

To Noah's surprise, Detective Jeff Baines was already seated at the window table when he walked into Peace and a Cup of Joe. Natty business garb had been replaced by equally fashionable black cord slacks and a gray turtleneck of soft wool worn beneath a burgundy hooded wind breaker.

"You undercover?" Noah asked.

"One of the wonders of the modern world. A day off with no court appearance. And yet here I am, squandering these precious minutes with you."

Noah shrugged out of his mackinaw and draped it over the chair back. "The least I can do is spring for the coffee."

"That's what I was thinking. And you could surprise me with a cinnamon donut to go with it."

Noah returned carrying a tray with two cups of coffee and accompanying donuts on paper plates.

Baines slid two folded sheets of paper across the table.

"As requested," he said and attacked his breakfast.

The first page was a grainy arrest photo of a black man with a pockmarked face and piercing eyes. Below the picture was typed a physical description and personal history of the man. The two dark dots at the top of the page confirmed to Noah that the page was a photocopy of the man's arrest sheet taken from the police file.

"You have any trouble getting this?" Noah asked as he scanned the data.

"Me? None. I couldn't go near that squad room without that asshole Masterson hearing about it. I asked the lovely Detective Taylor to do it."

Noah gave him a questioning look.

"She wasn't thrilled about it, but—mission accomplished and no casualties. That's all that matters."

The man in the arrest photo was identified as Rufus Jones, with an alias of Spike Jones. Age—fifty-three. No permanent address.

"This is the man who confessed to stabbing Jason Jefferson?" Noah questioned.

Baines, intent on pulling a piece of sodden donut from his coffee cup, nodded.

"Am I right?" Noah asked. "The murder weapon was never recovered."

"No mention of it in the file and it's not entered into evidence."

Noah set the sheet aside and picked up the second page. It contained only a name and street address in Baltimore's Highlandtown neighborhood.

"What's this?" He asked.

"The name of the resident at the address where that puke Rollie Corbett drove Detective Taylor on an interview of the wild goose chase variety, while this arch fiend was confessing."

"Joseph Kusicki. Does that name mean anything?"

Baines smiled and ran a paper napkin across his chin. "I'll let you decide," he said. "Kusicki is Detective Corbett's brother-in-law."

Noah picked up the first sheet and studied them together. "So we were right. The interview *was* bogus. A ruse to get her out of the way while they bullied a confession out of old Spike here."

Baines picked up both empty cups. "This round is on me."

When Baines returned, Noah, scribbling notes in the space below the Kusicki address, mumbled, "Thanks."

Baines sat and stirred the contents of a packet of Sweet'N Low into his coffee. "Looks like you have a plan."

"A start anyway." Noah put his pen away and lifted his steaming cup in salute. "I have an idea which is too rudimentary to be called a plan. Does Mister Spike have an attorney yet?"

"I doubt it very much. Who in their right mind is going to represent a streeter unless he's court-appointed and has no choice. As far as I know, Spike hasn't been arraigned. What do you have in mind?"

Noah tapped on Spike Jones' photo. "This case is a real dog. No murder weapon; I doubt they can show a motive. Any decent counsel can get the confession tossed; they got nothing. Before the cops can take it to the state's attorney, they're going to have to dress it up pretty good. No way around it. Which means somebody will be committing perjury."

"There's a couple of problems."

"Go ahead."

Baines reached over and tapped the photo. "This guy is going to wind up with a teenager from legal aid for an attorney. Said teenager will jump on an opportunity to plea bargain this hound away. Whichever assistant state's attorney gets stuck with it will no doubt be thrilled to make said teenager an offer which can't be refused. No one will ever have to get on the stand and raise his hand."

"I thought of that. I have a friend in one of the big firms in town. They have a policy of donating a certain number of hours a month to pro bono work. I'm pretty sure I can get him to see Spike's defense as a worthy cause."

"I hate to spoil your fun—just being the devil's advocate here. Isn't there a good chance that your old office will refuse to take this loser to court? Especially if they're going up against a hotshot defense counsel."

"I think I can work something out on that end."

Noah could see Baines' mind churning.

"Let me see if I understand this," said Baines. "You want this to go to trial so a couple of my brothers in blue will be forced to lie under oath. To do that you have to get an expensive lawyer to represent Spike here for nada."

Noah nodded. "Two things. Spike may not be much, but he is still a human being. If we let him get herded into a plea bargain, it will not only send the poor bastard to prison for the rest of his miserable life; it will also mean that the case is not just closed, it's nailed shut. And the actual killers get away with these crimes and any other shit they are pulling. I can't sit still for that, can you?"

Baines replied, "And you will be the puppet master pulling the strings on both sides; the defense and prosecution."

"Puppet master is a little strong. Just trying for a little justice here."

Baines opened his mouth to protest but Noah cut him off.

He asked, "Do you believe that VoShaun's lieutenant is bent?"

"Masterson? Probably."

"Would justice be served if we took what we suspect about Lieutenant Masterson and his merry band to Internal Affairs?"

Baines shook his head. "Doubtful. Very doubtful."

"I would like your help, but I understand if you don't want to be a party to this. Just say so and I'll go my own way."

Baines stared into his coffee cup, sighed and looked over at Noah. "When you lay it out like that it doesn't sound like fun anymore. Still, it has to be done. What do you need from me?"

Noah told him.

28

Marvel was dozing in a white molded plastic lawn chair when Noah and Corky entered Red Emma's on St. Paul Street. The door, two steps below street level, opened into a cluttered bookstore and coffee shop.

Marvel roused himself and joined them at the counter.

"You can order here and we'll take our breakfasts over to them three chairs I set up in that corner. The stuff they serve is mostly all 'organic,' whatever that means. But it's still good. Somehow I missed breakfast this morning so I'll have me one of them bagel rolls. The one with cinnamon and raisins, toasted up real nice and spread all over with some of that *organic* cream cheese. And I'll require a big coffee, o'course."

After ordering, Noah took in the room. Directly across from the counter, two plate-glass windows faced onto St. Paul Street at street level. Below the windows sat tables and racks displaying an assortment of used books and magazines. The floor, overlaid with a thin carpet, was strewn with a random collection of uncomfortable-looking wooden and plastic chairs.

Noah realized that, though scattered about, the seats generally faced a separate row of four chairs.

Looks to be set up for some sort of performance. Most likely local musicians or a reading of original poetry.

The back wall, where Marvel had arranged their chairs, was lined with book shelves offering more shabby reading material.

The place would be right at home in San Francisco's Haight - Ashbury District during the 1960s.

Marvel was saying, "If you're thinking I'm going to pay, you're out of luck. I musta left my wallet back at my packing crate."

Noah realized that a heavy set-woman glared at him from behind the counter, her hand out. He passed a bulging brown envelope to Corky and paid the scowling woman.

No name tag. Wonder if that is Red Emma?

There being no table, Marvel balanced his roll and coffee on his knees. The streeter gnawed away a large chunk of bagel, creating a bulge in one cheek as he chewed. "I reckon you fellas never heard of this place. 'Red' in the name don't come from the color of the brick building. It's commie red, from the old days. As for Emma, she was a rabble-rouser way back when. Any FBI or poleece comes around they get run off. If you noticed there ain't no security cameras on this street corner. Emma's won't allow it."

Noah saw no reason to tell Marvel that he was already aware there were no security cameras mounted at the corner of St. Paul and Madison streets. Following his meeting with Jack Douglas, Noah had scrolled through a website listing the location of nearly every security camera in the city and had wondered how frequently those planning criminal activity bothered to visit the same site.

Noah had decided that from now on, where possible, he would meet at locations free from camera coverage.

They could be using the cameras to watch us. Why not? They're city employees and it's likely they have at least one cop in their pocket.

Marvel washed the last of the bagel down with a gulp of coffee. "If you noticed, I wasn't real comfortable when we was up to the Lexington Market. Too many up there ready to run a fella off. Emma's is one of the few places in town that treats us streeters like real folks."

Noah sat his coffee cup on the floor and motioned Corky to hand over the envelope. He withdrew three sheets of paper and said to Marvel, "When you are finished with your breakfast I want you to take a look at these."

Marvel nodded and wiped both hands on his cape.

"This here one is Spike," he said, holding the first sheet. "But I guess you know that. Word is he got locked up for killing that boy. Must be so."

He looked from Noah to Corky and hastily added, "I mean it's so that he got locked up—not that he's a killer. It don't make no sense. Spike's a little daft, but he wouldn't hurt nobody."

Marvel motioned with one arm. "The folks in this place is right about those damn poleece. If they was looking for somebody to frame for murder there's more likely pickin's out there than old Spike."

"Where does Spike hang out?" Noah asked.

"Most days he works the War Memorial Plaza. He does pretty good at the parking garage across Fayette."

Noah pulled out a notebook and pen adding to his to-do list for Baines.

Marvel said, "Some days he makes his way over to the Vet Center on High Street."

Check for security cameras—War Memorial & Vets Center—High St. If present—Baines review. Any VA records on Spike?

Next, Noah showed Marvel the picture of the white city-owned car from Jason's thumb drive. "There are more copies of each picture in here to give out to your people."

He stopped, assured himself that Marvel was paying attention and added, "You must stress to anyone who gets these pictures that they are to do nothing except report what they see and hear to you. It could be dangerous if they were caught snooping around on their own. The people we are looking for are killers."

Marvel scratched at his beard with dirty, talon-like fingernails. He glanced toward the counter before saying, "There's some folks who won't take it kindly if they know we was helping the cops."

"They aren't going to know from us. That's why we're meeting here, remember. Our agreement is, I take anything you get to the cops and they won't know where it's coming from."

Marvel nodded and picked up another picture. "This the boy was killed?"

Noah nodded.

"Not likely we'll see him around then, is it?"

"Don't be a smart ass. We want you to show that picture to every streeter you can think of. Can they remember seeing him?

We're hoping someone saw something that will help. Maybe Jason meeting up with some stranger. Where and when? Write it down. It's important that we know the time and day, as well as the location."

"Where'd you get this?" Marvel asked as he studied a copy of the picture of Doctor Musk from Jason's computer.

"Do you know him?" Noah asked.

"Seen him around the clinic on Fayette Street. Believe Wise Eddie knows him. He's a nasty one, keeps to himself. He do it?"

"We're hoping you can help us with that. Maybe one of your tribe has seen him arguing with Jason. Something like that."

Corky pointed at the photo. "It looks like he's heading straight for the camera. Maybe that's when he stabbed Jason."

"Not likely," Marvel said. "That fella is walking in the 400 block of Fayette Street. East. Near the clinic."

"East Fayette?" Noah questioned. "You sure about that?"

"Yep. You walk these streets as many years as me, you get to know your way around. You figure he's hiding something?"

"Everyone is hiding *something*. The question is does this guy believe his secret is worth killing to keep?"

Marvel nodded. "Oh, in case you was wondering, I *can* read and write, but I'll need writing stuff for putting all this down."

Noah handed the envelope to Marvel. "There's a pad and couple of pens in there," he said and then placed another photograph in Marvel's hands. "This is the house I told you about on the phone. It's important that we find it."

Marvel studied the area in the picture pointed out by Noah.

"Yep. I see what you mean, pretty clever. Not many folks would a thought of that."

"Remember, when you find it call me right away."

"Gotcha."

Back in the car, the windshield wipers disposed of the damp snow that had accumulated while they were inside Red Emma's. With a gloved hand, Noah wiped the condensation from the interior windshield. "Where do you want me to drop you?" he asked.

"Pratt Street Pavilion." Corky hunched forward and peered out at the heavy clouds hanging just above the rooftops.

"I doubt that I'll stay very long, by the looks of that sky." He turned to Noah. "How long do you figure to be with Deacon?"

"Probably an hour—round trip."

"Would it be a lot of trouble to cruise by Pratt and Light on your way back? Maybe I could hitch a ride out to my car. If I'm not there it means I couldn't stand it and I already left."

"I can do that."

"I have to confess, I'm losing my enthusiasm for this life."

"It's easy to see why."

Corky brightened. "But I am taking a liking to this investigation business. And I believe I have a knack for it. I wasn't kidding when I said we should hang out a shingle when this is over. My wife—"

"Whoa. I hope you haven't gone and bought yourself a trench coat. I don't know what I am going to be doing after this is over, but I'm quite sure it won't be private investigations."

"Why not? From what I've seen you're damn good at this stuff. Be a shame to waste all that talent."

Noah did not want to discourage Corky, lest he might throw up his hands before they finished what they had started. Still, Corky had to face reality, at least as Noah understood it.

"You do know that you have to be licensed and bonded by the state. Unlike television, a PI almost never has a real need to carry a gun. But you need to be licensed in case it comes up. Do you think you would have a problem qualifying for a PI license and concealed weapons carry permit?"

"I—"

"Then the toughest part of all—competing with all the ex-cops and retired feds already out there. Picture a prospective client comparing your background with that of a twenty-five year veteran FBI agent when he's considering who to hire."

Corky slumped in his seat and said no more until he got out of the car at the Inner Harbor. "Don't forget me in an hour," he said and closed the door.

Noah headed east on Pratt Street toward Patterson Park to meet with Deacon.

29

Jack Douglas stood aside while the jailer admitted him to the cramped interview room at Baltimore Booking and Intake on Madison Street. Seated at the small metal table was Douglas' new client, shackled to a heavy chain bolted to the concrete floor.

On the man's head, a thatch of oily salt-and-pepper hair merged with the tangled beard covering his face. He watched warily as Douglas settled into the chair opposite.

He's probably awed by the presence of a man wearing an eight-hundred dollar suit.

It had been several years since Douglas had visited a prisoner in jail. His law practice specialty being white-collar crime anyone who could afford to hire him did not delay doing so until after being arrested.

Jesus. This guy could give low-life a bad name. Cassidy owes me big time. One dinner at the Prime Rib will not cover this.

"I'm Jack Douglas, Mister Jones—your attorney. Okay if I call you Spike?"

The man blinked, which Douglas took as a sign of consent.

"I would have been here sooner, but they had you on the circuit."

Spike ran his tongue over chapped lips and said nothing.

"They ran you around from lock-up to lock-up, making it harder to locate you."

Spike shrugged his indifference.

"Listen up, this is important. You may not remember having had another lawyer. The public defender assigned to your case says he was never able to catch up with you."

Like he really tried.

"We went before the judge this morning and I replaced him as your attorney of record. A happier man I have not seen in a long time. So it's okay for you to talk to me. I'm on your side."

Douglas, getting no response, said, "Do you know why you're in here?"

The man blinked again before saying, "They told me I killed somebody."

"They told you? Do you remember confessing to killing someone?"

Spike shrugged. "Hard to say."

"When you close your eyes, can you see pictures of you killing somebody?"

Spike had the look of a man struggling to grasp vague thoughts as they flitted around inside his head. Finally, he cornered one and spoke up. "They showed me a paper where I said that I sure enough done it. So I guess I did."

Douglas let that go. "You know that you've been locked up for several days."

This time the prisoner nodded vigorously.

"What's the last thing you can recall before the cops locked you up?"

Another struggle and then Spike said, "I got it now. Some citizen dropped a twenty in my cup. A twenty dollar bill. So I hied myself over to the store and got me a big bottle of Night Train. It must've done its job 'cause I don't remember nothing. Funny thing, though…"

"What's that?"

"My patch is around the plaza. The poleece said I done the killin' over to Penn Street up by Lombard. That'd a been a real hike for me, with my bum leg and all. So my question is, what would possess me to hoof it all the way over there when I never been there in my life, to kill somebody I don't know?"

"That is a very good question," Douglas said and jotted a note on a legal pad. "By the plaza, you mean the War Memorial Plaza in front of City Hall."

Spike nodded.

"That's near police headquarters."

"Yup."

"How long you been in business there?"

Spike's eyes searched Douglas' face. Was this lawyer gulling him?

"Hard to say."

I'm not trying to trick you, if that's what you're thinking. Remember, I'm on your side. It's important. How long?"

Spike's eyes showed that his mind was laboring. Eventually he offered, "Some years is the best I can do. Time don't mean much to a streeter. Holidays are no help. Christmas is the same as any other day except all the usual places are closed. Why you asking?"

"Over those years, you must have seen lots of cops come in and out of headquarters."

"I reckon."

"Do you know any of them by name?"

Spike shook his head. "Never was introduced."

"Could it be that it was one of them who put that bill in your cup?"

Furrows appeared in Spike's forehead. "I never heard tell of no poleece giving twenty bucks to a street bum. What're you gettin' at?"

"What did you do after you got the twenty?"

"I just told ya. Jesus boy are you paying attention? I hied myself over to the liquor store and got a big bottle of Night Train." Spike licked his lips, "I sure could use some right now. What of it?"

"Maybe it was a cop who dropped the twenty figuring you'd head for the Night Train."

Spike shook his head muttering, "That don't make no sense."

"It does if they wanted to set you up to confess to the killing."

"Set me up?"

"It's something to think about. Well?"

"Well, what?"

"Do you recollect anything? If it was a cop, it was likely a detective. Not a uniform."

"Wish I could say. I don't pay much attention to folks passing by. I found that if you look them in the eye it scares some of 'em away. I didn't hear no coins dropping so it took a minute to know that I had snared me a big one. See, I use one of them old-fashioned tin cups so's I can listen for the clink when a coin hits. I had a feeling somebody had stopped was the reason I took a peek and I couldn't believe my eyes. There sat a twenty dollar bill. I grabbed her up in case the citizen saw his mistake and tried to get it back. When I looked around, the street was empty. Sorry."

"Do you go anywhere else, besides your patch?"

Spike snorted. "Oh yeah. I'm forever being invited out. Where am I going to go?"

Douglas, seeing nothing to be gained by pointing out that his client was being a smartass, asked, "How did you hurt your leg?"

"Getting pretty damn nosy, aren't you?" Spike's effort to shift his left leg into his lawyer's view was stopped short by the manacle attached to that ankle. "Well, shit. If I could get it out here, you could see for yourself. You *could* say I was 'hurt'—my damn leg was near blown off."

"Iraq?"

"Afghanistan. Same war—different ragheads."

"You ever go to the VA?"

Spike grinned for the first time. "Oh, I see what you're getting at. Maybe I was at the VA when the killing took place. Pretty smart. Sorry I was so uppity before."

"Well?"

"Well, what?"

"Were you at the VA when that boy was killed?"

"Hell if I know. I'm not real clear on when it happened. But it'd be easy to check. I only go to the one VA that's just across the Jones Falls on High Street, I try to get over there two or three times a week. If it was nasty weather whichever day it happened, I was likely at the VA. They'd have my sign-in record."

Douglas finished jotting a note and said, "It can be quite dangerous out there on the mean streets. What kind of weapon do you have—for your own protection, of course?"

"Mean streets? That sayin' is a load of crap. It ain't the streets that's mean—it's the people on them."

Douglas smiled. "I stand corrected."

"It's true I carried a little pocket knife." The fog that had befuddled Spike seemed to be lifting. "A beaut, one of those Swiss Army knives. Real handy for folks like me. It'll open any bottle and most cans."

He stopped talking and studied Douglas. "If you're wondering— I didn't steal it. Saved up and bought it at Sunny's Surplus when they had a store on Baltimore Street."

"Then it should be in your property or held as evidence— though no way that was the murder weapon."

Spike stiffened and his eyes snapped. "Now I'm mad. Those poleece kept pushing me about what I done with the knife I cut him with. I answered 'em right back; the only knife I ever had was that Swiss Army knife."

Spike hunched over the table. "Then the one fat bastard gave me a big smile, turns to the other one and says, 'You hear that Bobby? He admits having a knife.' Then he goes on to tell me that I must have dreamed up that story about a Swiss Army knife, 'cause they didn't find one on me."

"You had that knife for a long time, right?"

Spike nodded. "Bastards stole it. That's what."

As Douglas made more notes he said, "One of them probably liked it and figured you wouldn't need it where you're going."

Spike's eyes narrowed.

Douglas smiled. "You did confess to murder—remember?"

30

Noah was deep in conversation with Jack Douglas when it occurred to him that Abba's hit song "Take a Chance on Me" was playing in his coat pocket.

"I love Abba," he said, retrieving his cell phone. "I was going to use "Dancing Queen" as a ringtone, but then I realized that being an unmarried man of a certain age, it might send the wrong signal."

He checked the phone's caller ID. "It's Marvel. You remember me talking about him."

Douglas nodded, striking a bodybuilder pose.

"Go ahead," Noah said.

"It's Marvel. I think we found what you want."

Noah dug a ballpoint pen from a jacket pocket. "Where are you?"

"On Harlem Street." Marvel gave him the nearest cross street. "They's no numbers, that's the best I can do."

Noah scribbled the street names. "Is the white car there?"

"They's no cars in the whole block."

"Walk a block east—that's toward downtown—and wait. I'm at the Starbucks on Eutaw Street; I'll be there in ten minutes."

"I know which way is east, for Christ's sake," Marvel snapped.

Noah pocketed his phone. To Douglas he said, "Let's take a ride."

"Would you please occasionally take your eyes off the mirror and put them on the road?" Jack Douglas chided. "The way you drive, nobody could be following us."

"We're almost there. If this *is* the place, I don't want them to know we found it."

Marvel was not in view as they approached the agreed-upon street corner.

"Maybe he got confused," said Douglas.

Noah shook his head. "One thing Marvel knows is streets. He didn't get confused."

The car drifted into an intersection and Marvel appeared from the recessed doorway of a long-abandoned mini-mart on the northwest corner. Noah pulled to the curb, Marvel yanked open the door and slid into the back seat. "Who's this?" he asked, glaring at Douglas.

"His name is Jack Douglas. He's Spike's lawyer."

"You should'a told me he was coming. I don't take kindly to strangers."

"I'll remember that."

Noah turned left at the next corner and Marvel fumed. "Hell you going?"

He leaned forward until Noah could feel the man's warm breath on his neck and pointed a grubby finger at the passenger side window. "The house is that a way—on Harlem Street, three blocks."

"We're going to sneak up on them."

"Who you sneakin' up on? I told you, they's nobody there."

The block they were now in was as desolate as the previous one. On either side of the street once-proud three-story row homes slumped in decay.

Noah noticed as they moved slowly along the street that nothing moved. No vehicles were parked, no children played, not a feral cat or rabid dog was to be seen. He thought it likely that even the rats had moved on. It was reminiscent of a scene from an apocalypse movie.

Noah turned right at the next intersection and drove slowly along a street which paralleled Harlem Street. To the left, another row of discarded buildings loomed. Through the passenger's side window, an entire block had been leveled. Slabs of concrete foundations and the occasional single row of cinder blocks were all that remained of a once-vibrant neighborhood.

Discarded mattresses and car tires dotted the acreage.

The desolation provided them with a clear view across the ruins to the buildings fronting Harlem Street

Marvel thrust his head between the two men in the front seat. "That's it! That's it!" he exclaimed, aiming a shaking finger at the line of attached houses on Harlem Street. "At the end of the row."

Jack Douglas considered the string of connected houses. "This may be a dumb question," he said, "but how do you know it's that particular house? They all look the same. Boarded up and deserted."

Noah chuckled and said, "Marvel."

"Look real close at that end house and the end house of the next row. What do ya see that's different?"

After another minute, Douglas shrugged, "I give up. What?"

At least for this moment, Marvel was smarter that this fancy lawyer in his rich man's suit of clothes.

With Douglas eying him in anticipation, Marvel pointed a bony forefinger out the window. "That end house is the only one in this whole neighborhood of dead houses that has electric lines running into it. And, if you was to go around back and look up to the top floor, you can just make out the edge for one of them sky dishes for the TV."

Noah nodded at Marvel. "Good work."

"Damn straight!"

Douglas turned to Noah, "Two questions. How did you think to look for the electric lines; and two, how can you be certain this place has anything to do with our villains?"

Noah rummaged through the manila document envelope on the seat beside him and handed Douglas a set of the photos copied from Jason's thumb drive.

"These were on Jason's computer. You know, the person your client, Mister Spike, is charged with killing."

Douglas held Jason's photo up to the windshield for a direct comparison to the row of houses on Harlem Street. "It's hard to tell this far away. You have a pair of binoculars?"

Noah shook his head.

Douglas lowered the photo. "Okay. Let's say it is the same house. How do we link whoever is inside to the killings?"

"Jason took pictures of two houses with power lines connected; both houses had the white city car parked in front. The second house is in a better looking neighborhood, not so run down. We're still looking for that one."

Douglas held up another photo.

Noah touched an index finger to the picture. "See that tag number. It's the same one that is on the car that's been following me—"

Douglas responded with quizzical look.

Noah jabbed a finger into his own belly. "I know it in here."

31

"I want you to drive Leonard back to that house in Dickeyville," Tony ordered.

"You mean that place where all the dicks hang out?" Vernon repeated their tired joke in a futile effort to cheer up his boss. Tony DiRosa was not in the mood and shot him a look that said so in no uncertain terms.

The two men were huddled in a cramped second-floor office Tony kept in the city housing inspection building on Reisterstown Road. The door was closed and the blinds drawn. They spoke softly.

"I want it done tonight!"

After a moment's hesitation, Vernon mumbled. "Gee, Tone, you know I do whatever you say," he shook his head. "But tonight's no good."

"And I don't want you using that city car. Got it?"

"Why? I switched the plates like you said."

"Why? Because it'll be night." Tony jabbed a forefinger at his own head. "Use your head. He sees a white car, he's already looking for trouble. He won't bother to get close enough to check the tag. He's never seen your SUV—use it."

Vernon kept his eyes on his shoes. "Anyhow, Tone, did you hear me say I can't do it tonight? My wife wants me to go with her to the kid's school. Anyone can drive the guy. How about Jimmy or Allen?"

Tony grabbed up a snow scene paperweight from his desk, for several seconds he sat poised to throw it. Vernon cowered in his chair, forearms shielding his head. "Come on, Tone," he pleaded. "What're you doing?"

Tony slammed the paperweight on the desk and buried his head in his hands. "This was supposed to be so easy," he moaned.

"Why can't that guy drive himself? He ought to know the way. You remember, I took him out there once already, the time he come back with that lawyer's computer. What's he want this time, the TV? Before that was the dead kid's house—same thing, he come around the corner with that computer."

Receiving no response, Vernon added, "We're gonna get caught, we keep doing this stuff."

Tony reached out and dragged a dented metal waste basket between his legs. "Watch your shoes," he moaned and retched into the basket.

Vernon scrambled away and stood behind his chair. "Jesus, Tone. What's the matter? You want me to drive you to the hospital?"

Tony waved him away, saying, "Just get me a bottle of water from that machine down the hall. I'll be all right."

When Vernon returned to the office, Tony was sitting upright, holding a handkerchief to his mouth. He reached for the bottle, "Pop it open," he ordered. Vernon unscrewed the top and placed the bottle in the open hand.

"You sit still while I bring the car up to the side door."

Tony swigged from the bottle, swished the water inside his mouth and spit it into the wastebasket. "Sit down; we're not going to a damn hospital."

Vernon hesitated at the door and Tony softened his tone. "Look, it's just an ulcer. You wanna help, stop aggravating me and do what I say."

Vernon, feeling pushed into a corner, returned to his chair and stood behind it. He feared Tony's reaction to his next question and, perhaps subconsciously, kept the chair as a barrier between them. In any event, he wanted to be in a position to flee if Tony made another move to hurl the paperweight.

Vernon twisted his hands. "I got to say this, Tone—that guy Leonard is scary. He gives me the creeps—"

"Dammit, keep your voice down!"

"Okay. Sorry. What do we need him for, anyhow?" Vernon whispered. "Things was better when it was just you and me. Remember?"

Tony shrugged. "It was never—just you and me."

"What you sayin,' Tone? Sure it was. I know we let a few of the guys in the party house," Vernon waggled a finger between the two of them, "but it was still—just us with the movie business."

"You better sit down Vern."

Vernon hesitated.

"Don't worry, I won't throw nothing. I swear."

Vernon came around and slumped into the chair, an awful churning in his belly.

"First," Tony said," I want you to know that I haven't lied to you, exactly—I just didn't bother to tell you some stuff. It was for your own good." He heaved a deep sigh and then continued. "When we started making those porn movies, I told you it was to make a few bucks peddling them to some friends of mine."

"What you said was that we'd be rich."

"That was the dream. But I had what you call a silent partner, almost from the get-go. He's the one who made me give Leonard a city job. Anyway, the movies were real popular and it wasn't long before my silent partner—"

"He's the reason we're not rich, right? This partner guy took our money."

Tony shrugged as if to say that was as good a reason as any other. "Anyhow this guy shows up one day with Leonard and says he will be peddling all the movies we can crank out."

Tony stared into the waste basket as if he were looking for a place to hide. "Funny thing is, I still didn't get it. It was already a done deal—I had no say about anything. I opened my mouth and Leonard slides between me and the guy and gives me a look that would freeze your blood. You know the one I mean."

Vernon nodded.

"'You heard the boss,'" Leonard says to me. "I knew that was it."

Tony took a drink from the water bottle and wiped his mouth on a sleeve. Vernon sat poised on the edge of his chair, rubbing his hands together.

Tony forced a grin. "They were a 'good hood bad hood' team. Where Leonard was nasty from the start, the talker was very friendly and all smiles on the surface, but you knew that just below was a whole lot of trouble.

"The talker says they represent a movie distributor who is going to be the sales agents for all—he repeated it, *'all'*—of the movies we can produce. I just nodded, yes. I wasn't going to argue—not with these guys. Then, he says that Leonard was the marketing rep for this area and would be staying on to 'assist with any distribution problems that might come up. He'll need a city job.'"

Tony looked up, real fear in his eyes. "Jesus, Verny, I almost said that Leonard would have to fill out an application. Lucky for me I was too scared to talk."

Vernon had watched enough cop shows involving organized crime to understand what he was being told. "These guys aren't from around here are they, Tone?"

Tony shook his head.

"I'm guessing, Philly."

Tony nodded.

"So it's not your call on what this Leonard does. Going into these houses and all."

Tony nodded.

"Still, you couldn't tell me, Tone?"

"I was protecting you. No need for both of us to be throwing up. The one thing I did right is put that detective on the pad. I'm hoping he can keep the cops from sniffing around the studio. Then this Cassidy guy sticks his nose in bringing us more trouble."

Tony doubled up his fists. "Why didn't he just keep the fuck out of our business? Jesus. The cops got that bum to admit killing the kid and that was supposed to end it. Still Cassidy keeps coming." Tony rubbed his hands together. "It's out of my hands. The bastard is going to be sorry he didn't stop when he could."

Vernon's mouth was suddenly dry, his left leg shook and he could feel his stomach roll over. In hopeful desperation he said, "Why would the cops sniff around? Right? Even if they did, making the movies is no big deal. Right? You said so yourself, remember? Those kids' folks know about it and they are okay with it. Besides, they're only bums. Who is going to give a rat's ass about them? It's not like they are a real family or nothing."

Tony sat shaking his head very much craving a cigarette and angry at his wife for badgering him to quit. "I'm gonna tell you all of it. I never meant to—" Tony glanced around the cramped office. "Certainly not here, but you need to know it—for your own good."

A stricken Vernon said nothing.

When Tony looked up again there were tears in his eyes. "I'm not a tough guy. I always figured I was tough, growing up in East Baltimore and all. I guess I was more of a bully. These guys from Philly are the real deal. Tough guys. I don't have the stomach for it."

"The stomach for what, Tone?"

"The killings!"

Vernon's head snapped. "Jesus Christ, Tone! Don't say that. You and me, we're not killers."

Tony, unable to look at Vernon, mumbled. "We are now."

Tony had kept Vernon in the dark about luring Jason to the address on Penn Street where Leonard was to relieve him of his camera phone using only necessary force. In his planning, Tony had not foreseen Jason's devotion to his phone or Leonard's enthusiasm for killing.

"I told Leonard there was no need to hurt the kid. He just looked at me with those dead eyes and I knew we were in for it. My stomach dropped and hasn't been right since."

Vernon's mouth was so dry his words were a whisper. "Remember I was worried about him going into those houses to steal those computers? You yelled at me about being a baby and said not to worry 'cause it was taken care of? What about that?"

Tony looked out the window. "That was straight," he said. "My cop had it covered when they were burglaries. But that wasn't enough for Leonard. He gets his jollies by killing the kid and then

Cassidy's landlady. And now he's a bulldog, he'll never let go." He shrugged. "We got no choice. It's us or him."

The color drained from Vernon's face. His palms were sweaty and bile rose in his throat. He yanked the waste basket between his legs and bent over. For a moment, his entire body convulsed with dry heaves. Afterward he straightened and stared across at his boss.

Tony said, "I know it's bad, but we can't cross these guys. You're still gonna have to drive Leonard out to that house in Dickeyville. Whatever you do, don't let on you know about the killings."

Vernon, voice quavering, asked, "What's he gonna do out there? I never knew any of this stuff was going on. But I was right to hate Leonard. I'm not driving him out there so he can kill somebody else."

"You got no choice, Vern. They don't trust you anyhow. I already saved your ass by swearing that you was solid. If you don't drive him...well you know."

Vernon, his fear fused with anger growled, "You want to know something, Tone. You haven't been protecting me—you been using me."

32

Detective Jeff Baines was sitting in his vintage Thunderbird, dozing behind the wheel when Noah pulled alongside. Theirs were the only vehicles in the vast parking lot A behind the idle Oriole Park at Camden Yards.

Noah waited while Baines cranked down the driver's window before saying, "Sorry if I disturbed your nap."

Baines checked the stainless-steel TAG Heuer on his wrist, "I have court in forty-five minutes. I get my twenty winks when I can. I say twenty because I never seem to get forty."

Noah admired the car. "That's a beautiful specimen," he said. "'57?"

"Very good." Baines switched off the engine. "I'm coming over there as long as you keep the heat on. This beauty is too cozy for two adult males."

Noah admired the classic auto as Baines slid in beside him and closed the car door.

"Hard to be discreet in that."

"I'm neither a married man nor a cop on the arm, hence I'm unconcerned about—discreet."

"Brilliant white with matching whitewalls. They must be hard to get?"

"Yes. But clearly not impossible. Now to business." Baines pulled a manila envelope from his pocket and passed it across to Noah.

"Meeting like this could look like a payoff, except the envelope is going in the wrong direction."

While Noah studied the copies of photos the detective had taken from security camera footage, Baines added, "This working nights is turning out to be a big plus for us. Nobody's awake to ask questions while I paw through security camera files or to get nosy about why I'm copying certain photos.

"What you are looking at is some footage from a camera on High Street near the Vets Center which might, according to your buddy, provide an alibi for his client. I have to say it is loathsome to be working for a defense counsel. I could never be a PI."

Noah held up a photo. "The center is on High Street. What's the cross street?"

"Gay Street on one end, but the Center is at the other end of the block at the corner of Low Street."

Noah looked over to see if he was laughing. "High Street and Low Street?"

Baines held up his right hand. "I swear."

Noah studied two photos before saying, "This looks like our man Spike."

"It doesn't just look like him, it *is* him. Nice of him to face the camera. He enters the center just before two p.m. on the day the kid is getting killed, about twenty minutes later and many blocks away."

"You don't waste any time. I just told you yesterday about the VA thing."

"You ain't seen nothing yet, brother."

Turning back to the photos, Noah selected another one and held it for Baines to see. "What's this?"

"It's hard to make out, but if you look at it through a magnifying glass, as I did, you'll see that it is some people getting into a car."

"Okay—?"

"It looks to be a family of four. They're coming out of the Center and getting into a white car. It's down the block from the camera; still it could be your mystery car. "

Noah drew the image closer. "How do you get that?"

Baines patted his stomach. "Just a feeling. Okay, it's a stretch, but I've seen longer shots come in. If you watch cop shows you know we do not believe in coincidence." He tapped the photo. "This would be one of those."

Noah scrutinized the picture while Baines checked his watch and admired his automobile through the passenger-side window.

"There's another problem," Noah announced.

"Only one? That sounds like good news."

"Even if this *is* a picture of four people getting into *that* car, what the hell does it mean? It seems very problematic that it has anything to do with our case. What goes on at this Vets Center that would involve our killers?"

Baines shrugged and opened the car door. "No clue. City housing car, homeless families? All I know is the center is a place for homeless vets. See your man Spike for further details. Maybe he can enlighten you on why the white car was there. Gotta go."

As he strode across the parking lot, Baines waived his car keys in the air and called out, "—Hi-ho Silver, away!"

After Baines drove away, Noah sat for a few minutes studying the pictures of the white car without gaining any further insight. He made a note to give a set to Jack Douglas for display to his client.

Noah pulled out of Lot A and, deciding to treat himself to a few quiet moments, turned north. On the drive up town he maintained a steady vigilance in the rearview mirror. Having reached North Eutaw Street without seeing anything to cause concern, he parked around the corner on Baltimore Street grabbed up the manila envelope along with his laptop and defied a fierce wind to the Starbucks on the corner.

Once inside, Noah plugged into the store's Wi-Fi and draped his coat over a chair back. When he returned from the counter with a doppio macciato he opened a Microsoft Word file as a repository for case notes on the Jefferson killing.

While the police considered Jason Jefferson's murder a closed matter, and the murder of Frau Wirtz a separate, though open case; Noah was certain that both victims were killed by the same hand and should be viewed together as one active investigation.

Had those responsible for the murder of Frau Wirtz's stopped with Spike's phony confession, the case would be over. Frau Wirtz would still be alive and there would be no Detective Baines to locate candid shots from security cameras. Noah would have nothing more exciting to occupy his time than renewing the research on his book and occasionally looking for gainful employment.

By killing his landlady they had gone "a bridge too far," as it were. That crime had provided additional incentive for him to pursue them and, through Jeff Baines, an avenue by which to do so. He hoped that he would get the chance to rub their ugly faces in it once they were finally behind bars.

Working from memory and his notebook, Noah proceeded to enter the significant events as he understood them, adding his thoughts on leads to be pursued.

Road Warrior website—Follow up on e-mail address. Re-examine his photos.

Can Professor Martin be of further use?

Follow up on Dr. Musk

White city car—who is driving? Is he the killer or just a chump? Should we try and approach him? Scare him?

Role of Lt. Masterson—Merely a bozo in blue—or something worse?

Spike's confession—what is the next move there? Hearing?

Jack—show him pics from center on High St.

What goes on there that would involve city car?

Noah drank some coffee, and then eagerly rubbed his hands together as he continued.

WHO DO WE WANT TO TESTIFY AT SPIKE'S HEARING? PERJURY???

Watch the house on Harlem St. How? Where? No cover.

Regular calls to Deacon

Noah paused and scanned his surroundings. He needed a refill but was reluctant to leave his computer while he went to the counter. He saw no one inside the store to worry him, and it was too cold for anyone to be loitering on Eutaw Street.

I'm taking no chances.

He disconnected his laptop from the power cord, toting it and his empty cup to the counter.

A cute barista smiled as she took his cup. "You with the CIA? She asked. Nodding at the computer under his arm she added, "Must be some top-secret stuff in there."

Noah reacted in mock horror. "You broke the code. Now I'll never be able to come back in here."

It took her a moment to understand that he was responding to her joke in kind and she laughed. Returning his cup brimming with foam she waved away any effort at payment with the statement, "No charge on refills for secret agents."

Noah had plugged in his laptop and was sipping his beverage when Abba began singing from his phone lying adjacent to the computer. A lady at the next table glanced up from her novel and offered an approving smile.

He picked up the phone. "This is Noah."

"This is Jen, wondering why she hasn't heard from Noah."

"Been busy."

"What was that? Been too busy to let me know that you're okay?"

"Well—you see—"

"I'm listening."

When there was no response she continued, "I see that you believe you are protecting me. From what is not clear. If it's Drew, you can forget that. We have closure."

"How—what—?"

"And, I received a promotion."

"Congratulations. But, what does that have to do with Drew?"

"We can talk about that tonight, when you come over for the celebration."

"I—"

"Listen up, Buster. I'm not finished. If you think that by staying away you are protecting me from those killers you are chasing—or is it them who are chasing you?—I get confused. Either way you can forget that as well."

"What's going on?"

"Does the name Rufus Jones mean anything to you?"

Wary of what was coming, Noah answered, "Should it?"

"You may know him by his street name, Spike."

How in hell does she know about Spike?

"What's going on?"

"I seem to have your attention. Come for dinner—oh, bring the wine—something red to go with Italian from the market. It seems like forever since we have celebrated, so first we'll celebrate and afterward we'll talk some business."

33

Lying beside Jen in her darkened bedroom Noah was calmed, his anguish over the killings eased.

In one motion, Jen flung her left arm across his chest, her left leg settled over his thighs and her head nestled on his shoulder. A simultaneous act that seemed to him at least as intimate as the one they had just shared.

"Now *that* was a celebration," she murmured.

Noah touched his lips to her forehead. "I was afraid I might have forgotten how to celebrate. Which begs the question—what is it, exactly, that we are celebrating?"

Jen lifted her head to better study his face. "I have no idea how long we will be together," she said. "Personally, I'm hoping for a good run. Whatever it is, let's agree that this room is reserved for acts of love and, occasionally, sleeping." She raised a hand and pointed toward the closed door. "Any talk related to work or other contentious subjects is restricted to the other side of that door."

"That sounds sensible to me, as long as we can have an encore celebration in here following any discussions out there."

"So ordered."

In the kitchen, while Jen prepared a quick meal of pasta, bread and salad, Noah rephrased his question.

"As a celebrant, it's only right that I know what we are celebrating."

She laughed. "Celebrating makes me hungry. After dinner, I'll be happy to talk until you beg me to shut up. For now, I would love a glass of wine."

Noah blinked. "I thought you didn't like it?"

"I've decided to become a woman of mystery. Keep you guessing."

The aroma from the steaming pasta dishes, accompanied by garlic bread just from the oven, successfully diverted Noah's interest away from Jen's news. They ate until both were stuffed.

With the dishes soaking in the sink, Noah refilled the wine glasses and took a seat beside Jen on the futon. They held their glasses up in a silent salute and drank.

Noah said, "All right, lady. You have been celebrated, wined and dined—in a somewhat unique sequence. And I have been patient, now it's time for show and tell."

Jen smiled and set her wine glass on the end table. She reached up and dimmed the light on the reading lamp behind her to equal the soft glow from the lamp's twin perched on the table at Noah's back.

"Yes. Your self-control is admirable. The first thing I want you to hear about is my promotion, which somewhat ironically, brought closure to my problems with Drew."

Noah nodded as if to confirm that he was listening.

Jen took a sip of wine and began. "The big man called me into his office to inform me that I was the new head of the Homicide Division, unless I could convince him that I shouldn't be. Of course I told him I could not think of a single reason and that I was honored to accept."

Noah drank some wine, saying nothing.

Jen nodded to the bedroom. "You seemed happy enough when we were back there celebrating, and you had no idea why. Now that you know why, you don't seem so jolly. No congratulations?"

"If I appear less than pleased, it is because I care about you— very much. It's a lot to process. Hard for me to separate my professional feelings from personal ones. Excuse the pun, but from what I saw when I was in that office, being chief of homicide can be a killer of a job." Noah raised his glass in salute. "Having said that, I raise my glass in toast to what you have accomplished."

Stretching across the futon he kissed her full on the mouth. Settling back he said, "As a citizen of the city, I can't think of anyone better suited to protect us."

Jen leaned across and gave him a lingering kiss. As she pulled back Noah said, "A kiss like that could give rise—as it were—to another celebration."

She laughed. "Patience. Meanwhile, back to my story. I took a victory lap around the office to give everyone a chance to swear their undying devotion."

"How did that work out?"

"About as you would expect. Most of the lawyers were in court or buried in the penal code. I thought it boorish to stick my head in each office inviting the occupants to admire me, so I slunk back to my cubby hole to make some calls." She brightened, "Hey. This means I'll have a larger cubby hole."

"You'll get Kramer's office. Right?"

Jen nodded.

"What's going to happen to him? He's been an ASA since the middle of the Ice Age."

"You haven't heard. The big man gave Kramer and a couple of others a one-way ticket to private practice. He's been like Paul Bunyan with a chain saw, cutting out the dead wood."

Noah nodded, "That's…"

"No interruptions, please, we've got a lot to cover. I made a list of folks to call and then started dialing. No, yours was not the first number I dialed. I called my dad and my Uncle Andy—he's a retired city police lieutenant. They were bursting with pride. Drew was next on my list, for the reason that I wanted to be able to tell you what he said, especially if it was bad."

Noah nodded his understanding.

"I began by telling him that in my new position there was clearly no way we could continue to avoid each other at work. If that was going to be a problem for him, I needed to know now. I had steeled myself for a gut wrenching battle. To say I was shocked is a huge understatement. He offered congratulations, and wished me well."

She took a deep breath, drained her glass and held it out for a refill.

With a full glass in hand she continued, "As proof of his good intentions, he told me all about his new girlfriend. She sounds nice, and I hope for her sake that he has changed. Just before we hung up he asked me to tell you to forget what he said. That 'it was the vodka talking.' What did that mean?"

Noah, not wishing to inject any angst into her celebration, answered simply, "Hard to remember—and best of all, it no longer matters. It's all in the past. I'm pleased to have that behind us. We have more pressing matters to concern ourselves with. Okay?"

She watched him, trying to decide if pursuing her question was worth the aggravation. She concluded that it wasn't.

"Someday you'll tell me."

"Of course," he said. "Is it because of this promotion that you think I no longer need to worry about your safety?"

She shook her head. "I never thought I needed special consideration from anyone. Besides, I believe we already had this conversation. Remember, single woman—living and working in the city. No assistant state's attorney, male or female, can be an effective prosecutor if they are afraid."

Noah threw up his hands. "You win! I guess I should start getting used to that."

He reached over and gripped her hand. "Let's move on. How did Spike Jones' name come to your attention?"

Jen laughed. "It seems former Deputy State's Attorney Kramer wants no part of an 'orderly transfer of power.' Marge, his secretary—I guess she's *my* secretary...I'll have to think about that—I may decide to take Helen with me... Anyhow, Marge brings me a stack of new cases for my 'attention.' Among them was the city homicide bureau's case charging Rufus Jones—a.k.a. Spike Jones—with the murder of Jason J. Jefferson."

"Was VoShaun listed as primary?"

She shook her head. "First thing I looked for. Do you know Detective Rollie Corbett?"

Noah said, "VoShaun described him as Masterson's 'lapdog.' I'll lay odds she doesn't even know the case was sent over."

"I'll see what she knows."

"Or, what she will admit to knowing."

Jen sighed. "This has all the signs of turning to shit. I hope she has her boots on."

"Does the file mention Spike's defense attorney?"

"Some tyro from the PD's office."

"If that's what it said, it's not up to date. Spike is now represented by former Assistant United State's Attorney Jack Douglas. I don't think you have met Jack. He is currently with the firm of Sachs Geotz Bennett & Bell."

Jen's mouth opened briefly and then snapped shut.

Noah feigned innocence with an exaggerated shrug. "Jack wanted to do a little pro-bono work. No big deal."

Jen looked away. Eventually she faced him and said, "I know you have a plan. Does my promotion fit into your grand scheme?"

Noah shrugged.

"Will I hate it? Your plan?"

"I don't see why."

"What do you hope to accomplish?"

Noah extended his right hand with barely an inch separating the thumb and forefinger. "What we all seek—a little justice."

34

Noah drove slowly along East Biddle Street.

"That's the one," Deacon said, indicating a corner house through the passenger's window.

Midway down the next block Noah pulled to the curb and parked.

Deacon twisted around in the seat, craning his neck for a view through the back window. "Riley, duck down. How you expect I can see through you?" He turned back and fussed at Noah. "Why you park here? A person has to twist himself all up to watch back thataway."

"Use the side mirror."

Deacon grumbled and, with an exaggerated effort, hunkered down while peering into the small mirror. "This don't make no sense."

Riley, still sunken into the back seat, grunted his agreement

Noah adjusted the interior rearview mirror. "On the contrary, it makes perfect sense," he said. "We can watch the house just fine through the mirrors. Not much chance that anyone who stops there will notice a car parked halfway down the next block. Biddle is a one-way street so when they leave the house, unless they turn at the corner, they will pass by us and we can sneak a peek at them."

"How long we gotta sit here?"

"It'll be dark in three-quarters of an hour and I want to see if any lights go on inside."

Noah hit a button, unlocking the passenger's door. "But you boys don't have to stay."

Neither streeter moved.

The corner house was the first in a series of narrow three-story rowhouses clad in the tedious Formstone siding which was Baltimore chic in the mid-twentieth century.

Noah noticed that, unlike the empty lots and desolate buildings on Harlem Street, it was difficult to distinguish an occupied home from one that was merely abandoned. The buildings lining both sides of Biddle Street were fully intact, including unbroken windows on the second and third floors.

Whereas 4x8 plywood sheets haphazardly covered all of the remaining doors and windows on Harlem Street, here shaped wooden panels fit snugly inside the door frame. Panels which, at a glance, could be easily mistaken for the door itself.

In a few of the houses, though the front door was sealed, curtains still hung in the windows of the second and third floors.

Why would these guys have two locations so many blocks apart? Because they can. After all they work for city housing. Maybe there are more than these two! Let's not get ahead of ourselves. We have no proof that either house is connected to the killers.

Noah saw movement in the rearview mirror. He turned slightly and watched an elderly black couple, huddled together against the cold, crossing the street in the middle of the block. Looking through the rear window, he saw them open a door and hurry inside. The entry looked to be in the center of two rowhouses joined with a façade of new bricks and decorated with small white crosses embedded on either side of the door. A hand-painted sign proclaimed it to be The Church of God.

Such a desolate area seems an unusual location for a church, Noah reflected. Maybe it's intended as a beacon of hope in a sea of despair. Or, equally likely, it's a con game.

Noah looked at Deacon. "What time was it when you saw the car?

Deacon pointed to his head. "I recollected that this here phone has a clock and I looked at it just as the one was walking up the steps. It was 2:30.

"But you didn't think to snap his picture."

Deacon shrugged and continued to stare out the windshield.

"You said 'the one.' Was someone else in the car?"

"Yup. The walking guy—a short white man—was the driver; the other fellow stayed sittin' in the front seat. "

"What did he look like?"

"Can't say. We was too far away." Deacon glanced at Noah. "Just so we clear, me and Riley got no intention of getting too close to killers."

From the back seat Noah heard, "Damn straight."

"No one wants you to put yourself in danger."

A moment later, Noah turned the ignition key. "But it does give me an idea."

He drove away from the curb, made a right turn at the next intersection and another right turn at the next corner. Now they were running parallel to Biddle Street. At the next corner, he turned right again and as they approached the alley behind the Formstone-sided corner house, Noah stopped in the middle of the street. Using his cell phone camera, he quickly snapped three pictures before continuing across Biddle Street. From there, he made a series of left turns, which put them back onto Biddle Street a block above their target house.

This time, as they passed the house, Noah ignored it, instead concentrating on the row of houses immediately across the street. He slowed and snapped more pictures as the car drifted and then continued on to their previous parking spot.

Deacon said, "Nice ride. Why'd you take all of them pictures?"

Noah switched off the engine and proceeded to bring up the pictures on his cell phone for viewing. He immediately regretted the implied invitation for the two streeters to move in for a closer look. The stench of Riley and Deacon had become stifling with the heater running inside the closed car. Now, with the hot stink from each man's breath, the nauseating air forced Noah to breathe through his mouth.

The picture on the small screen was one looking at the rear of the target house. "A few houses in this area have an electric hook-up running from a pole into the house. Now, see the cable supplying power for our corner house," he joined the thumb and forefinger of each hand into a circle. "It is much bigger than those going into the other houses."

"Damn," Deacon said. "If that ain't something. What do it mean?"

Noah, stifling a gag in his throat, buttoned the driver's window open. With great pretense, he adjusted the side mirror while giving serious thought to the question. "Hard to say," he finally answered. "Something is going on in there. Could be computers. Computers would require a lot of energy."

With his free hand, Noah scrolled to the first picture of the house directly across the street from the target house.

"I believe they chose this neighborhood because whatever they are up to requires people going in and out frequently. While some activity would not be unusual, there are no immediate neighbors to get nosy."

Noah tapped a finger on a picture of the third-floor front window of the house directly across the street. "Lucky for us this window is covered with plywood, not curtains."

"You about done fixing that mirror?" Deacon groused. "We get enough cold air every day. Looking for a little heat here."

Noah, hoping that sufficient fresh cold air had flowed in to sustain him, reluctantly ran up the window.

"We need to figure out what *is* going on in there."

"How do you 'spect to do that?"

Again tapping on the picture of the boarded window, Noah replied, "I need you and Riley to move into this place for a couple of days."

Jack Douglas was seated at the small metal table when the jailer brought Rufus Jones into the attorney's room, sat him down and secured his shackles to the floor.

"I reckoned you forgot about me."

Douglas shook his head. "I never forget a client."

"Last time you said you was getting me out. So—I been wondering…"

Douglas pulled some photos from the file folder. "You need to be patient. You did sign a confession, after all, which means they see no reason to let loose of you. It will take a miracle to get you out from under that confession. I can do miracles, but they take a little longer."

He spread the pictures across the table. "Take a look at these and tell me what you know about the people."

Spike studied the array of photos without comment.

Eventually he reached out a crooked forefinger and dragged one picture closer. "This looks to be the Vet Center on High Street." A nod from his attorney confirmed the truth of that statement.

"How'd you come by them?"

"There is a security camera up the block," Douglas said and nudged the remainder of the photos toward Spike. "Do you recognize the people in any of these pictures?"

Eventually Spike selected one which he continued to study at arm's length. "I don't have my specs with me, but I'll do my best."

Douglas dug around in his briefcase and handed a pair of drugstore reading glasses across the table. "I know how that is. I'm forever losing mine. Try these."

Spike put the glasses on and pulled the picture closer to his face. He nodded. "This is better, still a little blurry. Can't see the faces, but that don't matter, only one family of four in the place. The sergeants and their two girls."

Douglas jotted down the name. "Do you know their first names?"

"First names? I don't know any of their names."

Douglas paused. "You just said their name was Sargent."

Spike shook his head. "No, no. That's their rank, not their name. The folks was both sergeants in the Army."

Douglas made the correction before tapping his pen on the white car in the photo. "Tell me what you know about this car and the men in it."

Spike adjusted the glasses on his nose and pulled the picture closer.

"The only car like that I can recollect is a Bawlmer city car used to come around and pick up them four. Is this a city car?"

Douglas grinned. "You're doing fine, Mister Jones. What else?"

"Well sir, I'm taking from that grin that I'm right. That car has shown up at the center a few times that I seen. I'm only there a couple days during a week, it could be it's there more."

"Go on."

"Like I said, I seen the car a few times. Didn't pay much mind to it or who was in it. I can say there was always two of 'em. The driver kind of mousey lookin.' I thought it was funny—him being the driver and looking like he was lost. The other one stayed in the car—the mean one."

Spike shuddered. "He caught me looking at him once. He looked fierce straight at me and scared me so bad I never looked no more."

"Tell me what he looked like."

"Like I said, mean looking."

"What else did you see?"

"Real pretty hair hanging down his back. Earring dangling from one ear. What real man wears an earring? I wanted to call him on that, but I didn't."

"The hair. A ponytail?"

Spike chuckled. "More like a horse's tail."

Douglas finished making notes and asked, "What goes on in this center?"

"You got a nail?"

Douglas went back into his briefcase and came out with an unopened pack of Camel cigarettes. A non-smoker, he carried a few packs for jail visits. It was a habit formed during his days as an assistant United State's attorney.

Spike grabbed the pack and greedily tore open a bottom corner. He forced one cigarette onto the table and jammed the package into his shirt pocket, the cellophane seal still intact.

Spike picked the cigarette off the table and sat poised, waiting for a light. "Hope you got a match."

Douglas fished a cheap butane lighter from his case and slid it across the table.

Spike patted his shirt pocket and cackled. "See how I did that? Looks like a brand-new pack, so's I can tell them bums inside that

I'm saving them. If they spot an open pack they can get real nasty if you don't share."

"Pretty smart," Douglas said, as if it was the first time he had heard of that ancient jailhouse ruse. When Spike's cigarette was aglow, Douglas retrieved the lighter before his client could pocket that.

"Again. What goes on at the center?"

"Homeless vets can get a place to sleep there, get help finding a job and getting back on their feet. Get counseled if they need to."

"You have a room there?"

Spike shook his head. "I'm a Day-Dropper."

Douglas frowned and Spike explained. "The Day-Drop is a program for us vets to go inside during the day to get a shower, take a class or just sit around—indoors. The beds is for the 'residents' who are in a different program."

"Isn't it unusual for a whole family to be in a place like that?"

Spike cocked his head while he mulled the question. "It's not so rare for women and kids to be on the street. But you're right; you don't often see a father with 'em."

"If somebody was to go to that center and ask about the sergeants with the kids—the folks there would know who they meant."

Spike nodded. "They would know, but they wouldn't tell you nothing. They're all pretty tight-lipped about the residents."

Douglas pondered that until Spike added, "'Course I could easy find out all about them—if I weren't in here."

Douglas looked at his wristwatch and collected the photos from the table top. "I'll be back in a few days. We need to talk about your hearing and some motions I want to file."

35

Noah, unsure of why Jack Douglas had insisted on meeting here, parked on West Ostend Street, in the shadow of the Russell Street overpass, and switched off the engine.

Douglas, once certain that Noah understood the location, had abruptly disconnected their call, precluding any discussion over the meeting site.

Noah was preparing a tirade against *waiting forever* when Douglas's black Tesla Model S navigated the corner and floated silently to a stop, their driver's side doors mere inches apart.

The image Noah saw, as the machine approached, was that of the QEII berthing alongside a harbor tug.

Without a doubt Jack Douglas reveled in the esteem generated by the Tesla, in equal amounts, from readers of Motor Trend Magazine and contributors to Greenpeace. Yet, he maintained with a straight face, that the feature which sold him on the car was the cargo area.

"Check it out," he had exclaimed. "The most trunk space of any sedan being made. It will hold my prodigious collection of athletic equipment; golf clubs, balls and bats, basketballs—tennis racquets. I'll be ready to compete wherever I should materialize."

Noah, following Douglas' lead, buttoned his window open. "Why all the cloak and dagger?" He asked. "You suddenly ashamed to be seen with me in a nice warm coffee house?"

"There is that. However, this will be a quickie, hardly worth the trouble to find a parking place and walk inside. And what I'm about to reveal is for your ears only."

Noah nodded and Douglas continued. "I spent the weekend in Atlantic City, where a young lady of my acquaintance disclosed some choice tidbits of data during a lull in our activities. 'Pillow talk' I believe it was called back in the day."

"Is this that federal prosecutor from Philly you hooked up with at some regional conference a couple of years ago?"

"The same."

"I thought you said that was a 'one and done' due to her having a husband."

"Also what I thought. She called me from out of nowhere, reaffirmed that her husband still possesses no firearms and suggested a conference in AC. But never mind that—just listen to what she had to say."

"Please continue."

"She is currently counsel to an organized crime task-force for which she has procured court-ordered wiretaps on various Philly-area wise guys."

Noah held up a hand. "She shouldn't be telling you this—"

"—And I wouldn't be telling you if it was not of mutual necessity. I'm loath to admit it, but it seems the lulls between our workouts are, by necessity, a bit longer than previously. Private practice can be quite dull, so I sought to entertain her with the tale of my client Spike and our intriguing murder investigation. Of course, I started at the beginning with that college kid's murder, and when I uttered the words 'Road Warrior,' Vicki sat bolt upright in bed. "

"Vicki? I thought her name was Valerie."

"Damn it! Forget I said that and pay attention to this. A short time ago the feds intercepted a call to their target, one Johnny Gio— a.k.a. Johnny G—from a cell phone in Baltimore. The caller obviously works for G and reported that *'Road Warrior is no longer a problem.'*"

"Why—"

Douglas threw up a hand and gave Noah a silencing look. "Why did she tell me this very sensitive intel, you would ask. Somebody at the off-site screwed up. They didn't trap the incoming call and it's only a matter of time before upper-management learns about it and heads roll. They are desperate to avoid that scene.

"She was so wired after hearing the name Road Warrior she demanded I tell her every detail. If she could march into the off-site on Monday with the answer, she would be the legal equivalent of a rock star. I countered that as my client was charged with the Road Warrior's murder, and she being a prosecutor—albeit a federal one— I had said too much and could be disbarred if it ever came out.

"She continued to beg and eventually I countered with a menu of pleasures which, if she agreed to perform any two, I would tell all. In a matter of moments we reached a compromise. After she told me the rest of her story, she would perform act numero uno. I would follow with the missing details of my story, at which time she would perform the second act."

A broad smile spread across the lawyer's face. "Want to guess what that act was?"

Noah ignored the question. "What did you tell her?"

"Everything. It was only right. It was amazing. Better than talking dirty to her—you got to be careful talking dirty, some words can turn them off. However, telling me all about their case and hearing about the killings down here and my client's phony confession and arrest, got her as hot as I have ever seen a woman. Pity though, our last session was so good I doubt I'll ever see its equal."

Noah stuck a finger in each ear. "TMI, Jack, give me a break. After listening about your sexual prowess, I hope you have something that might actually be of help."

Douglas stared through his windshield without hearing. "I think I've made a great discovery," he said. "You've heard about revenge sex and make-up sex—now, I've discovered investigation sex or maybe—homicide sex." He shrugged and turned a grin toward Noah. "I believe this will require more scientific research on my part."

"My hero. However, I'm really only interested in *her* story, not yours."

"Being a former prosecutor, albeit a local one, you're gonna love this. She wanted to brag to me about it and, I must admit, I was a little jealous that she pulled it off. Johnny G is a mob enforcer with hirelings in the usual spots—L.A., Vegas, Miami. You know—all of the best places. For local jobs—like Baltimore, in this case—he contracts assassins out on a case-by-case basis. Gives a new meaning to the term 'working stiff.'"

Douglas wiggled his eyebrows. "Get it?"

"Jesus, Jack."

"Anyhow, the strike force tap is on a pay phone in a Philly cheesesteak shop frequented by G. Since the shop is open to the public, the authorizing judge restricted the overhears to instances when the feds could eyeball G going inside. So they wire the shop for sound, rent a third-floor room across the street and prepare to take down Johnny G. But, as we know, it's never that easy."

Noah nodded sympathetically.

"For openers, they hear enough chatter to identify G's voice and one or two others. The trouble is they're not talking dirty. The most they hear is the latest odds on the Eagles game or how great the rack is on some babe who wandered in for a sandwich.

"Every once in a while, in the middle of a conversation they hear G say 'Let's take a walk.' Next thing, G and his crony are standing on the curb talking a streak, hands going in all directions. Since G is no longer inside the shop the agents are required to shut off their inside mike. Minimization—you remember that from law school."

Noah waited.

"Well," Douglas continued. "Vicki said they knew G was standing out there in front of God and everybody, issuing orders for mob hits and getting reports from contractors, and the feds could do nada."

Douglas broke into a smile. "That is until Vicki recalled the feds case against John Gotti in the early nineties. She gets a court order to wire the parking meters on the curb in front of the shop. Again, they can listen in only when G is outside talking to one of the bad guys."

"So, they are about to take him down?"

Douglas made a face. "No. Though much better, they haven't heard enough yet and there are lots of loose ends, like the Road Warrior thing. They are getting crap like that from all around the country. She's all charged up that we can clear up some of the Baltimore stuff and maybe get one of these guys to roll over on the cheesesteak crowd and move the party along."

Noah, feeling the chill wind, ran his window partway up. "I thought you said this was a short story. I'm freezing my ass in here. Give me the *Reader's Digest* version of how we are going to 'clear up some of the Baltimore stuff' without either of you getting jammed up. Are you going to be her anonymous informant?"

Douglas, himself shivering, ran his window up half way. "We talked some about that. If it got out she was talking about their case, to a defense attorney of all people, she'd be lucky to find work writing wills in Topeka. That's if she stayed out of jail! The way we left it, she was going to do another Internet search, looking for even a shred connecting Road Warrior with our murder."

Noah shook his head. "If you recall, the cops never officially made the connection. There's no way the Internet, will have anything linking the Road Warrior website to Jason's murder."

"I was afraid of that. Plan B is for her to get the Philly FBI to send a lead to their Baltimore office asking them to query city homicide about Road Warrior. In that case, we're going to have to figure a way to connect the dots for them."

"I can see a problem with that," Noah said.

Douglas shrugged. "What are you thinking?" he asked.

"We are working on the assumption that the killers believed Jason Jefferson was the Road Warrior and they killed him to prevent him from revealing some lurid secret of theirs on his website.

"That is something only known to us and the killers. Masterson isn't going to share that with anybody. All an FBI inquiry will accomplish is to alert the bad guys to the fact that someone else has made the connection."

Jack Douglas nodded as he followed Noah's reasoning. "I see what you're getting at. If the federales start asking around the P.D. about the Road Warrior, the killers are going to learn of it and ask themselves, 'How the hell did the feds hear about that up in Philly?' And they may well come up with the right answer, a tap on Gio's phone."

"That's it."

"Not bad for a radio announcer." Douglas made a move to roll up his window. "I must make a call," he said as his window closed.

Before Noah shifted into drive, Douglas rolled down his window and motioned for Noah to follow suit.

"What?"

"Ask your detective friend to check for security cameras around War Memorial Plaza on the day my client was arrested."

"What are we looking for?"

"Somebody dropping a twenty into Spike's metal cup."

Noah mugged a look of admiration,

Douglas wiggled his eyebrows and sped away.

36

Corky Kilmark slid into the passenger's seat. "Where we headed?" He asked.

Noah gunned the engine. "We're going to have a look inside the house on Harlem Street. You up for it?"

"Well, uh...I guess.... You know it's going to be dark soon."

"That's the idea. If anybody is inside, light will be leaking around those boarded-up windows and we don't go in."

"Uh huh," Corky hesitated. "Don't you need a warrant or something to go into somebody's house?"

"The police do. We are not the police and this isn't somebody's house. So no. I checked online, all those buildings are owned by the city of Baltimore. We've got just as much right to be inside it as do the killers."

Corky was quiet for a couple of minutes before saying, "I guess you're carrying."

"No."

In answer to a perplexed look, Noah added, "I don't own a gun."

"What about when you were—"

"Prosecuting attorneys don't carry guns. Not even on TV."

Corky's anguish was evident in his voice. "What do you think we'll find in there?"

Noah shrugged. "No clue. But, I'm not sitting around waiting for the next murder. We are not getting answers to any of the questions in this case. Maybe we'll learn what they are hiding that is worth killing for. This is the quickest way to know if the answer is inside this house."

"What about that other house. The one Deacon found?"

"He and Riley are stashed across the street. People are going in and out at all hours—but no further sign of the white car. Anyhow, so far as they can tell, someone is always home. No point in us trying to get inside."

Out of the corner of his eye, Noah saw Corky's head slump to his chest.

"Heads-up. It's good experience for your career as a P.I."

Noah braked at a four-way stop. "Keep a sharp eye. Our target is halfway down the block on the right."

Noah let the car creep through the intersection, his eyes sweeping the area for any light, any movement or parked vehicles. Corky turned to stare out the passenger's side window, his body rigid with fright.

As they rolled passed their target, Noah broke the quiet. "That's it," he said.

"Jesus," Corky muttered.

"Keep your eyes on the houses we pass to the end of the block."

"I thought that was the house."

"It is, but we need to be alert for a fire or a lit candle. Unlikely, but these guys may have some streeters keeping an eye the place for them. "

Noah turned right at the next corner and extinguished the headlights before turning right again into the alley running behind their target.

"We're looking for parked cars—particularly our white compact. Also, check the houses across the alley for lights just to be safe."

As the car crept along the alley, Noah was uneasy about the engine noise carrying on a cold still night. The headlights were out; still anyone within two blocks could hear the motor. And the tires crunched as they rolled over broken glass.

The car emerged from the alley and Noah made two successive right turns, putting them back on Harlem Street. "We'll take another pass by our target. If we see no problems we'll park a block away and go in."

Once parked, Noah pulled two flashlights from the glove box, one of which Corky reluctantly accepted.

"What happens if somebody catches us inside there?"

"We're from the city sanitation department. Looking into a complaint about unsanitary premises."

"In the dark?"

"I would say that 'we're dedicated city workers,' but who would believe that?"

"What if they ask to see some ID?"

"We ask to see theirs."

"Why don't we park farther away?"

"Farther to run if we need to."

"What if—"

Noah placed his hand on the handle to the driver's door. "If you don't want to come, stay in the car. I took out the dome light, but if you are coming shut your door very softly. ... Well?"

At the back door, Corky nervously scanned the surrounding area as Noah tugged on the plywood sheet. To his surprise it swung open with ease. "I'll be damned," he whispered. "It's on hinges."

The original back door offered no resistance and, once inside, Noah hesitated, listening for any unwelcome sounds. To Corky he whispered, "Pull that plywood shut behind you."

After another moment, he switched on his flashlight and they both tiptoed through the kitchen and down a narrow hallway. They halted in the doorway to the next room and played their flashlights around the interior. Noah led the way into the living room. On one wall was displayed a huge flat-screen high-definition TV hanging adjacent to a stainless steel side-by-side refrigerator. Facing the TV, a plush leather recliner sat beside a fabric club chair.

"Sweet," Corky murmured.

Noah peered into the refrigerator finding only bottled beer and cans of Coke, Next he pulled open some cabinet doors which he promptly closed when the contents proved to be of no interest.

Keenly aware that they could not take the time to look in every nook and cranny in the house, Noah quickly checked the side pockets of the plush leather chair.

No doubt this chair belongs to the honcho.

Finding nothing, he straightened abruptly, almost knocking Corky's light from his hand.

"Sorry," Corky mumbled and took a step backward.

"It won't be much longer," Noah said. He shined his light across the wall to the front door. Inside the entry way an enclosed stairway led to the upper floors. He motioned Corky to follow.

At the second-floor landing, Noah flashed his light up the dark stairway leading to the top floor. "We'll be able to get out of here quicker if we split up."

He turned his light along the second-floor hallway. "You search this floor and I'll take the top."

Corky appeared unable to move, as if his feet were encased in concrete. "What am I supposed to be looking for?" he asked.

"Hard to say. How about the two computers they stole; anything that looks illegal. You'll know it when you see it."

Noah, his foot on the first step, said, "If I don't think you really searched, I'll have to do it myself. It'll take twice as long to get out of here."

On the third floor, Noah found a room with a desk and filing cabinet, neither of which were locked

Someone feels pretty damn secure.

Admittedly there was nothing, so far, to connect this place to the murders. Maybe the connection did not exist.

Noah chose to look in the cabinet and opened the top drawer which held a holstered automatic pistol. Vaguely familiar with handguns, Noah knew it was of a recent design and contained a loaded clip in the handle.

Still means nothing. Likely a legally registered weapon. A certain hunting knife could be a different story.

The second and third drawers were empty, but Noah stifled a yell when he opened the bottom drawer revealing two laptop computers stacked one atop the other.

Heart thumping, he lifted both out and sat them on the desk. He readily determined that the top computer was the one stolen from his apartment the night Frau Wirtz was slain.

Hands shaking, he prayed for enough battery life and pushed the on button of the second machine. The computer whirred to life, allowing Noah to quickly see that this was indeed Jason's stolen computer. Though sorely tempted to seize this evidence laying there in front of him, Noah returned both computers to the cabinet and closed the drawer.

While finding the two computers was a big step; in his mind it confirmed his theory that both of the killings were connected to each other *and* to this house. Still, they were no closer to identifying the actual killers

The middle desk drawer produced a couple of ballpoint pens, several loose postage stamps and a memo from the mayor's office. The memo was directed to several officials of the city housing department identified along the top left margin. He hastily counted at least fifteen names.

Across the bottom of the sheet someone had scrawled a one-word response to the memo's contents.

Bullshit

A city car following him is registered to the city department on this memo, two abandoned houses likely rehabbed sub rosa.

Come on!

Noah's gut instinct assured him that the name of at least one of the killers was on the list.

This guy may not be the sticker, but he knows who is.

The paper was dated in May, over six months before.

He played the flashlight around the small room confirmingthe absence of a copy machine.

There's no time to copy all of these names by hand...Would it be missed after all this time? I'm going to risk it. He folded the paper and slid it into his coat pocket.

Heart pounding he hastily opened and closed the remaining desk drawers. In the final drawer, lying on top of some papers, were copies of the photos taken from Jason's laptop. Among them were pictures of this house and the white car sitting in front of the Formstone house Deacon was watching. Many of the photos were identical to the pictures Noah had distributed to Marvel and Deacon's tribes.

The discovery was rattling.

Had some streeter sold them out?

If so, the damage was done. He tried to shake it off and riffled through the other papers.

Noah froze after picking up a document bearing his name and home address. When the print came back into focus he identified it as an original of a nationwide name search conducted on him by someone in the Baltimore Police Department.

Instinctively, he knew that he and Corky needed to get the hell out of that house. At once! Where the city memo was months old, and likely forgotten, this new document was dated three days prior and focused directly on him.

Noah quickly jotted down the data which should identify the police official authorizing the computer search, then returned the document to the drawer. Still shaken, he made certain the room appeared undisturbed and rushed out.

Their investigation was miles ahead of where they were before entering this house. Noah had come into possession of crucial intelligence, which trumped 'gut instinct' every time. He now had cards to play.

It was more urgent that they escape this place undiscovered.

Noah heard Corky moving around on the floor below and stifled an urge to call out that he was coming right down.

Corky was about to speak as Noah brushed past him. "Let's get the hell out of here!" he hissed and charged headlong toward the first floor.

Corky immediately returned to panic mode. Clamoring after Noah, he cried, "What happened up there?"

37

Noah stepped to his breakfast bar and poured two cups of coffee. "I'm afraid it won't measure up to the brew at Peace and a Cup of Joe," he said.

Detective Jeff Baines took a sip. "It is a lot better than precinct coffee. Now, what is so urgent to get me over here at this early hour?"

"There have been some developments which should be reported to the police. As it relates to Frau Wirtz's murder—at least I believe it does—I assumed you would rather meet during your shift."

"I'm intrigued and, yes, I would. Thanks for the consideration."

Noah pushed his cup across the bar and then came around to claim the other seat. He stirred his coffee and taste-tested it.

"I don't mean to steal your thunder," Baines said, "but I have a small news item. Let's get that out of the way."

Noah nodded and took another sip of coffee.

"As you are aware, this area—Dickeyville—is a somewhat unique neighborhood."

"It has been referred to as a 'quaint English village.'"

"Just so. And, while finding bodies on the Leakin Park side of Wetheredsville Road is as rare as finding Easter eggs on a certain Sunday morning—a body on this side of Wetheredsville Road is unheard of. Pigtown this is not.

"This is by way of saying that it raised no departmental eyebrows when I requested that the precinct inform me of any 'suspicious activity' reported from this area. In Pigtown stabbings and street corner drug deals in broad daylight are barely viewed as 'suspicious activity.'"

Noah interrupted with, "I'm beginning not to like where you are going with this."

Baines shrugged. "It may mean nothing, but I wanted you to know. Last evening one of the local ladies was walking her dog along Wetheredsville Road in the direction of Leakin Park. A little way past your place here she spots a car sitting along the road with no lights. She heard the engine running and didn't think much of it. Cold weather, likely kids parking or drinking beer. She kept walking in that direction, all the time getting more uneasy about the car. And she noticed the last two street lights before the woods are out. Apparently not unusual—vapor lights can act up for no known reason—still, it added to her discomfort.

"She is still a ways from the car when it occurred to her that it is also possible this car is there to dump a body in the woods. By now, her dog is barking and straining at the leash to get at the car. It's a struggle but she gets her turned around and they head for home. The dog is one of those annoying, yappy little things."

Noah nodded. "That would be Mrs. Sinclair and Ellie."

Baines checked his notebook. "That's right. You know the rest; she gets home and calls it in, but by the time the sector car arrived the mystery car was gone."

"She give any description? Not our white car?"

Baines shook his head. "It was a dark SUV and of course she didn't get a tag number. Off the record, were you home last night or away at a sleepover?"

"What difference…? Oh, I see. You are thinking that if I was home they wouldn't have waited around. They'd have come on in."

"And?"

"I was out until about midnight."

Baines checked his notebook. "The call was logged in at 21:53. I'll stop and talk to Mrs. Sinclair and Ellie after I leave here. Like I said, probably nothing. Kids necking or something."

"Nice try, but we both know they were here for me."

Noah got up to top off their coffee cups and give himself additional time to consider just how much he could tell Baines about last evening's foray into the house on Harlem Street.

As he and Corky fled the building, Noah had the presence of mind to ensure that the back door and its plywood cover were returned to their original positions before racing on to the car.

Noah was rattled by the discovery that someone in the police department was conducting an investigation of him and, in all likelihood, reporting his findings to the killers.

Though such a thought had occurred to him briefly, seeing his name and home address in print was chilling. He believed that if he and Corky were caught in that house, they would have been killed. And wanting nothing more than to be out of there, he had bolted down the stairs.

Once away from the house, Corky commenced to badger him about what had spooked him. Noah was hesitant to relate every detail, but with Corky's incessant jabbering he was unable to think clearly. Besides, he reasoned, Corky had risked as much as he had and was entitled to know how their gamble had paid off.

But Baines was different. At their first "unofficial" meeting, the detective had been adamant that he was not to be told of any sub rosa activities. Still, Noah was now in possession of information that was the first real revelation in the two murders. The detective had to be told enough to understand the significance but revealing too much might anger Baines. Would he consider their foray into the house a breach of trust?

You crossed the line.

The problem remained—where was the line?

The news that Detective Baines had just shared added to Noah's dilemma. There was little doubt in his mind that the car seen by Mrs. Sinclair was waiting for him to come home. Withholding vital information could prolong the investigation and they would keep coming for him and maybe others.

Even in her new position of authority, Jen could not proceed unilaterally to build a case against the real killers. Not only did the police have a suspect in custody, but that suspect, Spike Jones, had signed a confession. Any venture to bring new charges in a closed case would provoke sensitive questions.

"Ms. Stambaugh, with the case closed and no detectives assigned, how were you able to collect this so called—evidence?"

"Who authorized this rogue investigation?"

Noah had no way of knowing how pervasive was this particular corruption of the city government. Once again the bane of his professional life—local politics reared its ugly head.

Noah filled both mugs and returned to his seat. "After you hear what I have, we can talk about the next step."

Baines produced a notepad and a ballpoint pen, poised to write.

Noah began. "I received information which, in my view, confirms that the house we found on Harlem Street is connected to Jason's murder and to the killing of Frau Wirtz. My source says this place is a party house for some rogue city workers."

Noah wove the few facts he possessed with what he believed were well-grounded suspicions. He had to be careful here; his goal was to tantalize the detective enough to keep him in sync with Noah's plan. Lay it on too thick and Baines might charge ahead, making public accusations for which there was, as yet, insufficient proof.

On the other hand, revealing too little of what he knew could render Baines impotent; unable to proceed in a straight line to a timely arrest.

Noah swirled his coffee and continued. "I am told that inside the Harlem Street house there is a ground floor with pool table, plush chairs,flat-screen TV, big refrigerator. I'm guessing here, but it's likely this was paid for from city funds."

Stealing from petty cash is a far cry from murder, but Noah employed a well-worn prosecutor's trick; throw all the shit you have against the wall and see what sticks.

Baines laid his pen beside his note pad and flashed a questioning look that said, "Is that it?"

"It gets better," Noah responded.

"It would have to."

"My source has been through the place. There are a couple of rooms on the second floor. One is set up with a classy poker table and a couple of slot machines. There are twin beds in the other room. There are three rooms on the third floor one of which is used as an office with a desk and filing cabinet. My source was in the office but not the other rooms. In one of the desk drawers, source saw copies of pictures taken off of Jason's computer."

Baines arched his eyebrows and jotted a note. "With no one to tie them to, that's not much. What else?"

Saying it out loud, Noah realized how weak his "revelation" was. So far there was no proof of anything except that city employees were likely having a good time which might be at taxpayers' expense.

"Two lap tops were in the bottom drawer of the filing cabinet."

"So? Why wouldn't there be laptops in an office?"

Without being able to affirm that these laptops were the ones stolen from him and the Jeffersons, Noah's information was essentially meaningless.

"The description jibed with mine and Jason's."

Detective Baines put down his pen. "How so?"

"Uh. Well, source reported that they were the same brands. You know the same general description."

"You are taking great care to conceal the gender of your 'source.' Let's make it easier on both of us and refer to 'him' with the caveat that you are not admitting gender."

"Fine."

"Is he, your source, a computer whiz? The same computer whiz that broke the code on the thumb drive?"

Damn! It looks like Jack Douglas was right; playing music on the radio has dulled my wits. I stepped into that one. Any effort to obfuscate here will be obvious.

"Please understand that I'm trying very hard to honor your edict that some actions I undertake remain obscured to you, while endeavoring, at the same time, to accelerate our investigation into these killings."

Baines stared into his mug, studying the dregs at the bottom of his cup. Finally, he looked at Noah. "Yes or no—can you say to a degree of certainty, that the computers in that house are in fact the ones that were stolen?"

"Yes."

"Yes or no—to the best of your legal knowledge were anyone's civil rights violated to obtain this information?"

"No."

"No 'fruit from the poisonous tree?'"

Noah shrugged.

"What does that mean?"

"Who knows how some wacko judge may twist the law? Under current rulings, entirely admissible."

Without producing the document for Baines to see, Noah described the Housing Department memo pointing out the obvious connection to the mysterious white car.

Baines scrawled some notes. "I hope you know what you are doing."

38

As soon as the door closed behind Baines, Noah put in a call to Corky. He was anxious to determine the other man's frame of mind. Had he been strong enough not to reveal last evening's activity to anyone? Not even his wife?

"This is Corky."

"How are you holding up?"

"I'm okay. I didn't feel up to going to work. Too cold, anyway."

"What happened when you got home?"

"I was still pretty shook. I usually fix the drinks, but my hands were shaking and she had to make them."

"What did you tell her?"

Corky brightened. "I did alright. I said the cops were nosing around and you took me in to talk to them. Straighten it out. Told her they were satisfied; still it was a scary experience. I hated doing that to her—she was so upset she knocked her drink over, but she bought it. I told myself it was for the best—the truth is a hell of a lot scarier."

If you only knew, Noah thought. He was forced to keep Corky in the dark about Jack's bulletin that they were dealing with a hit man for the Philly mob. And, for Noah, any question about a whether a Baltimore cop was actively working with the killers had been answered.

Noah could not bring Corky fully into the loop. There was too much at stake and he was not at all certain how Corky would hold up under another grilling from either the police or his wife.

"I know it's tough on you not to tell her. But you did the right thing. Last night was a big break for the good guys—that's us, in case the description was unfamiliar. Now I'm beginning to see the end."

"Tell me, am I still alive then?"

"Let me take another look. Yes—that looks like you standing on your street corner."

"You need glasses. If I'm around at the end, I won't be standing on no street corner."

"Did you tell her about leaving the street?"

"No. I'm saving it for when I need it."

"Need it?"

"The next time you scare the shit out of me and I can't fix the drinks. She'll be so happy to hear that I'm off the streets, she'll forget to question me."

"Let's hope there are no more of those nights. I don't like them any better than you do."

Corky said, "It's too cold for the streets but I'm up for a meet at Joe's later on."

"Let me see how the day goes. I'll call you if I can make it."

Noah stared at the silent phone and sighed heavily as he reached for the coffee pot. After filling his cup, he retrieved the Harlem Street memo from its hiding place. The document, from the Office of the Mayor, City of Baltimore, Maryland, was addressed to Housing Authority—Code Enforcement.

The memo forwarded a citizen's complaint regarding a piece of property in the Edmondson Village area of Baltimore. The original recipient, likely adept at passing the buck, had scrawled "DeRosa Handle" beneath the letterhead. It seemed probable that DeRosa had complied by scribbling Bullshit just below and deposited the paper in the desk drawer, where it was promptly forgotten.

We know the white car is assigned to a branch of the city housing authority and it looks like this DeRosa guy, though a manager, is somewhere down the chain. Could be that he is one of the killers. Unless he in fact passed the memo on down the chain to someone who inscribed his own feelings on the paper and also drives a white car and, unknown to DeRosa, also plays hooky at the place on Harlem Street. Seems a stretch.

Noah jotted down some thoughts for follow-up. Next, he turned to the information he had copied from the background check the dirty cop had run on him. What concerned him was not just the fact that a search had been conducted; it was the audacity of the act.

The bastards had the temerity to run his name through the FBI's National Crime Information Center. It was a bold and reckless move. Perhaps a desperate one. Surely they knew that he had been a prosecutor and the likelihood of finding anything on him was nil.

And unlawful use of the federal records system was a criminal offense, as some former local cops and private investigators could attest.

Yet they had done it.

He could think of nothing that would stop them from committing a third murder.

Why am I saying third? If one of them is a hired assassin, three could be a very low number. And, last night they were waiting for me.

39

Noah was headed across town to the Biddle Street house being watched by Deacon and Riley.

He had left Jen's early and driven home. Before leaving his apartment, he contacted Detective Jeff Baines and gave him the name DeRosa, of the city housing authority.

Baines dutifully inquired as to the source of this information and Noah duly responded that it came from his confidential informant. Baines did not press the issue, merely saying he would look into it, and rang off.

As he drove, Noah likened their charade to a variation of the "Don't Ask Don't Tell" policy invoked by the U.S. military. And, in the end, it would probably prove to be just as effective.

Deacon and Riley had been secreted in the abandoned rowhouse directly across Biddle Street from the target house for most of three days. Late yesterday, Deacon, using a pre-arranged code, messaged Noah asking that he come to the lookout. The simple code, easier than trying to explain text messaging, was utilized to save prepaid minutes.

Deacon was to call Noah's cell, allowing it to ring three times before disconnecting. A one ring response from Noah meant that the message was received and he would make an appearance the following morning. Deacon had complained that he needed more than the one ring to hear "Hit the Road, Jack." Noah, ended the discussion by saying there could be no Ray Charles songs overheard coming from a vacant house.

Noah parked two blocks above the Biddle Street address and approached along the alley at the rear of the lookout. The gifts he bore consisted of two breakfast sandwiches, two large containers of coffee, two packs of unfiltered cigarettes and one pint of Jim Beam— for warmth, or so he had been told. Deacon had been firm that he and Riley would occupy the lookout for no less.

Do they have information, or is Deacon anxious for his gifts? Noah wondered as he squeezed through a gap between the back-door frame and a sheet of plywood splashed with random obscenities.

Outside banks of grey, snow-laden clouds hovered just overhead casting the structure's interior in a heavy gloom. Fortunately, the plywood sheeting over the first-floor windows had been haphazardly applied, permitting faint light to leak in at the edges.

Regardless, Noah was not reckless enough to chance that a moving light would be seen by someone outside the house. He had been emphatic in forbidding his spies any form of artificial light and would not himself be guilty of the same offense.

Once through the door, Noah gagged on the putrid smell of decay as he lingered while his eyes dilated. He then groped his way to the staircase and commenced his cautious climb toward the third floor. Given the condition of the house, he considered himself fortunate to be seeing so little of it.

At the second-floor landing, he glanced upward and was dismayed to find the going even murkier ahead of him. He resisted an impulse to call out and started up.

The two streeters must have heard him on the stairs and were mindful of his instructions not to call out in the event someone else wandered into the place. The only sound coming from the floor above was the scurrying of four-legged animals. To his dismay, they sounded too large to be mice. Deacon and Riley were in for additional gifts for enduring such appalling duty.

When he reached the third-floor landing, Noah paused to orient himself. He was at the back of the house, and the two streeters would be in the front bedroom at the far end of this hall.

The door to that room must be closed, or there would be some light showing through the peep-hole which Deacon had notched into the plywood covering the street-side window.

Noah moved toward the front of the house, feeling his way along the wall as he went. Not for the first time, he was grateful to be wearing heavy gloves. The idea of sliding a bare hand along these walls was repulsive.

Finally, at the end of the hall, Noah paused at the door. Now it was safe to identify himself in a low voice, otherwise a startled Deacon might deck him as he entered the room.

He scratched on the door and said, "It's Noah. I'm coming in."

That he received no response was a little troubling. *If they had said "screw this" and taken off, I couldn't blame them.*

With trepidation Noah turned the knob. The moving door was abruptly blocked, giving rise to the specter of Frau Wirtz's lifeless body as he forced his head around the door.

The ray of light seeping through the peephole was all the illumination necessary. Noah gave an anguished cry and pushed the door enough to allow him to squeeze into the small room.

He quickly confirmed that both men were dead, and likely had been so for some hours. Producing a penlight, he scanned the area around the bodies, searching for Deacon's cell phone, or anything of evidentiary value. In doing so, he was sickened by the realization that he stood with both feet in a glut of blood which had pooled between the two corpses.

Something stirred in the room and Noah reacted to the glow of two pairs of eyes glistening from one corner. Rats!

Unwilling to chance seeing the violation already inflicted on the two streeters by these vermin, Noah averted his eyes, breathed through his mouth and completed his search of Deacon's pockets. This confirmed his fear that the man's cell phone was missing.

Shit! It is programmed with my cell number.

Noah straightened and gulped in air, hoping to quell the fierce pounding in his chest.

Get hold of yourself. It's terrible, but there's nothing you can do for them now. Think!

What will happen if I pull out my cell phone and call it in? Even if I do it anonymously, it's only a matter of time until they trace the call to me. Either way I will have to explain to the cops what Deacon and Riley were doing here and— more troubling—what I am doing here.

Their questioning of him would be relentless. "Oh I see, you are running a vigilante investigation—which has, so far, cost two lives."

Three, if they connect Frau Wirtz's killing, which they will do when Baines hears about this.

Inevitably the authorities will demand to know on what evidence this rogue action was taken. Noah would be forced to talk; compelled to tell them everything. Even then it made little sense. Moreover, in all likelihood, he would be telling it to the cop working with the killers. Perhaps not in person, but the bastard would certainly get his hands on the report.

The killers would be alerted to everything that he knew; the value of Jason's thumb drive, the fact that he was onto the white car and the location of both houses. Including that Noah had in his possession a city memo with, he was certain, the name of one of the killers.

Noah was adamant that he not betray Jack Douglas and Douglas' bedmate, who had revealed the organized crime connection to Jason's killing. To do so would inevitably result in her being fired and possibly prosecuted.

Noah himself would be open to charges, several of which would be felonies. Obstructing a police investigation, burglary, and whatever else they could dream up. He knew from experience that Baltimore cops were very creative when the need arose.

I might be able to keep Corky out of it.

The most damning result would very likely be an abrupt halt to any further investigation into the murders.

Nice work, Cassidy. You've mucked this up so bad the only one prosecuted out of this mess will be you.

None of that is going to happen!

It was now clear to Noah that he must get out of there, leaving no trace that anyone, except the killer, had been there. He was thankful that in his initial shock he had held on to the plastic bag containing Deacon's gifts. Making sure that the lids were secure on both containers of coffee, he slid one into each overcoat side pocket. He found a place for the pint of Jim Beam and the cigarettes in various pockets of the sport coat he wore under his top coat.

Unwrapping both breakfast sandwiches, he stuffed the wrappers in a pocket and heaved the food toward the eyes glowing in the corner of the room.

It's not much, but it's all I can do to keep them away from Deacon and Riley. At least for a while.

This is not the time to be squeamish, he thought as he maneuvered his left foot out of a shoe and placed it in the middle of Deacon's back.

I'm not leaving a trail of bloody shoe prints back to my car.

The tainted shoe he placed in the plastic bag, repeating the procedure with his right foot. In stocking feet, he balanced himself precariously on Deacon's corpse clutching the bag containing his two blood-soaked shoes.

Gingerly, Noah stepped from Deacon's back onto the area of dry floor in the doorway. There, he hesitated for a last appraisal of the room in the dim light.

Resisting the urge to fling the whiskey bottle at the rats in the corner, Noah wedged himself through the door. Once in the hallway he closed the door behind him and was instantly overwhelmed by a suffocating dread.

Blundering toward the stairs, he despaired of escaping this miserable crypt. Of bleeding to death in this hideous place, while rats bided their time, eyes glowing in anticipation.

Plunging down the stairs, Noah stumbled onto the second floor, barely avoiding a fall. Heart racing, he braced himself with one hand against the wall and breathed deeply, before rushing ahead.

At the back door, he paused to scan the surrounding area before venturing into the alley in his stocking feet.

Safely behind the steering wheel, Noah shook so violently he found it impossible to insert his key in the ignition. He pulled one of the containers of coffee from a coat pocket and drank deeply of the tepid brew.

Noah found himself several blocks from the house before he was rational enough to consider his next actions. His impulse was to find a telephone and make an anonymous call.

Calm down! Calm down! Think!

He realized that he could drive for hours and not find a working pay phone on the street.

In the lobby of one of the downtown hotels? Possibly, but I can't walk around town in stocking feet.

Then he comprehended that there was no need for urgency.

Thirty or forty minutes are not going to make a damn bit of difference to them, or to the investigation.

Mindful of the traffic laws, Noah carefully headed across town to Dickeyville. There he scrutinized the neighborhood, including the road leading on to Leakin Park, before parking on the macadam surface at the foot of the stairs to his apartment.

Inside his front door, Noah emptied his pockets. The cigarettes and whiskey bottle he set on the breakfast bar and then poured the remaining coffee down the sink. Quickly he slipped on a scruffy pair of loafers, scooped up the empty containers and headed back downstairs to his car.

Within ten minutes he had deposited the plastic bag containing the bloody shoes and empty cups in a dumpster behind a 7-Eleven store and was parked in one of the vast lots surrounding Security Square Mall.

Inside the mall, he checked the map and proceeded to the location he sought. There, Noah paid cash for a disposable cell phone and walked back to his car.

Before getting in, he scanned the area for a dark SUV or a white car bearing the Baltimore City crest. With chagrin, he comprehended that this was the first instance, since leaving Deacon and Riley, he had been sensible enough to check for a tail. Satisfied that he was not followed, Noah sat behind the wheel and sharply jabbed the 911emergency number into the phone.

That done, he drove south to Frederick Road, turning east toward Irvington, an area just inside the Baltimore City limits. He pulled over at a Royal Farms store and discarded the phone in the store's dumpster. Minutes later he was parked in front of the Half Mile Track, a dim bar where he was unknown.

.

40

Jack Douglas appeared at his office door; Noah brushed past him and slumped into one of the leather client chairs facing a massive oak executive desk.

Noah had spent the previous night in the gloom of his apartment, languishing in his chair, agonizing over his discovery of the two dead streeters. His torment heightened with the thought that, with a cavalier disregard for their well-being, he had, in essence, sent them off to be butchered.

First he had called Jen, certain she was still at work, and left a brusque message not to expect him. He ignored her ensuing calls to his cell phone and allowed the machine to answer any calls to his apartment number.

It became apparent to Noah that he needed to unburden himself to someone. He had already ruled out Jen; besides his feelings of guilt about the two streeters, his confession would put her in a terrible position, professionally. The basis for disregarding Detectives Taylor and Baines was apparent. No serious thought was given to confiding in Corky.

Around 9:30 he roused himself, grabbed the bottle of Jim Beam from the breakfast bar and fell back into the chair. Before taking a drink, he raised the bottle in tribute to Deacon, repeated with a tribute to Riley and, gazing at the place by the door where her body had been located, mumbled a memorial to Frau Wirtz.

Just after midnight the thought that the killers could again be lying in wait outside on Wetheredsville Road stumbled into his consciousness. "Don't wait, you bastards," he called, "come on in and let's be finished with this."

To himself, he added, *I don't give a damn how many of you there are—I'll fight you all to the death—and I really don't give a damn which of us dies.*

When he woke it was daylight and the last thing he recalled was vowing to seek Jack Douglas' counsel without delay. Besides being his only real option, Douglas also had the most to lose personally from any disclosure to the authorities.

It's my fault he's in this.

Noah then roused himself, downed two cups of hastily brewed coffee and headed into the city.

Douglas settled into the companion chair in front of his desk and, correctly reading his friend's body language, refrained from his customary banter.

"You don't look so good, pal," he said.

"You won't either when I'm finished talking."

Douglas heaved a sigh. "Let's get it over with, then."

Noah reached beneath his overcoat, secured his wallet and dug out a five-dollar bill which he handed over.

"One of those, eh?" Douglas said pocketing the retainer. "Okay you are on the clock. Go."

Noah spoke for almost three-quarters of an hour during which Douglas ordered in coffee and Danish.

Noah listed the items of evidence he had located during the search of the house on Harlem Street. This was followed by the basis for his belief that the place on Biddle Street was equally crucial to their investigation.

"The same white car has been in and out of there. Lots of people coming and going and the heavy power cables connected to the back of the house. Besides, being the clever bastard that I am, I figured those two streeters had nothing better to do than spy on the place. And, thanks to them getting murdered, we have a solid connection between the killers and that house."

Douglas frowned. "Solid seems too strong a word. What am I missing?"

"It was too dark in that house to determine their cause of death, but I'm betting an autopsy will find that it was the same blade used on Jason and Frau Wirtz."

Douglas patted the pocket where he had deposited Noah's retainer. "I have a bad feeling that I'm going to earn this."

During the silence that followed, Douglas rose and walked around his oak desk to the matching credenza beneath a wall of glass which offered a stunning vista of Baltimore's Inner Harbor. He pulled out an open bottle of Glenlivet and held it out as an invitation. Noah shook his head and Douglas returned to his chair lacing his coffee with a generous portion.

"It is a bit early for this, but by the looks of it, you have at least a furlong on me. Did you drink all night?"

Noah responded with a slow shake of his head, "I had to quit when the bottle was empty."

"Do you have a plan?" Douglas queried. "Any kind of a plan?"

Noah met his gaze. "Do you agree that we can't go to the police with this?"

Douglas sipped slowly from his spiked coffee before answering. "I feel compelled to mention that my priorities are, of necessity, at variance with yours. I, on the one hand, will do whatever is required to keep secret Veronica's role in our melodrama. While you—I'm just guessing here—are probably concerned for yourself. Staying alive. That sort of thing."

In spite of his best efforts, the trace of a smile appeared around Noah's mouth. "My apologies if I appear selfish."

"Apology accepted. Now, let us put together a plan with a view to achieving both of our goals."

Noah was mulling several options in his head when Douglas jumped from his chair and hurried back to the credenza, which to Noah's eye stretched below the plate glass like the Great Wall of China. Posing a question would prove fruitless, and Noah watched in silence as his friend yanked open one small door after another, muttering as he went.

Douglas cried "Aha!" and ceased slamming doors. A few quick movements took place behind the desk and Douglas returned, holding a bulging 8x10 manila envelope, which he presented to Noah.

"This may help with making your dream come true—the one where you don't die."

Noah dug into the envelope and pulled out a small handgun. "And I didn't get you anything," he said.

"I know you don't have a firearm, but it sounds like you should."

While a prosecutor, Noah had spent a single afternoon at the Baltimore City police firing range with several fellow prosecutors. Each of them had fired two full clips from a Glock .40-caliber.

Now he gripped the handle with a finger at the trigger guard. This gun was tiny compared to the heavier Glock.

"What is it, a .25?"

"It's a .32 auto," Douglas replied. seven in the mag and one in the chamber."

He leaned forward to emphasize the significance of what he was saying. "Don't expect to bring anyone down at long range. Fortunately, our killer works with a knife—even close in the stopping power of this little gun is problematic. If you are forced into a corner and must use it, aim for his chest and keep pulling until it's empty."

Douglas shrugged. "If he is still on his feet, throw the damn thing at his head and scamper away."

Noah, his eyes on the small automatic in his hand, said, "I was awake most of the night and, among many other thoughts, it occurred to me that I should get a gun and a carry permit. Then it dawned on me that with all the red tape, it could easily be at least two weeks after my funeral before I could legally possess it."

Douglas gestured with both hands. "I cut through all the red tape—and you're welcome."

Noah gripped the pistol, his finger now moved to the trigger. "I have resolved not to wait around for them to come for me. I'm going to force their hand."

"I'm pleased to see that you are not going to let a little thing like an unregistered firearm stand in your way."

Noah held up the undersized pistol. "You are correct, sir. Out of curiosity; if I am required to shoot somebody will the police be able to trace it back to other crimes?"

"You're not going to shoot anybody unless you are in mortal danger. Your life or his. At that point, the gun's history is the very least of your problems. Now about your plan."

Noah returned the automatic to its envelope and settled it on his lap. "One thing I do know, and that is I will not put any more lives at risk. I'm going it alone the rest of the way."

Douglas eyed him over the rim of his cup. "Brave or foolhardy?"

"We'll know soon enough."

41

During his session with Jack Douglas, Noah had decided that the safest course of action was to distance himself from Corky, Marvel and anyone else connected to the murders, however remotely. Even Jen. Especially Jen.

After leaving Douglas's office, Abba announced a call as he walked along East Pratt Street to his car.

"You see the paper this morning?" Corky asked. "Those two streeters getting killed over on Biddle?"

"Yes. Horrible."

"They didn't give no names, just said a couple of homeless men. Do you think it could be Deacon and his white pal?"

"Riley."

"That's it. Do you think it was them?"

"Anything is possible."

Corky was worried. "You're going to check though, right?

"Of course."

Corky said nothing further and Noah walked along in silence: unwilling to add to the turmoil building in the other man's mind.

Noah had decided to return to the house on Harlem Street based largely on a nagging inkling that Corky, in his fear, could easily have missed something important during their first visit. That, and the anguish over his own inability to think of anything else to do.

Anxious to fill the silence, Corky said, "It's been a while since we met at Joe's; since that night on Harlem Street. I'm sitting here at our table, why don't you stop in and we can plot some strategy."

"I'm already downtown. Had an early appointment and I have others. Got to find a job. You know how that is."

"What are we going to do about Jason's killers?"

"That's on the back burner for now. The cops aren't looking at you, so you don't need counsel. I've given Baines everything we could come up with," he lied. "Hopefully, they will stumble across the truth—eventually."

Corky said nothing and a vexed Noah blurted, "You know, I had a life before this case. I'm going up to my folks in Wilmington—you know, Thanksgiving. I'll call you when I get back."

"...Okay. Well, have a good one."

"Thanks. You too."

I'm not sure he bought it. But, hopefully he will understand when this is over.

Noah sat in his car, staring through the windshield, seeing nothing. His right hand rested on the bulging manila envelope on the passenger's seat.

Eventually, he was roused by the presence of a blue uniform at the driver's window. Jolted by the looming figure, heart pounding, he instinctively jerked his hand from the envelope and reached for the button to lower the window. His head cleared and he recognized the uniform of a meter-maid motioning at the expired parking meter in front of his car.

Noah waved as he started the engine and nosed into traffic. Making two quick turns, he was headed west toward Dickeyville. Galvanized by a single-minded determination, much needed to be done to prepare himself for tonight.

Noah left his driveway shortly after midnight and turned left on Wetheredsville Road. Around the first bend, he stopped in the middle of the road, with a view of the stretch leading to the Leakin Park gate. Two does eyed him from the other side of the gate before darting deeper into the woods. No vehicles.

He swung a U-turn and headed out of Dickeyville to Windsor Mill Road, which he followed into the city. The road was dark and narrow where it wound through the heart of Leakin Park. No one would dare follow him down this road without their headlights on. Even if they hung well back, he was certain to pick up any trailing lights in his mirror.

The pistol Jack Douglas had given him was in the pocket of an old, wool Mackinaw worn over a dark-blue sweatshirt. The gun was as he had received it, seven rounds in the magazine and one in the chamber. Ready for anything. He welcomed the warmth of the Mackinaw's quilted lining, regretting that the light plaid exterior was not a darker shade for what he intended.

He wore a pair of wrinkled khaki pants dug from the floor of his closet, the cuffs of which he jammed into the top of scruffy Wolverine insulated work boots, worn over heavy socks. He anticipated a long and chilly night.

Another thing that gnawed at him: what he would do if his search turned up no new evidence. He had been closer to the truth than he wished to admit, by telling Corky that there was little more they could do.

This morning as he summarized his case against the house on Harlem Street to Douglas, it sounded much flimsier than when he recited it in his head. Though dubious when spoken aloud, deep in his gut his conviction was as strong as ever.

The house on Harlem Street and the house on Biddle Street were somehow linked. And both locations were connected in some corrupt business with a Philadelphia organized crime family. Of this he was certain

"What do you expect to find that wasn't there the last time?" Douglas had asked a few hours earlier.

Noah's answer sounded desperate. "Something to tighten the noose around their necks—our computers, Deacon's cell. Something like that...Deacon's cell would clinch it."

"Except for the fact that you have no way to link his cell, or the computer, or that house to the killer."

"After I find everything I can, I'll wait there until someone shows up."

"Sounds like a desperation play. A hail Mary pass."

Noah had shrugged it off. "That's what you do when you're desperate."

They had sat in silence, both gazing down at the masts of the USS Constellation sitting magnificently at anchor in the Inner Harbor seven stories below.

Douglas reached over to his desk and splashed some more Glenlivet into his cup. "How about I go with you?"

He mimicked clawing a gun from a shoulder holster. "You know—backup."

"No!" Noah cried, with an emphatic shake of his head. He offered a quick smile to signal his gratitude for the offer and held up the manila envelope. "I'm carrying the gun."

"I can get hold of another one by tonight."

"Thanks, but this is a small, narrow house. I'd be more afraid of being shot by you than stabbed by them."

Noah believed that, by offering, Douglas was merely playing the role of dutiful friend and likely would rather be anywhere else.

"I mean it," Douglas replied.

"So do I. Anything else?"

For emphasis, Douglas drained his cup and sat it firmly on his desk. "This, I insist on. You will call me just before going inside the house. Then, while inside you will keep one finger on the last-number-dialed button. Hit that at the first sign of trouble."

"Sounds almost like a plan."

"Good. You keep your phone where you can press that button in an instant and I will ride to the rescue."

"Like Batman responding to the bat signal in Gotham City."

"Close enough."

Noah made his second pass by the house on Harlem Street. Seeing no sign of activity, he turned into the alley at the rear of the place. He had considered parking well away from the target and creeping down the dark alley.

Fuck that! And fuck these guys! If I don't find anything, I'll just grab a beer from the fridge, and sit in that leather recliner and watch the big TV until one of these assholes comes in. Yeah. Damn right! I have always wanted to get a good look at a mob assassin. I have my gun and all he'll have is a knife, What was Sean Connery's line in

The Untouchables? *"Isn't that just like a wop? Brings a knife to a gun fight."* I hope it turns out better for me than it did for Connery.

Noah, almost indifferent to being discovered, carried an ultra-bright Maglite. Too compact to be serviceable as a weapon, it hung easily at his side from a belt clip, giving him a free hand when needed.

Once through the back door, he proceeded cautiously into the kitchen. One hand held the flashlight, the other his gun. Though anxious to confront his enemy, Noah first needed to complete his search and had no intention of being ambushed. He moved cautiously, playing the beam along the floor ahead.

The small kitchen displayed the remnants of recent carousing. Piles of empty beer bottles and three discarded pizza boxes from a carry-out on Edmondson Avenue. Leaving the flashlight on, Noah hung it on the belt clip while he tore off a section of the box bearing the name of the pizza store and stuck it in the pocket of his jacket.

Might be worth checking at some point.

Noah retrieved the light and resumed flashing the beam along the floor and around corners as he made his way to the stairs. In the next room, additional empties littered the area.

Bastards! No doubt celebrating their killing spree.

He flashed his light to the top of the stairway.

Anything incriminating is more likely stashed in that office on the third floor. I'll start there and work my way down. Can I be lucky enough that Corky did miss something on the second floor?

Noah headed straight to the third-floor office, closing the door behind him. He secured the Maglite to the belt clip, letting the beam continue to illuminate the cramped room.

Noah's first stop was the metal filing cabinet. This time it was locked.

Did they somehow know I was here? No matter.

He produced a heavy-duty Craftsman screwdriver from a tool belt worn under his mackinaw and quickly popped the small lock from its housing.

With pounding blood roaring through his head, he pulled open the bottom drawer. They were still there!

With a feeling of elation, he lifted both computers from the drawer and sat them on the desk. The holstered revolver, which he pocketed, was the only other item of interest in the cabinet.

Though relieved by the recovery of the two computers, as a prosecutor Noah knew they were no help in identifying the killer. The recovery of Deacon's cell phone was still critical. He unclipped his Maglite and played it ahead as he peered into the murky hallway.

Noah whirled at a noise. Was it a creaking stair? And flashed his light toward the top of the stairs.

No one there. Get a grip, boy.

He moved along the hallway and found the door to the next room closed and locked. Briefly, Noah toyed with the idea of using his pistol to unlock the door..

Again, the Craftsman screwdriver made short work of the lock.

Inside the room he found two more locked metal filing cabinets. Sealed cardboard boxes were stacked four high next to the cabinets.

Returning the Maglite to his belt, Noah used both hands to open the top box.

Douglas would be tear-ass if he knew I didn't have my phone at the ready.

Now with the flashlight in one hand he quickly riffled through several file folders at the top of the pile.

Looks like documents of the Baltimore City Housing Authority. Strange place to store them.

One memo cover sheet contained the names of several departmental officials, which Noah folded and stuffed into a pocket.

We can come back for the boxes.

The second locked cabinet revealed a trove of compact disks, which Noah was certain were not music videos. He pocketed two of them and, following a thorough search for Deacon's phone, shut the drawer. The remainder of the drawers in the two cabinets contained a variety of gambling paraphernalia and sealed bottles of liquor.

Still no cell phone.

Though tempted to smash the bottles and allow the contents to spill over the decks of poker cards, boxes of dice and what he recognized as flash paper used by bookmakers to record bets, he left the drawers and contents as he had found them.

Noah moved to the door, shined the light up and down the hall and stepped across to the last room on this floor.

His heart sank. The room contained only a small unmade cot with a bare wooden chair at the head. Likely the chair served as a night stand for anyone using the cot.

Dismayed, Noah took the desperate measure used by many to locate a lost cell phone. Taking out his own phone, he touched the speed dial number for Deacon. If the phone was located on this floor, he should hear Ray Charles. If not he would repeat the procedure on each of the lower floors.

Almost immediately, Noah caught the unmistakable sound of Ray Charles singing *"Hit the road, Jack, and don't you come back no more..."*

It's not in this room but it is on this floor, an elated Noah reasoned and started for the door. Suddenly, he froze, the color draining from his face. Not only was the song playing on this floor, it was just outside the room and moving toward him.

Now frantic Noah focused on his cell phone jabbing repeatedly at the number pad. He disconnected his call to Deacon's cell and punched at Jack Douglas' direct dial button as a blistering pain seared his right temple.

42

Noah's eye lids fluttered rapidly in an effort to clear his vision. When the room shuddered to a halt around him, he squinted into the halo of light glaring directly into his face from an upturned desk lamp.

Instinctively, he tried to touch the aching spot on the side of his head but found his hands bound at the wrists behind his back. The room came into focus and he saw that they had returned him to the office. He was seated in the desk chair and then shoved forward, legs completely under the desk, his stomach hurting where it was jammed against the middle drawer.

On the desk in front of him the two laptops sat stacked as he had left them. Without moving, he knew that both handguns were no longer in his pockets; his cell phone gone. Disks gone.

The pounding in his head barely equaled the anguish he experienced with the realization that they had stripped him of the vital evidence he had uncovered. Without knowing what the compact disks contained, his gut told him it would have devastated the defense's case during the prosecution of a murder trial.

Movement at the periphery of the halo of light caught his attention.

Though unable to define a human form he called out, "What did you hit me with?"

"Nuthin.'"

"It doesn't feel like nothing."

"It wasn't me. Leonard done it," the man replied, his voice quavering.

Noah moved his head to the right trying to see into the gloom. "Speak up, Leonard. What's going on?"

"You can save your breath." The voice was still a tremor. "He ain't here."

"How long was I out?"

"I don't have no watch."

The absent Leonard must be the stronger of the two, the one calling the shots. Noah surmised that any chance of getting out alive lay with the man Leonard had left to guard him.

"This thing is way over your head. You're in deep shit and getting deeper."

The man snorted. "You're the one in trouble mister. You broke into our place and you was carrying a gun."

Noah shook his head to clear it and recalled that it was more difficult for a captor to kill you if he got to know you. "I'm Noah. What's your name?"

The man issued a nervous cough, but said nothing.

"So Leonard left you to do the dirty work. To take the rap for killing me."

"You got it all wrong, man," his voice shrill. "I'm no killer. Not in my nature to kill a living thing."

"Okay. I get it, pretty diabolical. He left you alone, figuring I would try to escape and one of us would kill the other, leaving less work for him. That leaves only the survivor for him to kill."

"Huh? I don't know what that *die-o-bol-i-cal* means. But Leonard wouldn't do me that way."

"Then where is he? I guess he just stepped out for a smoke break."

"It's important where he went. He'll be back directly. You better not try nothing. "

"If I'm the one in trouble he should be calling the cops to come and arrest me."

"Yeah. I guess. He said he had to make a real important call."

Noah speculated that the voice in the dark belonged to the flunky who had followed him in the white car. And Leonard was almost certainly the killer the feds overheard on the Road Warrior call from an unknown assassin somewhere in Baltimore.

Right now the Philly FBI is listening to a discussion about how I am to die with no clue where the call is coming from.

Noah figured he had nothing to lose and flung the dice. "We know all about you and Leonard. He's the mob's hired killer from Philly and you are the poor sap who drives him to all of his murders."

"Jesus! Oh, Jesus!" The man groaned. "How did—? You're wrong. I didn't know he was killing them people. Tone didn't tell me nothing until way after!"

"You been following me, so you know that I was a prosecutor, and I'm telling you that you are just as guilty of murder as he is."

"Oh God! Oh God!" The voice was pitiful.

"You are smart enough to know that mob killers don't leave any witnesses. Leonard isn't on the phone to the cops; he's calling to get the okay to kill us. *Both* of us. Make it look like we killed each other...He didn't give you a gun, did he?"

The man moaned.

"No. Of course he didn't. He doesn't trust you. Untie me. It's the only chance we have. Only chance you have."

When there was no reply, Noah pressed on recalling the other man's reference to Tone—short for Tony? Tony DeRosa a manager identified on the city memo. "The cops are out picking up your boss, "Tony," right now. You still have time to save yourself."

"Tone's in jail?" He whined.

"He's on his way. And next they are coming for you and Leonard."

Noah scoffed. "You don't think I came here without backup do you?"

With the man's torment as a distraction, Noah worked his legs to slowly push himself away from the desk. "As a prosecutor, I can see that you don't have the stomach for killing. You were only following Tone's orders. You are as afraid of this Leonard as I am. Tone's afraid too, isn't he?"

The voice was stronger now. "None of this was my doing. Tone wanted to make a few bucks selling them movies to a couple of his friends. Next thing Leonard shows up and we been like two drowning men ever since. We knew we was both in trouble, but what could we do? Tone said they would kill us if we was to back out."

Movies and the mob could only mean one thing—porn. Noah, the pumping adrenalin clearing his head, made some more connections. The family from the Vet Center. Kids. Child pornography.

"It was you that picked up that family from the Vet Center," he snapped, "and drove them out to the house on Biddle Street. You know what they do to child pornographers in prison?"

The man grabbed his head with both hands, his moaning louder now.

Noah, his legs clear of the desk, stood and wobbled as he gathered the force required to rush his captor.

An uproar erupted two floors below. Men shouted curses at each other and then a single gunshot echoed up the stairwell followed immediately by screams of pain.

Driven to frenzy with hands still bound behind his back, Noah knocked the lamp to the floor, the beam flooding his captor. Now in the shadows, Noah poised to rush him.

The man, head buried in his hands, swayed back and forth wailing, "Oh God! Oh God!"

Noah pulled up. This man was no threat; the real danger would soon be coming up the stairs. He stumbled over to the wall and secreted himself as best he could behind the open door. He could think of nothing else to do.

Through the pain throbbing at his temples Noah tried to fathom the sudden tumult on the first floor. And the screams of pain following the single shot.

Someone must have entered the house and confronted Leonard. Not likely it was the police. They would have torn the doors off, shouting POLICE! as they stormed in. And there would have been a lot more shooting. In Noah's experience, cops never missed an opportunity to shoot at a live target.

If, by some bizarre circumstance, Jack Douglas had ridden to the rescue—"leading the charge"—as he had put it, and encountered Leonard, a single shot from Noah's gun, now in the killer's hands, would be all that was required. Ironically, the pistol Jack had given to Noah for his protection.

The sound of footsteps on the stairs penetrated the ringing in Noah's head. Through the crack of the open door, he glimpsed the thin beam from a small flashlight playing around the floor, while the figure holding it edged toward him along the far wall.

Noah was desperate to slow his breathing and quiet the pounding in his head. His captor, head still in his hands, appeared oblivious to the turmoil around him. The best Noah could hope for was that the man, perhaps cowed by Noah's words, was too stricken to be of help to Leonard when he came.

Still, Noah reasoned, he was unarmed with both hands bound behind him. It was doubtful Leonard would require any help.

Noah calculated that his only chance would be to throw himself against the door just as the assassin entered the room. The impact might dislodge a weapon—gun or knife—and Noah could somehow grab it up before his adversary could retrieve it. However slight the chance; at least it *was* a chance.

He cursed the fact that light from the desk lamp was enough to alert Leonard that Noah was not seated behind the desk. His timing would have to be precise.

The footsteps hesitated at the door. A flashlight beam darted about the room.

Noah caught the glint from a pistol barrel.

NOW!

Noah launched his right shoulder against the door, sending it crashing into the form. "Uh!" The breath rushed from the intruder as he caromed against the door jamb before stumbling backward into the hallway. Something metal bounced along the floor, a flashlight beam skittered in a different direction.

Noah avoided the rebounding door and leapt into the hall. The man was still on his feet and Noah steeled himself for a charge to head-butt his adversary into submission.

The other man steadied himself and clamped a firm hand on Noah's head, stopping him in his tracks. "Whoa, big fellow," he ordered.

Noah halted his charge and stepped back. "Jack?"

"You sound surprised. You did ring for a rescue, did you not?"

Noah turned around displaying his bound hands. "Cut me loose and tell me what the hell is going on. What was that shot? Where is Leonard? Where are the cops?"

Douglas produced a pocket knife. "Another fine mess you've gotten me into," he said as he severed the plastic ties from Noah's wrists.

While Noah rubbed feeling back into his hands, Douglas stooped to pick up the pistol and retrieve his flashlight. "The cops are on the way," he said.

"How did you get here ahead of them?"

"I had placed two of the fitter attorneys I know—we play in the lawyers basketball league—on alert. They were thrilled to come. Couldn't keep them away. As for the cops, I didn't call them until we pulled up in back."

"What…?"

"I promised my buds some fun. What fun can you have when the place is crawling with cops?"

"Wait! Are your 'lawyer buds' with Leonard?" Noah moved toward the stairs. "We gotta get down there."

Douglas stuck out an arm blocking him.

"I assume Leonard and the man who pointed your gun at me— the one given to you for protection—are one and the same. If so, not to worry. My compadres are sitting on him—literally."

Douglas' words triggered Noah's memory of Detective VoShaun Taylor's admonition. *If you were sitting on the killer with the knife and a confession, the police might be able to do something.*

No confession—yet. Still two out of three ain't bad.

Noah led Douglas into the office and nodded at the ashen figure still seated in silence. "You can explain in here. There is still one handgun unaccounted for and, while I don't expect any trouble from him, there is no point in taking unnecessary risks."

The moaning man, his head still cradled in his hands, ignored Douglas as he approached. Douglas, his pistol held in a batting grip, took several leisurely swings near the man's head. "What's your name, fella?"

The man lifted his head slowly and gazed at the gun missing his head by mere inches without comment.

Douglas increased the speed of his swings closing the gap between the gun's barrel and the man's face.

The man threw up his hands to shield his head. "Jesus! I'm Vernon, okay? Vernon. I didn't know what they was doing!"

Douglas withdrew the weapon from Vernon's face and grinned. "Listen up, Vernon, you'll get a kick out of this, too."

To Noah he said, "You. Sit down before you fall down."

When Noah was seated, Douglas began his story, looking at each man in turn. "I invited a couple of adventurers out for an evening of revelry. After we had reveled for a time, I told them of your adventure and, as I said before, you couldn't keep them away. Though good chaps, one practices real estate law—an incredibly boring existence—"

"Jesus, Jack get on with it. I hear sirens."

Douglas cocked his head, shrugged and continued. "Soon as I got your call we headed for my car, the trunk of which contains a vast assortment of implements, some suitable as weapons. Rich selected a shiny chrome four-way wheel spanner. Quite fortuitous, as you will shortly see. Donny grabbed a sand wedge and I brought Black Beauty, my trusty softball bat."

"You brought a baseball bat to a gunfight?"

"In my defense, I was thinking knife. I failed to consider that you would furnish weapons to the enemy."

"Jack!"

"Okay. We get here, call for backup, of a sort, and swept in through the open back door and charged down the hall. Anyhow, Leonard's on a cell phone when we come thundering down this narrow hallway, hollering and cussing—straight at him. He drops the phone and is trying to get the gun out of his pocket when Rich lets go with the wheel spanner. It was a thing of beauty. Four arms of gleaming chrome spinning end over end like a boomerang.

"The gun had just cleared Leonard's pocket when the spanner caught him in his chest. He got off a shot into the floor as he stumbled backward, that's when Donny swung from the heels. The sand wedge caught our assassin on his gun arm and nearly took his hand off at the wrist. You must have heard Leonard's yowling up here. The gun slides along the floor, leaving old Leonard cussing and holding on to his dead arm.

"This Leonard is like a Rottweiler. Snarling and getting ready to charge us." Douglas took a level swing across the desk top. "I stepped to the plate and swung Black Beauty from the heels sending several of Leonard's ribs into deep left center. He finally went down and my buds jumped on him."

He lifted the gun and pretended to aim along the barrel at Vernon. "I swapped my ball bat for this and rode on to your rescue."

Douglas glared in Vernon's direction. "Had I known you were being guarded by a jelly roll, I would have left the gun with the other X-Men."

Noah shook his head. "You're certifiable. Did you know that?"

"Lucky for you."

Noah pointed at Vernon. "I hear the cops downstairs. Grab Vernon there and march him downstairs in front of us. In case the cops are irate over not getting to shoot anybody."

43

After dinner, Jen insisted that they take the wine bottle to the sofa, where Noah could resume his account of the melee two nights before. The dishes could wait until later, or better yet, tomorrow morning.

They were settled in, with wine glasses full, when Noah was interrupted by the Bee Gee's energetic "Stayin' Alive" sounding in his jacket pocket.

"It's Corky. I'll be quick."

After a hello, Noah listened briefly and then said, "I'm looking right at her and, yes, we both really do want to come. What can we bring? How about a bottle of wine?"

He rolled his eyes at Jen. "Fine. Rum it is."

He listened another minute. "Saturday night at 8 you will find two beautiful people standing on your porch. That will be us." he said and powered off the cell phone before returning it to his pocket.

"I heard the Bee Gee's," Jen said. "Are you tired of Abba?"

"Never." Noah shrugged. " 'Stayin' Alive' seems apropos for the present."

She nodded. "So what was it this time? Don't tell me he is still worried that we won't show."

"He has had no experience at hosting a power couple." Noah pointed to Jen and himself in turn. "That's us, in case you weren't sure. He once told me he has no real friends."

"It's more than that."

"What do you mean?"

"He looks at you as some sort of hero. This case is the most exciting thing that he has ever experienced. Killings, the Mafia, and hired assassins—real life, not on the television. Being followed by a mysterious white car. He may have been terrified being inside that house with you, but he survived. Now he doesn't want it to be over. Especially as any actual danger has been removed from the equation.

"Come Monday he will be telling his story to any streeter who will listen. You can take odds that his part in it will grow like Jack's beanstalk."

"I don't know about the part where I'm a hero, but he'll need to find another audience for the rest of it."

Jen gave him a quizzical look.

"He told me that he is not going back to the street. Any allure attached to that life is gone. More to the point, his wife demanded that he get his 'ass off the street and get an actual job.'"

"Does he have any plans?"

Noah laughed. "That's all he has. At present he is going to enroll in an Internet course for private investigators. There is also a good chance that come Saturday night he will grill you about a career as a paralegal."

"Does he know that you are not going to be his partner in the gumshoe business?"

"I've told him, but he doesn't listen."

"Yes, but does he know that you have actually decided on something else?"

"If it comes up, I'll tell him."

Jen held out her empty glass, but Noah's mind seemed elsewhere, so she poured her own wine.

"Uh, sorry," he said and took the bottle from her.

"If you are back from your trip, I want all the gory details about your close encounter. Following which, I have some news items of my own.

"For starters, can you explain why on earth Jack's friend picked a wheel spanner for a weapon? He must have been told that they could be facing armed killers."

Noah shrugged. "I asked Jack the same question. You know what a wheel spanner looks like? For changing tires."

Jen pantomimed the size of the spanner's four arms.

"Close enough. Jack told his cronies what I had said about the layout of the house. Narrow halls, a closed stairway, small rooms. No gunplay expected—we were a little off there—

"His buddy, Rich, had recently seen a kung fu movie where, during one of the endless scenes of close combat, the hero and the bad guy were trapped in a tight place. The hero grabs a spanner and hurls it, knocking out several bad guy teeth and shattering his jaw. When you think about it, those things are heavy, and you just can't ignore one of them hurtling at you end-over-end when there is no place to hide."

"Whatever works, I guess."

Noah continued with his narrative, answering each of Jen's questions as honestly as he dared. He omitted entirely Jack Douglas' Atlantic City adventure with the federal prosecutor. Not only for the sake of Jack and his bed partner, but indirectly he was also protecting Jen. It was highly unlikely that the other woman's indiscretion would become an issue, but if it did Jen could not be accused of withholding a material fact. Maybe someday—if they were still together—he would mention it.

Were Jen to ask him directly if he was the one who found the bodies on Biddle Street, he would be compelled to admit it. But she didn't. She laughed when he told her of Jack Douglas's reference to himself and his two cronies as X-Men. For the most part she listened intently.

That night, at the Harlem Street house, the X-Men had given their statements to an incredulous uniform officer. When Douglas was satisfied that Noah had no need of them, he motioned to the others and they left. Noah remained behind while the uniforms originally dispatched to the scene tried to convince headquarters to send out two detectives.

While waiting for the detectives to arrive, Noah had concluded that Corky, Marvel and Deacon were not germane to the events of this evening and would be omitted from his account.

It was nearing 3 a.m. when a plainclothes pair arrived. The detectives, intermittently yawning and rubbing their faces, were undoubtedly grouchy at having been roused from their slumber.

It was immediately evident to them that Noah was to blame for the disruption of their rest. Consequently, they took turns at badgering him as he gave his account.

The older of the pair interrupted Noah with disbelieving questions, leaving no doubt that, in his opinion, Noah was, at the very least, a liar and likely complicit in whatever had gone on here tonight. Eventually, Noah responded by pointing out that, as a former prosecutor of major felonies, he knew what the hell he was talking about and they better start paying attention.

That was when it dawned on the detectives that this case had the potential to be "a big one." Front page headlines in *The Baltimore Sun*. A case involving the Philly mob and hired killers. Possibly an interview with that cute TV reporter on Fox 45 news and the necessity for them to review porn films for investigative and evidentiary data. They seemed indifferent to the fact that they would be viewing pornography involving children.

Noah led them to the third floor, where he explained the relevance of the two laptop computers and described the roles played by Vernon and Leonard in the murders, as he saw it. He told them that Vernon had voluntarily blurted out that his boss in this criminal enterprise was named Tone. He then produced the city housing memo from his pocket and pointed to the name Tony DeRosa.

Noah voiced his belief that Vernon would roll over on Tony and Leonard to save his own butt. This was all contingent on the detectives' ability to get Vernon's story before he received a visit from a mob lawyer or another assassin. In either case he would be done talking.

Noah had urged them to contact Detective Baines regarding Frau Wirtz's murder, but said nothing about Detective VoShaun Taylor or her lieutenant. Baines could play that card however he saw fit.

Almost an afterthought, Noah had mentioned the likelihood of corruption inside the city's Housing Authority.

Noah drained his glass and reached again for the wine bottle. "You're still awake," he said.

"It would make a helluva book," Jen noted.

"That thought had crossed my mind."

He motioned with the wine bottle and she shook her head, "You drink while I talk," Jen said.

Noah saluted her offer and filled his glass.

"First," Jen said, "Let me point out that your friend Jack sounds like something of a loony toon."

"As he said, 'lucky for me.' He saved my life—a fact which he will never let me forget."

"*Touche.* You have had your fun, now I have to construct a prosecutable case out of the shambles you have left."

Noah again saluted her with his wine glass. "A woman's work and all that."

Jen made a face before saying, "Hollywood Baines came to see me about putting together a case charging them with premeditated murder in the killing of your landlady..."

"Frau Wirtz. Premeditated—that's a real long shot."

Jen shrugged. "Let's see what Vernon has to say."

Noah raised his face and sniffed the air in exaggerated fashion. "Vernon was so scared that night that he literally crapped his pants. You know your job, but I would be remiss if I didn't say something here."

"Go ahead."

"It will immediately occur to Leonard's bosses that if their hired assassin gets buried, pun intended, under murder indictments, he might co-operate. Bad for them, thus bad for Leonard. That probably only happens if Vernon testifies against him. They can't afford to take a chance on that so they will hire a good criminal attorney to represent him. An attorney whose only function will be to get Vernon out on bail so he can do his time beside some other snitch in Leakin Park."

Jen nodded. "The FBI has already been in to see me to offer their assistance in the prosecution of Leonard Lindeman, aka 'Stallion.' What a strange name, I guess he is *big* with the ladies."

"Sorry to disappoint you, but the name is more likely because of the magnificent ponytail which hangs down his back. It is the color of the mane on a palomino. It is a rather bewitching sight. Jack wanted to take it."

"Scalp him?"

Noah laughed. "Not the whole scalp, just the ponytail. It would go nicely in his trophy case."

Jen studied his face to see if he was joking. She was learning that most anything was possible when discussing Jack Douglas. She gave it up and merely said, "It is still a strange aka for a killer. I'm thinking something like 'Leonard the Blade.'"

"You were saying about the FBI. Do they have a plan?"

Jen nodded, "Surprisingly the 'big law' laid it all out to me, a lowly assistant State's Attorney. According to them, Leonard is a mob hit man, probably good for many more killings than the two in Baltimore."

They don't realize that Leonard also did Deacon and Riley. Again, up to Baines.

Jen was saying, "The bureau wants to bury Leonard under so many indictments, he will have no option but to strike a plea deal, testify against the bosses and disappear into the federal witness protection program."

Noah nodded. He surmised that the FBI had not told her of the Task Force wiretap and he had to be very careful not to say anything that could reveal the fact that he was aware of its existence.

Jen said, "What I can't figure out is how the FBI connected Leonard to the Philly mob so fast."

Noah was determined not to lie to her. "They have their moments," was all he said, hoping that the look on his face was not a giveaway.

Jen was thinking of something else. "Oh, that reminds me, of another question. Why didn't Leonard kill you in that room? Instead he leaves that fish to watch you? Was it just luck?"

Noah shook his head. "We can't discount luck entirely, but there were other factors. It's very likely that he did not expect me to come to as soon as I did. As you have said, I'm pretty hard-headed."

Jen nodded with a smile.

"Probably more significant was their desperation to get their hands on Jason's thumb drive, which they figured out I had. Yesterday I talked to an FBI agent who gave me a short course on mob protocol.

"There are rules for a hit man, which if he doesn't follow, he ends up on the wrong end of a hit himself. In my case, in addition to getting their hands on Jason's memory stick, Leonard was required to check in with them to see if I had more intrinsic value alive than dead."

"Value? Were they taking bids on your ears, or a kidney?"

Noah laughed. "I hadn't thought of that. Given all of the mob hits around the country they are missing a profitable sideline in organ harvest.

"The agent said that as a former prosecutor I would have value if I could be 'persuaded' to go on their payroll while I charmed you into revealing 'state secrets.' They might have hoped to convince me to re-up with the state's attorney while working for them.

"It is also likely that Leonard was quoting them a price on a twofer, me and Vernon. This would require him to leave the room before making the call. Vernon is a dolt, of that there is no doubt, but even he might catch on while being discussed as one of the menu items in Leonard's two-for-one price hit package. "

Jen mulled the horrors of those details and then sat her empty wine glass on the coffee table. "That's about all I can absorb in one night."

She yawned and stretched her arms. "I got a couple of more things. You up for that?"

"I'm still wired from all that's happened. I'm up for anything."

"You can tell your friend, X-Man Jack, that we will be dismissing all charges against his client, Rufus 'Spike' Jones."

Noah nodded. "That brings to mind another aspect of this case, the stench of police corruption from Day One."

"You are not going to like this. VoShaun passed along the news that her lieutenant—Masterson—has suddenly put in his retirement papers. Telling everyone he got an offer he 'couldn't refuse.' Some security job with one of the local casinos."

Noah grimly shook his head. "That sounds about right. It gets him out of the glare if someone decides to shine a light on police corruption. Internal Affairs doesn't usually bother with ex-cops in those things."

Jen shrugged. "It would be a damn shame if he got away from this untouched."

"All is not entirely lost. If you can work on Tone—Tony— Vernon's boss, he might roll over on Masterson. Assuming that Masterson was involved and his sudden resignation was not a mere coincidence." Noah wiggled his eyebrows. "I wonder if this Masterson knows that the local villains paying him were doing the Philly Shuffle with organized crime."

"Maybe somebody should tell him."

Noah smiled. "That's what I'm thinking. Let the sonofabitch start looking over *his* shoulder. Why should he get out of this without being scared shitless? I didn't."

Jen reached out and took Noah's hands in hers and stood. "I'm through with my story, how about you?" She tilted her head toward the bedroom. "Keep in mind the house rule against any discussion of business once that door closes."

Noah stood, "I'm about to thank you for another wonderful day."

44

"We're back! You are tuned to *Ben Simon Reports* on WINF, all information radio at 108FM. We are in the final segment of our discussion with Noah Cassidy. Taking your questions and comments today concerning Noah's riveting account of how he and a band of Baltimore street people uncovered corruption in city government and captured a mob assassin."

"Noah, it sounds particularly depraved, even for the mob. The cold-blooded murder of a brilliant college student and a defenseless woman, your landlady, to protect their trafficking in child pornography.

"Our next caller is Linda from Glen Burnie. Linda, you are on 108FM with Noah Cassidy."

"Ben, thank you for taking my call. Mister Cassidy, I am fascinated by your story. It struck me that while the rest of us were at home eating dinner or watching TV, you were out in the streets becoming a target for these killers. It's not like you had to do it, it wasn't your job. So why did you do it?"

"Linda, thank you for taking the time to call in. As to your point about it not being my job; I didn't see it that way. As an attorney, I did what I believed was required for my client."

"All due respect, Mister Cassidy, how many defense lawyers do you know who have faced up to a contract killer on their client's behalf? Admit it; you were in it for the thrill."

"Noah and I appreciate your thoughts, Linda. Next up, Martin from Highlandtown. You're on 108FM with Ben and Noah."

"Hi Noah, it's a real pleasure to talk to you. An eye-opener. Guys like Leonard are the pit bulls of the underworld. If they weren't on a short leash it would be open season on anyone who peed them off.

"Mob people live in a different world that the rest of us. Thanks for giving us a peek into it. You should write a book.

"Before I hang up let me say that Linda has a point about the excitement. Earlier you announced that you will be hosting a talk show on this station weekdays from 3-7. Won't that be a snooze after what you have been doing—prosecuting vicious criminals in one of the murder capitals of the country, facing down hired mob assassins?"

"Martin, I can tell you that I have had enough danger and excitement to hold me for a long time. Besides, keeping abreast of callers like you will be plenty of challenge."

"What's the theme of your show? If you told us, I missed it. Sorry."

"No, Martin, thank you for your interest. The show is called *Legalese*. We will discuss all facets of the law. Listeners' thoughts and questions on everything from local ordinances to issues before the United States Supreme Court. State and federal laws on gun control, abortion, immigration, drugs, just for starters."

"Sounds interesting, Noah. Will callers be able to get help on their own legal problems? Say, how about this for a catchphrase—'If you have a radio, you have a lawyer!'"

"I'm not going to be Judge Judy, if that is what you are asking. I will do a triage on a caller's legal situation. After hearing the facts, I hope to be able to steer him or her toward a solution by identifying the legal specialty that fits their problem.

"Sorry, but your catchphrase will not be applicable. I won't be offering specific answers to legal questions and any referrals I make will be generic in nature."

"This just occurred to me, Noah. Has there been any discussion about putting up some kind of memorial to the two streeters, as you call them, who gave their lives, Deacon and Riley?"

"Not that I have heard of, but it's a great idea."

"It seems to me that those two did more for this city than some of our 'esteemed' politicians who have had a building or a park named in their honor."

"No argument here. We'll add that to the list. Thanks for your call."

"We are out of time. Where did it go? Noah thanks for this riveting account. For you listeners, Noah returns on December 12th with his own show, *Legalese*. With any luck, you may be able to induce him to reveal even more details of his personal war with the mob."

CPSIA information can be obtained
at www.ICGtesting.com
Printed in the USA
BVHW03*0425290918

528818BV00002B/9/P

9 781626 466913